SEIZE THE PARALLEL

ROBIN BRANDE

SEIZE THE PARALLEL
Parallelogram Quartet, Book 3
By Robin Brande

Published by Ryer Publishing
www.ryerpublishing.com
Anniversary Edition © 2026 Robin Brande
www.robinbrande.com
All rights reserved.
Cover art by William Mahnken and Mykira/Dreamstime
Jirawan, Rezzz, Likanis_flares, Kikmat Studios, vetortradition,
Rizkreativ, Icons8, DGJ, goodprintsshop, Sketchily, Sinaelgicon, and
Marie Dautel/Canva
Cover design by Ryer Publishing
Ebook ISBN: 978-1-946627-14-8
Paperback ISBN: 978-1-952383-23-6
Hardback ISBN: 978-1-952383-70-0

ALSO BY ROBIN BRANDE

YOUNG ADULT STANDALONES

Evolution, Me & Other Freaks of Nature

Doggirl

Fat Cat

Replay

Young Adult Series

~ Parallelogram Quartet ~

Into the Parallel

Caught in the Parallel

Seize the Parallel

Beyond the Parallel

~ Bradamante Saga ~

Book of Earth

Book of Water

Young Adult Self-Help

What If You're Doing It Right? For Teens

SEIZE THE PARALLEL

I can't blame Halli for what she did. She knew she was dead. I know now, too.

What do you do when your real life is over, and all you have left is this one? You do the best you can. And if you're Halli Markham, you do a better job than I've been doing, pretending to be her.

"I'm not like you," she told me. "I can't be you." I know that. Any more than I can be her.

But that's what we're doing, both of us. Living our opposite lives, messing them up in so many ways, maybe improving them in others.

So I don't blame her, for most of it.

Just for that one thing.

But that one thing—I'm not sure I can get over it.

2

When Halli was growing up, she and her grandmother, Ginny, did a lot of dangerous things: exploring the Amazon; climbing the Himalayas; rowing across the Atlantic; trekking to the North and South Poles. The list goes on from there—Ginny Markham was a world explorer, a world adventurer, and she took Halli everywhere with her from the time Halli was a baby.

But even though their adventures were dangerous, Ginny always emphasized two things: one, that preparation is the best defense against everything that can go wrong. And two, when everything goes wrong anyway, face up to it and keep on going from there.

So Halli learned to anticipate. And Halli learned to

adapt. To look at her situation with a cold, hard eye, and not wish things were different than they were, but to deal with exactly what was happening at the moment.

So if a rope failed, a bone broke, if Halli and Ginny were lost somewhere in the middle of a violent storm, Halli learned to be quiet. To stop. To assess her condition, her surroundings, her options.

Is it any wonder, then, that once it sank in—the conclusion that Professor Whitfield and I had come to that the real Halli was dead, and I hadn't saved her from that avalanche at all, but instead had split off a new parallel universe where the only Halli who had ever existed was this new Halli 2, the one who was actually *me* inside Halli's body, and there would be no way to reverse it because the original Halli was gone, that connection severed forever—was it any wonder that a calm came over Halli, and she started thinking about what she had to do?

Especially once I disappeared again, ripped out of the body—my old body—that I'd been able to visit temporarily and share with Halli somehow. Now I was gone, and no matter what Halli and Professor Whitfield tried over the next several hours, they couldn't bring me back.

So as night fell, and my mother was calling to the daughter she thought was me, asking her what kind of takeout she wanted, and Professor Whitfield told Halli they'd have to try finding me again in the morning, Halli was already thinking about what to do next.

Because just like Ginny said, if things go wrong, you have to be able to rely on yourself. No point clinging to a rockface after your climbing partner has just fallen, and crying because it's all so sad and frightening. You'd better figure out a way to save yourself. You can cry about it later.

So Halli began making a plan.

3

M eanwhile, me.

Rushed to a London hospital and immediately pumped full of drugs.

Drugs that made me hallucinate. Drugs that kept me
in this kind of twilight sleep, never really dreaming,
never really awake, but just floating in this sort of sick
haze, unable to swim my way to the top of it or force it
out of my system. My brain was gooey. Muddled. Limp
and useless.

"Halli?" I could hear Daniel saying to me, and if no
one was around, "*Audie?*" I tried to form his name, but it
was too hard. My mouth felt too heavy. I don't think I
even got the D out.

Then other voices—Jake, other people—all of them
shouting "Halli," trying to get me to answer, but I was

too deep and far away. And why come back when it was all so noisy? What I needed was quiet. And for someone to come dig me out. To grab me by the hair and keep me from sinking further into the deep. To sweep away all the haze and the gunk, and help me clear out my mind again.

"She needs rest," I heard a woman say. "Miss Markham needs her rest. Clearly she's exhausted."

No, Miss Markham needs to find the real Miss Markham. Miss Markham is Audie Masters. She'd like to go home now. Her mother brought her some soup. She was just about to see her mother when suddenly Jake and Sarah and that reporter burst into the room and ruined everything. Now where am I? What have you done with her? With me? What's happening?

"Audie," Daniel whispered. "We're doing everything we can. I hope you can hear me."

I can. I could. Then it was back into the deep dark void for me.

4

Halli rose at dawn and went for a long run. It was Sunday, the day after my miraculous and all-too-brief visit, and Halli needed to mull over everything she had learned. She always did her best thinking when she was on the move.

Over the past week she'd gone running at least twice a day: in the morning, as soon as my mom left for work, and again in the afternoon before my mom came home. In between, Halli spent hours cooped up in my room, talking to Professor Whitfield and his lab assistant Albert, alternating between trying to bring me back and learning everything she could about how to pretend to be me.

And part of that involved pretending to be sick.

My mother understood immediately. She had been

expecting it for weeks. She kept warning me I was pushing myself too hard, not getting enough sleep, never taking a break from obsessing over getting accepted into Columbia University. My application was due November 1, and I kept promising her I'd relax after that. But she knew in her heart that it would all finally catch up to me, and when it did I would crash hard.

So when she came home from her business trip and found Halli—theoretically, me—coughing and sniffling and dragging herself out of bed, my mother declared that school and my job were off-limits for a few days, and I was to stay home and do nothing but rest. Halli nodded meekly, let my mother heat up cans of soup for her and fuss over her a little, and then leapt out of bed as soon as the coast was clear and took off running every chance she could get.

And it was fine for that one week. Halli figured it was temporary. She would work with Professor Whitfield to find me and reverse what had happened, and then she'd be back to her old life in no time.

Meanwhile, it was interesting to learn about this other universe she'd dropped into: how the technology worked, how the people lived, what everything looked like. It wasn't so different from experiences she'd had many times before, visiting new countries and learning the language and the customs.

But mostly Halli was interested in the terrain.

Ginny had taught her that was the first and best way of getting grounded in a new place: find out where you are and where everything else is around you.

"I need maps," Halli told the professor.

"Maps of what?" he asked.

"Everything."

"Halli, we need to keep working—"

"I need maps."

She was so insistent, he finally gave in. Showed her how to access maps on my computer. "But don't do it now," he told her. "We have to keep working. Come on, Halli, we need your complete focus."

Reluctantly, she agreed. And returned to the more tedious business of mapping out my life.

"See if you can find any identification numbers," Professor Whitfield and Albert suggested. "Passwords ... her driver's license ... bank information ... notes ... e-mails ... pictures..." Anything and everything that would let Halli slip into my life and pretend to know what I should know.

Albert had the bright idea of using my social security number and student ID to hack into my school records. That way they could find out what classes I was taking, what rooms they were in, and what my teachers' names were, in case Halli had to take it all a step further and go to school as if she were me. She couldn't just stand there in the hall and ask someone passing by, "Excuse me? Do you know me? Where do I go?"

Halli took one look at my class schedule and didn't like what she saw.

"Physics? World History? English Literature?" she said. "I won't know any of those. Don't you think people will notice?"

"We'll coach you through it," Professor Whitfield promised. "And maybe it won't come to that. Let's keep working."

The problem wasn't just that Halli had never been to school in my universe, it's that she'd never been to any school, period. Ginny taught her everything she needed to know: foreign languages, navigation, survival skills. Halli never spent a day of her life sitting in some classroom taking quizzes or writing essays. And the only thing she knew about physics was what little I'd taught her so far. That wouldn't help if Mr. Dobosh called on her and asked her to explain some esoteric principle that I would clearly understand. Halli was right—people would be suspicious.

With all the work involved trying to learn to be me, it's no wonder Halli had to take as many breaks as she could to go out running. I'll be the first to agree that having to cram in someone's life in just a few days—not to mention having to learn as much as you can about how to function in a strange place in general, with technology you've never seen, around people who expect you to know who they are—can be totally mentally exhausting.

On the other hand—and I don't say this just because I'm jealous—it was pretty convenient for Halli to have a team like the professor and Albert helping her through all that. Even little things like suggesting she carry my laptop all around the house so they could see our appliances on the screen and explain how they all worked.

I understand that was best for everybody since it meant fewer things for my mother to get suspicious about, but don't you think I would have loved some help like that when I suddenly had to start pretending to be Halli? I was thrown into her life as abruptly as she was thrown into mine, and I didn't even have time to properly freak out before there was a knock on her door and some guy standing there who looked exactly like the one I've been in love with most of my life, telling me his name was Jake instead of Will, and that he was there to fly me back by private jet to Halli's parents' private island, where I was supposed to be the star attraction at a company board meeting I knew nothing about.

Not to mention that Halli's parents are horrible, her world is confusing, and I never once, no matter how many times I tried, managed to figure out how to work the holographic tablets they have over there. So yeah, I would have appreciated a little help.

I'm not saying Halli had it easy, just in some ways easi*er*.

While she sorted through all my stuff those first few days, searching for clues about how to be me, Halli couldn't resist cleaning up a little as she went.

I've never really minded living in chaos. I know where everything is in every pile in my room, so it's never seemed important enough for me to take the time to clean. If I'm in there I'd rather be studying or sleeping. But I can understand someone else coming in and needing to bring some order to the place, to sort out what's useful and necessary from what's not.

Halli brought that kind of cold calculation to my closet one afternoon. She was sick of having to sort through all the clothes I crammed in there, just to find things that fit. I still had a lot of clothes from back in junior high, and maybe even a few from elementary school. What can I say? I've been busy the last few years.

But Ginny never would have let me get away with something like that.

"If you have something, use it," she used to tell Halli. *"If you don't use it, don't have it."* That applied to clothing, gear, equipment—everything. Despite all her wealth, Ginny liked to live very simply. She could fit all the essentials of her life into a duffel or two, and be on the move at a moment's notice. Halli developed that same skill.

By the time she was done cleaning my closet and my room, Halli had filled five garbage bags full of clothes, shoes, odds and ends—anything she couldn't see an immediate use for and that didn't suit her regular style.

Gone were some of the pants and shirts I let my best friend, Lydia, talk me into getting over the years, but that never really fit me right. Gone were the flowery skirts my mother always gave me for my birthday. Gone were all the beat-up, worn-out flats and sandals I've worn for years because my shoe size hasn't really changed.

But Halli kept any T-shirts, sweatshirts, sweatpants, all my jeans, my shorts, my sneakers—any kind of clothing a person could run in or hike in or generally not have to fuss with. And she especially loved my cargo pants: comfortable, sturdy, practical with all their pockets—just the kind of thing she liked.

She stowed all the bags in our storage shed. She wasn't about to permanently throw out anything of mine that I might come back and want. Then she settled back into a bedroom that looked more like her clean, sparse house than the place I had left behind.

It looked nice. I'll admit I was shocked—and maybe even a little hurt—the first time I saw it. But the truth is everything Halli did needed to be done. Nobody can be as ruthless about purging your stuff as somebody else who's never been attached to any of it. I'm actually grateful that she did it.

And my mom was absolutely stunned.

"Audie, what ...?" My mom stood in the doorway of my bedroom, staring around her in shock. I doubt she had ever seen it that clean since the day we first moved into the house.

Halli glanced up from where she sat on my bed, back propped against the wall, my laptop balanced on my legs. She gave my mom a shrug. "I felt a little better this afternoon. Thought I'd do some cleaning up."

"But..." My mom just shook her head. "Wow."

Halli smiled politely, then went back to studying the map currently up on my screen.

And even without meaning to, just by that small act of cleaning up my room, Halli already set the stage for everything else to come.

5

When Halli returned from her run, she found my mom sitting in the kitchen drinking coffee and reading the Sunday paper.

"Oh!" my mom said, looking up. "I thought you were still asleep. Were you ... outside?"

Halli quickly put on the sweatshirt she wore tied around my waist. She didn't need my mother to see how sweaty my T-shirt was.

"I felt so much better when I woke up," Halli said, "I thought I'd go out and get some fresh air."

"Oh." Since that's not the sort of thing I do normally —ever—my mother gave her a puzzled look.

And Halli decided right then and there that it was smarter to make up a longer-lasting excuse than to have to keep sneaking around.

"I was thinking about it the whole time I was sick," she said. "I realized I need to start taking better care of myself."

"Well, I agree with that," my mom answered, as Halli suspected she would. "I always say you need more sleep. And honey, I know you don't want to keep hearing this, but I really think you have to stop pushing yourself so hard about Columbia."

"Hm." Halli nodded without saying more.

"Are you hungry?" my mom asked. "I think there are still some waffles."

My favorite Sunday morning breakfast—mainly because I can make them myself. Just pop them in the toaster and wait. That's about the level of my cooking skills.

"Actually," Halli said, "I was hoping we could go to the store this morning. There are some things I'd like to get. Now that I'm feeling better."

"Okay, sure," my mom said. "I need to get a few things, too. Let me just finish my coffee and we'll go in a little while."

"Good," Halli said. "Thank you." Then she smiled.

And right there, I'm surprised my mother didn't catch it: the insincerity. A kind of forced smile that only involved Halli's mouth—my mouth, technically—and never traveled all the way up to my eyes. The kind of smile you give a stranger who apologizes after accidentally bumping into you. *Sorry.* *No problem.* Fake smile.

When I asked Halli, during that short visit I was able to accomplish before being dragged off to the hospital, whether she talked to my mom, Halli's answer was, "As much as I can."

At the time I thought she meant she talked to my mom as often as she could—as in, she really wanted to be around her.

What I realize now is that she meant, "As much as I can stand."

Because the truth is, Halli has never had a proper mother. And by this point in her life, I can't blame her for not wanting one. Her real mother is awful: critical, shallow, materialistic, and mean. And her father isn't much better. I spent a whole weekend with them, and it was clear from the start that neither of them likes her.

Plus it's hard to get past the fact that they abandoned Halli as soon as she was born and let her be raised by her grandmother. Not that Halli wasn't better off because of it, but something like that doesn't exactly create the kind of close parent-daughter bond my own mom and I have.

So I understand that having to share a house with someone who looks just like her own mother must have been hard for Halli. And pretending that she loved her the way I really do love my own mother? Well, impossible.

But Halli tried—or at least she tried to do a good job

of faking it. For my sake and for the sake of her own situation. And I appreciate that.

Halli left the kitchen and went to take a shower. She stood under the hot water for a long time. Thinking.

All during that first week, she had thought of my body as mine. As something she was temporarily stuck in until I could figure out the physics and take it back.

But now...

She drizzled shampoo into my hand and scrubbed it into my hair. She'd gotten used to feeling the shorter haircut as it slid through her fingers, the same way she had to adjust to all the other differences between our two bodies. We might be parallel versions of each other, but anyone looking at us side by side would be able to tell we weren't the same person. Halli's body—the one I was currently occupying—was strong and athletic. Mine was ... not. But at least it hadn't completely broken down during all those long runs Halli took it on. That gave her some hope.

There's nothing special about the body, Halli could hear Ginny telling her in a memory from long ago. It was one of the worst conversations she ever had with her grandmother, but also one of the most important. It helped mold Halli into the kind of person she was now.

It had been Ginny's way of telling Halli she should always be prepared, no matter what. But now Halli realized the lesson meant so much more.

She had been thinking about it for the past twenty-four hours—ever since she listened to the professor and me discussing whether or not her old body was gone. Ginny never could have predicted that one day her granddaughter would end up in the wrong universe, inhabiting some other girl's life. But the lesson still applied—maybe more now than ever.

There's nothing special about the body.

Halli hoped her grandmother was right.

6

Halli was six when Ginny took her on her first really long backpacking excursion: three weeks high in the Colorado mountains. It was early fall, and the leaves on the aspens had already turned yellow. The temperature fell below freezing at night, and they always awoke to frost on the outside of their tent. But the days were still brilliantly sunny, so Ginny and Halli could hike for miles every day.

It was hard work, carrying all their gear and food on their backs as they trudged up and down steep terrain all day long, but Halli loved it. Ginny made sure she would. She'd introduced Halli to outdoor life almost from the very start. By the time she was six, Halli was strong for her age. She had already spent years learning to hike, horseback ride, paddle, and ski. I think of my own first six years and I can't even imagine how Halli did all that she did. But Ginny made it seem so fun and normal. Halli wouldn't have known any other way to live.

They mostly walked in silence. Ginny taught Halli that was the best way to see wildlife: elk and deer grazing along the hillsides; nervous marmots chirping in alarm, then diving into their dens; hawks gliding overhead, their wings bent up at the tips as if someone had folded them along a crease.

And bears sometimes. Always from a distance, running away once they caught sight or scent of Halli and Ginny.

"Won't they attack us?" Halli asked.

"Only if they don't feel they have a choice," Ginny told her. "Especially if we surprise them."

It was why they talked loudly and even sang sometimes if they had to navigate through the thick willows that grew along the streams.

"They won't be able to see us in here," Ginny explained. "Let's give them a chance to get away. They don't want to meet us any more than we want to meet them."

By the end of their three weeks, Halli was so used to the routines of the day and the feeling of being out in the wilderness all the time, she stopped worrying about any of the dangers.

Which was a mistake she learned not to repeat.

It was their last morning, and after a breakfast of hot, spicy tea and oatmeal with dried fruit, they packed up their tent and gear one last time and took to the trail. The air was cold enough that Halli could see her breath. She'd had a strange dream the night before, and was lost in thought, trying to remember all of it, when suddenly Ginny thrust out her arm to keep Halli from moving another inch.

In front of them, just a few feet off the trail, were a giant bull moose and his equally giant mate. They were larger than any animal Halli had ever been that close to—bigger than even the biggest horse. The bull's rack stretched out on each side of his head in a span as wide as his body was long. The two animals stared at them, both on high alert, their nostrils flared, ears erect.

"Back up," Ginny whispered urgently. "Don't run. Start backing up. *Now.*"

Halli obeyed instantly. She knew they were in trouble. Ginny had warned her about moose: how they weren't like deer or elk, who would just take off if someone approached. Moose stood their ground. They defended themselves. They could easily trample a person to death—and would, if threatened.

Halli's heart pounded. She followed Ginny's lead, backing up one step after another until they were out of the moose's line of sight.

"Now turn around," Ginny whispered. "Walk quickly, but quietly. Go."

Halli didn't argue. Didn't speak. She knew better. All she wanted was to get away. She hurried without running, keeping her boots as silent as she could against the dirt, looking back over her shoulder every few seconds to see if the moose were following.

Finally Ginny whispered they could stop. She led Halli off the trail to a clearing up ahead of them where they could remove their packs and rest.

"We'll give them a chance to wander off," Ginny said. She spread out a few items of extra clothing to help insulate them from the cold ground. Then the two of them sat down to wait.

Ginny smiled at her granddaughter. "Very good, Halli. You did well back there. I'm proud of you."

Halli blew out a long, cold breath that ended with a shaky smile. She liked the praise, but her pulse still pounded.

Ginny seemed perfectly calm.

"Weren't you scared?" Halli asked her.

Ginny thought about it for a moment. "No."

"Why not?" Halli asked. "I was!"

"It was just a situation we had to manage," Ginny said. "And we did. That's all you ever have to do, no matter what happens to you."

"But how?" Halli asked. "You don't know what will happen all the time. What if it's something really bad?"

"What if it is?" Ginny answered. "Let's say one of us got hurt just now. What would we do?"

"Hurt ... how?"

They had played this kind of game before. *What ifs* were Ginny's favorite way of teaching.

"Let's say that moose attacked you and broke your arm," she said. "Now what do we do?"

"Well ... we'd have to fix it," Halli said.

"How?"

Ginny made Halli go through each of the steps, from how she'd get away from the moose while still protecting her arm, to finding the proper materials to set the broken bone, to figuring out how to carry her pack so they could continue hiking out of the wilderness.

"So you could manage it," Ginny said when Halli finished.

Halli nodded. She actually felt much better now—calmer, more in control of the situation.

But then Ginny took it another step further. "What would you do if I died?" she asked.

Halli's eyes widened. She shook her head, not wanting to even consider the question.

Ginny asked again. "Halli, what would you do if I died this morning? What if that moose had killed me?"

Halli couldn't help it—no matter how tough she was already, she was still only six. Tears sprang to her eyes. "I don't want you to die!"

"I don't want to, either," Ginny said. "But I want you to think about what you would do if I did."

Again Halli shook her head.

Ginny wasn't having any of that. She wasn't raising a weak, scared little girl. She was raising a woman just like herself.

"Halli, I'm not saying it will happen any time soon, but it might, and you have to be prepared. I need to know that you'll be smart and brave and you'll do what's necessary to survive. Do you understand?"

Halli gulped back her tears and nodded.

Ginny smiled. "I love my life—especially since you came along. But if I died today, you could go on, couldn't you?"

Halli shook her head. A single tear escaped and rolled down her cheek.

Ginny sighed. "You could, Halli, of course you could. You know that and I know it. You're strong and brave, and I know you'd make me proud. So what would you have done this morning if I died?"

Ginny wouldn't let up. She made Halli go through each and every moment—from surprising the moose to watching them suddenly charge forward and attack her grandmother.

"What would you do?" Ginny demanded.

"I'd help you!" Halli cried.

"No, you'd have to run away," Ginny said.

"No, I'd stay and protect you!"

"You're too small," Ginny said. "You wouldn't be able to help me."

"But I couldn't just leave you!"

"Yes, you could. And you'd have to," Ginny said. "I'm counting on you to always protect yourself if I'm not here to do it—do you understand?"

Halli stared back at her miserably.

"Halli, do you understand?"

The little girl nodded.

Ginny made her resume the story: how she'd run away, hide, and wait for the moose to leave.

"And then what?" Ginny asked.

"I'd go back and find you," Halli said.

"Why?"

"To see if you were all right."

"And what if I wasn't?" Ginny asked. "What if I was dead?"

"Then I'd bury you!" Halli cried. It was the worst conversation she'd ever had in her life. But still Ginny persisted.

"No, you wouldn't bury me," Ginny said calmly. "That would be foolish. You're too small, and it would take too long. Then it would be dark out, and you'd be vulnerable. Think, Halli. What are the three most important things to have in the wilderness?"

Halli wiped her nose on her sleeve. At least she could answer that question. "Shelter, water, and safety."

"Not food?" Ginny quizzed her.

"No, you can go without food for several days," Halli recited. "But you have to stay warm and dry, and you need water. And you have to make sure you're safe."

"That's right," Ginny said. "So what would you do? You've come back and found my body, I'm dead, so what do you do?"

Halli wasn't crying anymore. The worst of the shock was over. Now it was just a lesson.

"I'd look for your pack and find the tent."

"Good," Ginny said.

"I'd get the water bag, too, so I could carry that."

"Good. And then?"

Halli sniffled. "I'd cover you up—can I at least do that?"

"It depends," Ginny said. "Is it close to dark? Do you have someplace safe to go?"

"I don't want the wild animals to get you!"

And then Ginny said the words that she couldn't have possibly known would be so important to Halli now, eleven years later.

"I wouldn't care," Ginny said. "Do you understand? I'd already be dead. And there's nothing special about the body. Once I'm gone, I don't care what happens to it. All I want is for you to keep going and be safe."

"How can you say that?" Halli argued. "That thing about the body? You always say we should be as comfortable as possible. You make me stop and put on extra clothes if I'm cold. Or fix something if it's hurting me— my boots, or the strap on my backpack—"

"We should always be comfortable," Ginny said. "I stand by that. Because as long as we're in these bodies, we should treat them well and make them feel good. It's a nice thing to do. But once we're done with them—once we're dead—it doesn't matter anymore. Do you understand that? It's just a body. It's like those clothes you're wearing. One day you'll outgrow them, and you won't need them anymore."

Halli thought about it. And even though she hated everything her grandmother was telling her, she couldn't say it wasn't right. Or that it wasn't true. Even at that young age, she knew how to be rational and practical.

And now the grown Halli stood in front of the mirror in my bathroom, brushing a set of teeth that belonged to me.

There's nothing special about the body. Once we're done with it, it doesn't matter anymore.

Halli spit out the toothpaste and leaned in closer. She looked into my eyes. She tapped their reflection in the mirror, to see who was home.

Nothing special about the body. Her body was gone. This was her body now, in the same way she had inherited all the clothes in my closet.

Treat it well and make it feel good. It's a nice thing to do.

She intended to. She already was. But beyond that? What was she supposed to do with this body of mine? Not just with my body—with this whole life of mine?

Use it. Mold it. Make it your own.

Halli knew that's what Ginny would say. What Ginny would do.

Her grandmother wouldn't have hesitated for a moment. She would have immediately accepted the reality of the situation, no matter how unreal it felt.

"I'm in Audie's body now?" Halli could imagine Ginny saying. *"All right, then, fine—what's next?"* Then she would have taken control of the situation right away—managed it. She wouldn't have spent a week waiting and hoping I'd return and make everything right again.

Halli went to my room and dressed herself the way she wanted to: cargo pants, sneakers, a long-sleeved T-shirt. She fanned her fingers through my wet hair.

"Audie," my mom called, "ready?"

Ready enough, Halli thought. It was time to put the first phase of her plan into action.

It was time she seized control.

7

"I'll get us a cart," my mom said, but Halli was already heading off in her own direction.

"Oh, okay," my mom said, clearly surprised. Usually the two of us walk the aisles together just to keep each other company. But Halli neither knew about that nor cared.

"I'll come find you," my mom called after her. "I just need to pick up a few things..."

Halli didn't bother listening. She was on a mission.

Because she knew if her plan were going to succeed, she needed to get to work on my body right away. It had done all right for her so far whenever she took it running, but she was about to start putting a lot more demands on it, and for that she needed strength.

And for that she needed proper food.

No more takeout, no more microwavable vegetables smothered in cheese, no more chips or sugary cereals or any of the other junk my mom and I love so much. Halli needed fresh food. Home-cooked food. And good coffee—she was a snob about that. I remember her taking a whiff of the cheap coffee my mom always buys, and telling me, "We're better than this."

So she scooped up a basket from the end of one of the checkout lanes and headed toward the right. She had been in that store once before, and knew exactly where she wanted to go.

She'd gone in one morning while she was out on one of her runs. She had a craving for fruit—not something we normally keep in our house, since it usually goes bad before my mom or I remember to eat it—and she was curious what kinds of food she might find.

But Halli wasn't in the habit of bringing any money with her, and she forgot that in my world she couldn't just step up to a cashier and have the person wave a sensor over the microchip beneath Halli's collar bone, and punch in a code to have the purchase deducted from one of her accounts. Not only do our stores not work that way, but my body doesn't come equipped with a microchip.

As Halli walked out of the store that day without the banana and kiwi she meant to buy, she made a note of that. Not of the fact that she needed money to purchase food in my world—that was obvious—but of the fact that she didn't have any money of her own, and would have to ask my mother for anything she wanted.

Halli didn't like that one bit.

It had been different with Ginny: the two of them were a team. Halli never had to beg or negotiate with her grandmother. They both understood that if either of them needed anything, they would just get it. It had always been that simple.

Of course, it helped that Ginny was rich—very rich. And when she died she left everything to Halli. Money was never a worry in Halli's life—not like in mine at all. My mom and I have been basically poor my whole life. And that was the life Halli stepped into.

When she searched my room those first few days, looking for clues so she could impersonate me, Halli found my wallet and the whopping $27.52 I had in there. She also found the bank statements showing a little over $2,000 in my savings account—money I'd been accumulating over the past several years to help my mom pay for college.

But that wasn't Halli's money. At least not in her eyes.

Yes, she could have gone into my bank at any moment, shown them my ID, and withdrawn every penny I had, but she wasn't like that. What was mine was mine, what was hers was hers.

And at the moment, nothing was hers.

But she had a plan to change that. One she had been

thinking about ever since she learned the day before that she might be stuck exactly where she was.

It was why she was currently loading up her shopping basket with several pounds of potatoes, squash, beans, bananas, apples, parsnips, turnips, onions, carrots, greens—

"Audie," my mother said, staring in shock at Halli's overflowing basket. "Honey, we can't get all that."

"Why not?" Halli was genuinely perplexed.

"Well ... we'll never eat all that. It'll just go to waste."

"No it won't," Halli said. "I'll eat it."

"But ... who's going to cook it?" my mom asked. She tugged at the bunch of Swiss chard. "I wouldn't even know what to do with some of this."

"I do," Halli said. "I'll take care of it. Don't worry." She patted my mom on the arm.

My mom laughed at her. "Honey! Listen, I think it's great that you want to start taking better care of yourself, but we can't just waste money like this. Now why don't you go put some of that back, and let's think about what we can realistically eat over the next week."

Halli took a deep breath and held her annoyance in check. She smiled as politely as she could. "These are the foods I want, and I know how to cook them. Nothing will be wasted. I'll make food for you, too. You'll like it. Trust me."

My mom gave her a look like I'd suddenly sprouted an extra head. Or like I was suffering from amnesia. We both know neither one of us has a clue how to cook. It's the whole basis of our takeout lifestyle. And it's why we're always so thrilled whenever Will and Lydia's mother, Elena, invites us over to their house for dinner.

"Everything will be fine," Halli said. "I promise. And if I need to, I'll pay you back."

"Don't be ridiculous," my mom muttered. "Come on."

My mom stood nervously watching the cashier ring up Halli's purchases. But she paid without saying anything more.

As they loaded bags into the trunk of our car, Halli took one more stab at reassuring my mother.

"I'll make us something for dinner," she said. "You'll see. You'll like it."

My mom shook her head. "Audie..."

She reached out and hugged me. Who she thought was me.

Halli stiffened. Then she caught herself. She tried to relax, and ended up giving my mom a couple of friendly pats on the back. Then she pulled away.

"I'm ... excited about you trying to cook," my mom said.

Halli just smiled. She couldn't tell my mother that she had cooked for herself most of her life: in fancy kitchens and primitive ones, in many countries and on every continent, on mountaintops, in jungles, on the deck of a wildly pitching boat, while suspended from ropes on the side of a cliff, and huddled next to a sled on a field of sea ice while Ginny guarded against polar bears.

No doubt about it, Halli would be doing a lot more than "trying."

8

"Miss Markham?" I could hear a voice calling to me. Female, with an accent. Not British, but something else. "My name is Dr. Rios. Can you hear me?"

"Mmm," was the best I could do. My mouth was dirt dry, my throat raspy and sore. My eyes felt crusted over. I tried to pry them open.

The doctor lifted one of my eyelids and shined a light into my pupil. Pain rocketed through my head. I jerked away.

"What does that mean?" I heard Jake ask. "Is she all right?"

"It could be a reflex," Dr. Rios said. "She's still heavily drugged. We're continuing to scan the brain to search for any damage."

That didn't sound good. I tried to open my eyes again.

"Halli?" Jake said. "Can you hear us? Halli, say something, *please*."

Too much trouble. He had no idea how much effort it took.

And I didn't feel all that motivated to do him any favors, considering it was his fault I was even lying there in the first place.

I couldn't remember everything, but I could remember enough:

Daniel and me together in a dark, quiet room at his parents' production studio. Me trying to contact Halli for the second time that day.

The first time hadn't ended well. A woman named Olga and her daughter Christine showed me how to calm my mind, how to let it drift while I felt for the energy of Halli out there in the vast ocean of time and space. And then, once I found her, how to dive down and rejoin my own body back in my own world.

But all it took was Halli's exuberant greeting to pull me out of the moment. I lost control. I don't know if it was because I came out of it too abruptly, or if something else went wrong, but for whatever reason it was like someone ripping my skin off and turning me inside out. Like spikes driven into my head. It was the worst pain I'd ever felt in my life.

Until it happened the second time.

Everything had being going well: I'd been able to talk to not only Halli, but also Professor Whitfield. We were getting somewhere. He had a theory about how it was I ended up in Halli's body, and she ended up in mine. Neither one of us understood how I'd jumped ahead three days in the process, but we probably could have figured that out if we had time.

And then I heard my mother coming in the front door of our house. I hadn't seen her since the whole thing happened, and I was desperate to look at her face again, to give her a hug, even just to hear her voice. She called out that she had soup for me. I started to run to her.

But then it all blew apart.

The door to Daniel's and my private sanctuary burst open, and in rushed Jake, Daniel's sister Sarah, and the reporter who'd been following us around. And then it was utter chaos: shouting, fighting, screaming. The screams were mine. I'd been ripped out of my real body once more, and this time the crash of pain felt like an explosion inside Halli's head. My screaming only made it worse, made Halli's brain feel like it was splitting down the center, but I couldn't stop myself. The sound just kept coming.

Daniel tried to protect me. I could hear him yelling at the three of them to get out, to leave us alone, but then Jake started pushing back, and finally punched Daniel in the face.

I couldn't worry about that—I just wanted the pain in Halli's head to stop. But the next thing I knew, there was more shouting, a bigger crowd, and I was being wheeled along on a gurney and then loaded into an ambulance. I remember poor Red, Halli's big yellow Labrador, trying to jump up in there with me, and being kicked away by the medic. And I remember looking over and seeing Daniel's bleeding face. I remember flashes of it all, each one more horrible than the next.

And now waking up in the hospital, in this prison of a drugged mind. I was going to have to convince somebody to stop feeding that into my veins. My only salvation would come from having a clear head again so I could travel back to my own universe. I needed a mind free to figure out the physics, and this gooey mind wasn't capable of it.

"Halli, open your eyes," Jake tried again. "Please. Come back to me. I love you."

I mumbled something. Couldn't get the words out. Couldn't tell him what I really wanted.

Which was for him to go find Daniel for me, and then get out of my life forever.

9

By the time Halli and my mom got home from grocery shopping, the phone in our house was ringing.

"Can you get that?" my mom called. She went back to the car to bring in more groceries.

Halli had been avoiding the phone all week. She knew there wouldn't be anyone calling that she wanted to talk to. The only people she wanted contact with were Professor Whitfield and Albert, and they always handled that by video chat. Even more important, Halli assumed that whoever was calling would expect her to know who they were. Even Caller ID wasn't any help, since Halli had never met any of those people in her life and wouldn't exactly know what to say to them.

This time the Caller ID said *Stamos-V*. That

narrowed it down to someone in the Stamos-Valadez family: Lydia, Will, or their mom, Elena. I'd shared details about all of them here and there in my conversations with Halli—including my sad, secret, unrequited love for Will—but it still wasn't really enough for her to fake knowing any of them. On the other hand, she couldn't think of a good excuse for not answering the phone when my mom had just asked her to. So she picked it up and waited.

After a moment of silence, the voice on the other end said, "Hello?"

"Yes?" Halli answered.

"How come you never called me back? I've left you like four messages."

It was Lydia. She didn't bother saying so, since obviously I'd know her voice.

"Oh," Halli said. And she left it at that. Not only had she not been answering the house phone or my cell phone, she had no way of ever accessing my messages, even if she wanted to.

Because even though her search through my desk drawers and notebooks had turned up quite a few of my passwords, she never would have found the code for my cell phone. That's because I had no need to write it down. I'll never forget it: it's Will's birthday.

I know, pathetic.

Apparently Lydia didn't care that Halli hadn't offered a full explanation, because she just went on with her message. "My mom says for you two to come over tonight. She's making enchiladas."

Halli hesitated. Should she say she was still sick? Avoid any social situations for as long as she could, in hopes that she never had to deal with any of them?

No, because realistically, she was going to have to move forward one way or another. And that probably meant showing up at school the next day and doing her best to pretend to be me. At least until she could come up with some better solution.

So if that was inevitable, then she might as well smooth the way by meeting at least a few of the people she would be expected to know.

Besides, Halli was curious about a certain person.

"Will Gemma be there?" she asked.

"Probably," Lydia answered with a certain tinge of disgust. Neither of us particularly cares for Will's obnoxious, hair-flipping, boob-thrusting, eye-winking British girlfriend. I, of course, hate her more, and would hate her even if she were the greatest person in the world. But Lydia doesn't know that. I've never told her about my feelings for her twin brother. That would be a disaster all its own.

But Halli was curious about Gemma for her own reasons. While Halli and I were hiking in the Alps, we met a party of three Brits: Daniel, who eventually became my sort-of boyfriend; Daniel's friend Martin; and Daniel's sister, Sarah. Halli and I both ended up adoring Sarah. She could be a little outspoken some-times, a little wearing in her need for attention, but she was also a fun and lively girl who turned out to be a good friend to both of us.

And yes, Sarah was partly responsible for the whole episode that ended up getting me dragged off to the hospital, but she had no way of knowing that. She thought she was just helping out some friends.

Sarah, as I'd explained to Halli, had a parallel version over in my universe. That girl was the hideous Gemma. I had described all of her hideousness to Halli, but now she was curious to see it for herself.

"What time?" Halli asked.

"Dinner's at six," Lydia said. "I have to teach, so I'll be there a little late."

"Teach ... yoga?" Halli remembered me telling her that Lydia did that.

"Uh, yeah," Lydia answered, in a tone that said *obviously*.

"Can I come?"

Lydia wasn't expecting that. Why should she? She's been trying to talk me into taking yoga ever since she started. I've always said no.

"Sure," Lydia said. "But why?"

"I want to," Halli said, and left it at that. "What time?"

"Four-thirty."

Lydia still sounded skeptical, so Halli knew she had

to be careful with her next question. Should she ask for the name of the yoga studio so she could look up the address? Or was there a sneakier way to do it?

"My mother has to use the car," Halli said. "Can I go with you?"

"I'm taking the class before that," Lydia answered. "Then teaching the four-thirty right after."

"That's fine," Halli said. "I'll go to both of them."

"You'll what? Audie, what's going on?"

"Nothing," Halli said. "I just feel like getting some exercise today."

"Did you hit your head or something?"

"I've decided to make some changes." It was an explanation that was going to have to do—for a lot of things. Halli decided she might as well be upfront about it. People were going to start seeing some of those changes soon enough. Doing several hours of yoga on a Sunday afternoon was as good a start as any.

Lydia must have been shaking her head over on her end. "Sure. Whatever. I'll pick you up at two. But if you hate it after the first class, you're going to have to get a ride home."

"I won't hate it," Halli said. "I promise."

10

My body is my body no matter who happens to be inside it, so it took a little coaxing to get it to do what Halli wanted. But the yoga studio is always kept pretty warm for just that reason, to let people unclench, and so by the end of the first class Halli found what she was looking for from my limbs and my joints and my whole skeleton in general.

Lydia seemed amazed.

Not so much that I could do it, but that I even tried.

"Are you sure you want to stay?" she asked Halli after the two of them finished the first class. "I mean, you did great, but it's a lot of yoga for one day. You shouldn't try to push yourself or you'll be sore tomorrow. Then you won't come back."

Lydia had seen it before with people who came to

the studio all ready to change their lives, and went limping and groaning out, never to return.

But Halli had her own reasons for wanting to stay. Not just to do another round of yoga—she'd had her fill, and could have happily run home right then, since the studio was just a few miles from our house, and now she knew the way—but because she was avoiding someone. Two people, in fact.

Professor Whitfield and Albert were all hot to continue looking for me. And that required Halli. They wanted her to sit in my room and meditate to see if I made contact again.

But Halli had been thinking about it. Or really, feeling about it. She trusted her instincts, and this time her instincts told her it was no use. She had devoted hours over the previous week doing everything the professor suggested, trying to bring herself into some sort of resonance with me, but none of that had worked.

When I finally did show up, Halli knew she had nothing to do with it. She was just about to go for a run, when suddenly I dropped into my body and greeted her. She knew without a doubt she hadn't even been thinking of me at that moment.

She figured it was like a one-way valve: I could come in any time I wanted, but she couldn't go out. She couldn't send any kind of signals to reach me, and she couldn't leave my body. The professor and I had said as much, too. The former way Halli and I communicated was gone. It had died with Halli in that avalanche. Whatever new universe I'd created, I also formed some new path of communication that Halli wasn't in control of. It all rested with me.

Halli had tried to explain her feelings about that to Professor Whitfield the night before, but he didn't agree. He wanted her to keep trying, as many hours as she could every day, until she found me again.

So instead of arguing with the professor, Halli decided to just keep herself unavailable. She had her own strategy for what to do next, and it didn't involve sitting in my bedroom for hours upon end calling to me with her mind.

Halli was tired of her mind at the moment. What she wanted to do was move around in a body.

And besides, she was curious about Lydia. Halli knew from me that Lydia and I have been best friends since we were little, but that's mostly because our mothers are best friends. Lydia and I don't really have that much in common. Not the way Halli and I do.

But Halli saw something in Lydia that I've never really appreciated: a devotion to training her body in a particular way. I've always viewed Lydia's yoga obsession as sort of silly and impractical. What good is spending hours every day contorting yourself and sitting there trying to meditate, when you could be reading physics books and really feeding your mind?

Of course, that was before I took home one of the meditation CDs Lydia mentioned off-hand one day, and through that, accidentally ended up solving one of the biggest mysteries in physics by not only proving that parallel universes exist, but by actually going to one. And then even taking it one important step further by finding Halli, my own parallel self. So I guess yoga does have its uses. As long as you pair it with physics.

But in the same way I know Halli would have loved that two-hour insane workout this man named Ferguson put me through over on Halli's parents' island, I'm not surprised Halli really took to Lydia's yoga. It was another way of blocking out the noise of life for a while and just focusing on the pure mechanics of moving her—or my— body just right.

At the end of the second class, Halli was drenched in sweat, and smiling. She hadn't felt better all week. She finally, for the first time, felt almost like herself again. Even though she could see in the mirror all during class that she was clearly a different girl.

When Halli emerged from the yoga room, Lydia stuck out her hand. "Who are you? I don't believe we've met."

Halli froze for a second. But then she realized it was a joke.

"You're a good teacher," she said, shaking Lydia's hand. "Thank you."

Then she walked outside to cool off in the fresh air.

When she looked back through the glass doors, she could see Lydia watching her with a kind of confused look on her face. As if something felt … off. We all get used to how our friends talk, what they say, how they act, and if suddenly they seem down or nervous or different somehow, we pick up on it. At least if we're not totally self-absorbed, which I'll admit I've always secretly thought about Lydia. But maybe I've been wrong about her. Because maybe she did notice some subtle change that afternoon—something beyond just me deciding to try yoga all of the sudden.

But that change was nothing compared to what Lydia would see later that night.

11

I t was 6:30 by the time they arrived back at Lydia's house. My mom was already there, chatting with Elena in the kitchen. Will and the disgusting Gemma were in the living room, mildly bickering over some detail that had to with her parents' upcoming ball.

That's right, an actual ball. As in fancy dresses, men in tuxedos, a private orchestra, a ballroom, the whole thing.

Because her family is as ridiculous as she is. And as pretentious. A surprise 50th birthday for "Daddy" couldn't just be like a regular party. It had to involve engraved invitations to the right people, who would then have to spend crazy amounts of money for the proper clothes and some sort of extravagant gift that would justify having been invited to such a gala event.

Gemma let slip about the ball one night while we were all hanging out at Will's and Lydia's. It was clear Gemma hadn't intended to invite any of us except Will, but once she talked about it in front of us, even she knew she couldn't be so rude as not to invite us all. My mother and Elena politely declined, but not me. I was all over that invitation.

Why?

Because Gemma also let slip that her older brother, Colin, would be flying in from England to surprise his father. And in the same way that Gemma is a parallel version of Sarah, I knew this Colin would be the parallel version of Sarah's brother, Daniel. I just had to see what he was like—the whole idea of it was too juicy to pass up.

"You *will* wear the hat," Gemma was telling Will in her prim and proper British accent.

"If I have to wear it, I'm not coming," Will answered in a friendly, sort of teasing way.

Gemma gave him her best pout, then flipped her hair and pressed her chest into Will's side. It was the first time Halli had seen that particular move, so it didn't annoy her nearly as much as it always does me. Still, she could already tell Gemma was going to be quite the spectacle to watch.

"Lydia," Gemma said, seeing them come in, "you *must* tell your brother to do as I say."

"Do as she says," Lydia said dully. She didn't care

what Will did or didn't do. She usually didn't want to get involved in any of these discussions with Gemma.

"Audie girl, what are *you* wearing?" Gemma asked in her usual disdainful tone. "Something suitable, one hopes. Just this once." Then she tossed her hair again and winked.

And right there, Halli could see what I'd been talking about: that disgusting combination of meanness, superiority, and then the weird attempt to cover it up by looking cute. But instead of Halli wanting to stab out that winking eye with a plastic fork the way I usually want to, the whole display secretly cracked her up. From then on, it's like she settled in for the show. She wanted to see what this strange girl who looked like Sarah would do next.

Halli reached into the bowl of nuts Elena had set out on the coffee table, and popped some into her mouth. She gazed at Gemma with the same kind of neutral, emotionless expression she'd seen on camels' faces while they chewed their cud.

Gemma narrowed her eyes. "I'm quite serious, Audie. There will be important people at this ball—people my mother has invited. I'd like to be able to assure her that any of *my* guests will be dressed appropriately."

"I'm sure you would," Halli said. She scooped up another handful and chewed some more.

"So what are you wearing?" Gemma persisted. "I'd like to know."

"I can see that," Halli answered.

Will suppressed a smile. Lydia went ahead and snickered out loud.

"Will, make her answer me!" Gemma said.

"What are we talking about now?" Halli asked in such an off-handed way, it made Gemma even crazier.

"The ball! You know that!" she snapped. "And I am *asking* you—politely," she added for Will's benefit, "to assure me you'll buy, or if necessary *rent*—" She said it with such a tone of distaste, it was as if she could barely stand the idea of even knowing people who might have to rent their ball gowns. "—a dress that will not embarrass me in front of my parents or their friends."

Halli gazed back at Gemma coolly. And picked up another handful of nuts.

"Will, TELL HER TO ANSWER ME!"

Will reached over and squeezed his girlfriend's hand. "Gemma, enough," he said quietly. He gave Halli an apologetic look. "I'm sure Audie will look fine."

But Gemma still wasn't getting the message. Either that, or she just couldn't stop herself from constantly picking on me.

But Halli is not me. And Halli hadn't spent a year with this girl, putting up with all sorts of humiliation for the sake of getting to hang around Will.

Halli didn't care about Will. She didn't know him

any more than she knew Gemma. She had absolutely no stake in this game.

So when Gemma went on with, "It's a simple question, Will, and I think she can do me the courtesy of answering," Halli smiled. That same fake smile she'd been giving my mother.

"You're right," Halli said. "Courtesy is important. You should try it."

12

Halli left the living room and wandered back into the kitchen to see if she could help Elena with any cooking.

My mom and Elena had been eavesdropping the whole time. They both welcomed Halli with big grins and silent thumbs-up.

Halli shrugged. Considering everything she's been through in her life, it was no great achievement to stand up to some bratty girl—even though I've never managed to do that even once in the year since Gemma has been hanging around. Halli was just sorry to see how Gemma basically ruined Sarah's personality. Halli would have liked to spend time with her if she were normal.

"Do you need anyth—" Halli started to ask, but

Elena held her finger to her lips. The fight was still going on.

"She's *your* friend," they could hear Gemma saying. "If she can't act properly, she can't come!"

Will mumbled something Halli couldn't hear.

"I didn't *invite* her," Gemma said. "The girl practically invited herself! It's no surprise. She has no manners or taste."

"Shhh," they heard Lydia say.

"You did invite her," Will said. "Remember? I was here for it."

"Only under duress," Gemma answered. "The way she was *looking* at me."

Halli chuckled to herself. Gemma was everything I'd described, and worse.

"This is your fault anyway," Gemma continued. "Always trying to foist that girl on me, as if we have anything in common—"

"Just let it go," Will said. "I've told you: Audie is my friend. And Lydia's."

"Yes, and now who pays the price?" Gemma said. "Does that girl even *own* a proper dress?"

My mother made a face. "I forgot all about that," she whispered to Halli. "I meant to go shopping with you when I got back from my trip. But then you were sick—"

"She can borrow one of mine," they heard Lydia say in the other room. "Calm down."

"I suppose *you* have suitable clothes?" Gemma asked, a little more nicely.

"I won't embarrass you, if that's what you mean," Lydia answered.

The next thing they knew, Lydia turned up in the kitchen. She rolled her eyes at the assembled eavesdroppers.

"Hairball," she muttered, using our favorite nickname for Gemma.

"Where are you going?" they heard Gemma demand.

"To the bathroom!" Will answered. "If that's all right."

Lydia and the two moms snickered.

"And by the way," Will added, "I'm not wearing a top hat to this thing, so you can just forget it. I don't care what your friends from England are wearing. I live in Arizona, in the twenty-first century. We dress normally here."

"Will..." she whined.

"I'm renting a tux, and that's enough. But if that's not good enough for you, then maybe I shouldn't come, either." Then they all heard the bathroom door slam shut.

A few seconds later, there was a clattering against the wood. It sounded like Gemma had thrown a handful of nuts at the door.

"You know, honey," my mom said now that the

show in the living room seemed to be over, "we really do need to do something about a dress."

"No, we don't," Halli said, leaning comfortably against the counter. "I'm not going to whatever that is she's talking about."

"Excuse me?" Lydia said. "Of course you are! I'm not going by myself."

"You won't be by yourself," Halli pointed out. "Will and Gemma will be there."

"Very funny," she said. "You're going, Audie. Don't even think about trying to get out of it."

"I have better things to do with my time," Halli said.

"You have nothing to do with your time," Lydia said. "You're going."

Normally Halli had very little tolerance for being bossed. But she'd had a fun afternoon with Lydia, and so she was willing to overlook it.

"Why don't you show her your dress?" Elena suggested. "Dinner's still going to be a little while—you have time."

Lydia lit right up at that. "Come on." She tugged at Halli's sleeve until she willingly followed along.

Halli sat on Lydia's bed while Lydia pulled the dress out of her closet and modeled it on the hanger.

"Very nice," Halli said. The dress was light green, made of a delicate-looking fabric that fell in layers all the way to Lydia's feet. With her olive skin and long black hair, she'd look like a Greek goddess in that outfit.

"I still need shoes to go with it," Lydia said. "Now, what about you?"

"What about me?"

"Stand up," Lydia directed.

When Halli didn't comply right away, Lydia pulled her by the hand. Halli shook her head as she rose, faintly amused.

"I think I have a few that might work," Lydia said.

She fished in her closet for more long dresses and held up several of them in front of Halli. One was from the prom a year ago, two were bridesmaid dresses she had to get for two different cousins' weddings.

"Here," Lydia said. "Look." She was holding up the second bridesmaid dress. It was light blue, sleeveless, and didn't look half bad.

Halli pressed it against my torso and looked in the mirror. True, the dress wasn't awful. But that didn't change the fact that the ball itself sounded like a colossal waste of time.

"Why do you need me to go to this thing?" Halli asked.

"I don't *need* you to, but you said you would. Come on, I thought you said you wanted to see what her brother's like."

Now Halli remembered. I'd mentioned something about that—about Colin flying in for the party. And since Colin would be a parallel version of Daniel, now Halli was curious, too. She liked Daniel. She wouldn't mind seeing what he was like over in my universe, as long as it didn't interfere with her plans.

"When is this supposed to be?" Halli asked.

Lydia rolled her eyes. "You know when. This coming Saturday. Stop trying to get out of it. You know you really want to go."

"Frankly, I'd rather chew rocks."

"But you'll go," Lydia said.

"Yes," Halli conceded, "I'll go."

Lydia beamed. "Excellent. You can take the dress home tonight."

Halli handed it back to Lydia for the time-being, then headed for the door.

"Hey, what was all that, anyway?" Lydia asked. "That thing with Hairball?"

"What do you mean?"

"Don't get me wrong," Lydia said, "it was great. I'm all for anything that makes that girl's head nearly explode. Even Will looked like he thought it was funny. But I'm just ... surprised, you know?"

She looked at Halli as if waiting for some easy explanation. Like I'd been faithfully taking my Stand-Up-to-Gemma pills this whole time, and they'd finally kicked in.

And in a way, Halli's explanation was easy—it just wasn't what Lydia expected.

"People are interesting," she said.

Lydia waited, but that was all that Halli offered.

"And...?" Lydia tried.

But unlike me, Halli wasn't about to sit around and gossip about Gemma. It wasn't her style.

"And I'm hungry," she answered, opening the door.

"Audie?" Will said as soon as she emerged. "Can I talk to you?"

13

Halli suppressed a sigh. She wasn't very enthusiastic about talking to Will about anything—she really was hungry, for one thing, and would have preferred heading back to the living room for some more of those nuts—but she crossed the hall anyway and followed Will into his bedroom.

He closed his door behind them.

"Listen," Will said, keeping his voice low, "I'm really sorry about Gemma. She's been pretty stressed about this party, but it's no excuse for being rude to you."

Halli shrugged. It's a wonder how unoffended you can be when you don't really care about people's opinions.

And that went for Will's opinion, too. He seemed nice enough, even though he clearly had horrible taste in girlfriends. It was hard for Halli to respect someone like that.

Still, it was decent of him to say something, even though he wasn't the one who should apologize.

Halli looked around his room. It was full of laptops, monitors, and other computer equipment. Will owns his own business, doing house calls to fix people's computers. Sometimes he buys people's broken hardware so he can use it for parts, or fix it and resell it later.

Halli picked up a smartphone she found on one of the tables. Professor Whitfield had one just like it. She had watched him use it often during that day she spent with him in Colorado before she had to fly home and start pretending to be me.

"Just got that one this morning," Will said. "Owner dropped it in the toilet."

Halli quickly set the phone back down.

Will laughed. "I've already disinfected the case," he said. "Don't worry."

"What will you do with it?" Halli asked.

"Dry it out. Fix it. Sell it."

Halli didn't hesitate a second. "Sell it to me." She didn't have any money yet, but she had some ideas about how she was going to get it. And having a small tablet like that smartphone might be useful for her overall plan.

"I thought you didn't want one," Will said.

He was right. In fact, he and I had had a specific discussion about it not that long ago. He was teasing me about still using a flip phone. I explained that I didn't need all the fancy features of a smartphone—at least, not for the price.

But it wasn't just the price of the phone that held me back. I probably could have bought a used one from Will at any time. The problem was I couldn't justify in my own mind having our monthly cell phone bill go up, just so I could have a cooler phone. My mom needs hers because she travels so much, and it's easier to check her email and use the Internet without always having to carry her laptop with her, but what was my life like? It couldn't have been more basic: school, work, home. There was always a computer nearby. I didn't need an upgrade.

But Halli didn't know anything about that conversation. So all she could do was bluff. "I changed my mind. So how much do you want for it?"

Will tilted his head. "Come on, Aud. You seriously think I'm going to charge you? It's yours."

"No, you don't have to do that—"

"It's done," Will said. "Give me a few days with it and I'll turn it over."

Halli smiled. "All right, thanks. That's nice of you."

There was a knock on the door. Without waiting for an answer, Gemma stuck her face in.

"What are you two up to, then? Secret plans, hmm?"

She winked at Will and gave him an extra-energetic flip of her hair.

Halli didn't say anything. She just stood there expressionless, waiting for Gemma to leave.

"I've decided to forgive you," Gemma said to Will. "And no, you don't have to wear a hat. There. Better?" She made a pouty face. "Now please come back out and sit with me. I'm terribly bored."

Halli gave a snort. She had heard the Sarah version of this girl complain of being bored plenty of times, but somehow when Sarah said it, she sounded charming and fun. Nothing about Gemma was either charming or fun.

"We'll be out in a minute," Halli said, then she slowly started closing Will's door. Gemma had no choice but to back up into the hallway. As soon as Gemma's feet were clear, Halli shut the door in her face.

Will looked at her in amazement. Then he couldn't help but chuckle.

"Like I said," he repeated quietly, "I think she's a little stressed lately."

"Piece of advice," Halli said, not bothering to whisper. "I've seen girls like that before. Insecure, and the only way they can feel better about themselves is to try to make everyone else around them look bad. It's boring. You seem like a nice guy. You could do a lot better."

Will continued to stare at her in wonder. "Audie, what's going on with you tonight?"

"Nothing." She patted him on the arm. "Sometimes things just need to be said." Then she jerked open the door.

Gemma stumbled back. She caught herself, then gave Halli a furious look.

Halli turned back to Will. "Thanks again. I owe you a favor."

She didn't even bother acknowledging Gemma as she strode right past her.

Gemma muttered her one-word assessment of what I was.

"Gemma," Will said wearily. "Just don't."

14

When Halli and my mom got back from dinner, Halli found several urgent messages from Professor Whitfield. She waited until my mom was in the shower before she called him back.

His face popped up on the screen after only a few rings.

"Where have you been?" he asked. "We've been calling you all day. Has something happened?"

"No, I had things to do."

"Things to ... Halli, don't you understand? We need to establish the connection again. As soon as possible."

Halli sighed. She'd been avoiding this conversation because she knew the professor probably wouldn't understand. Or agree.

"I don't know how to explain it to you," she said, "but I just know: It has to come from Audie this time. There's nothing I can do to contact her. It's like you said yesterday—we have a new kind of connection now. And I'm telling you, no amount of me sitting here and concentrating is going to bring her back. If she ever does come back, it's because she's done it on her own."

The professor was quiet. He stroked his beard. Then he closed his eyes for a moment and pinched his fingers against them.

"I don't know," he finally said. "You might be right—I just don't know. But it doesn't feel right not to keep trying."

"I know," Halli said. "I thought so, too, at first. But the more I think about it, the more I think I'm right. I'm sorry, Professor," she added. "I don't want it to be this way, either."

Now it was Professor Whitfield's turn to sigh. "So what do you want to do next?"

Halli almost laughed at that. Her list was long.

But she dealt with the most practical problem first.

"Do I really have to go to Audie's school tomorrow? Is there any way out of it?"

"Not if we're going to convince people you're her. And buy ourselves some time."

Because the professor had a problem—a huge problem. Halli didn't understand all of it, because it involved issues that never would have come up in her world. But if it had been me talking to the professor, I would have understood right away.

I was a minor. I wouldn't turn 18 for another few months. And that meant Professor Whitfield needed my mom's permission to do all those tests he ran on me the previous weekend when I came to visit him at his college in Colorado.

The truth is, I tricked him. I told him my mom knew all about it—I even let him buy her a plane ticket to come with me. But all along I knew I'd be coming alone, and that I'd bring a forged letter from her saying she gave him permission to test me.

Because up until then, I still didn't have the courage to tell my mother anything about what was going on— that I'd found a parallel universe, that I'd found my parallel self, that Halli and I were having the times of our lives, or at least my life, doing things like hiking together in the Alps. It was an amazing sequence of events, and I was afraid to tell her about any of it. Because I was pretty sure she'd stop me from ever doing it again.

So when Professor Whitfield suggested my mom and I come out to Mountain State College where he had loads of intricate equipment that he could use to test my brain function and physical reactions and all sorts of other things while I was interacting with the parallel universe, I said yes, of course. In part because I wasn't going to pass up the chance to learn more, but also because I was hoping Professor Whitfield would verify for me that everything I was doing was safe. Then once I had that assurance in hand, *then* I would tell my mother.

But of course it all fell apart. During one of the experiments I managed to cast my mind three days into the future, where I watched Halli about to be killed in an avalanche. I didn't have time to say goodbye to anyone, I just reacted: I used the laws of physics—or maybe twisted them, depending on how someone sees it—and catapulted some aspect of me out of that room where I sat with Professor Whitfield, out across the blinding white snowstorm where Halli was about to die.

But now I know I didn't save her. Not really. I saved some essence of her, which was now stuck inside my body in a universe where Halli didn't belong. And at the same time I appeared to have created this new parallel universe where I was currently a prisoner, too. Not exactly the result I'd been going for.

But the problem for Professor Whitfield was that if he couldn't find a way to help me reverse the whole thing, and return myself to my own proper body, he was going to have a lot of explaining to do one day soon. Starting with why he conducted tests on a 17-

year-old girl when he'd already started suspecting she might have lied to him about her mother.

Lose his job? Of course. Find himself arrested? Who knows? But no matter what, if the truth came out, he knew his career would be ruined. My mother might even sue him for losing her daughter somewhere out in the ether, and then he'd lose everything he had.

And aside from all that, Professor Whitfield just honestly wanted to fix this. He wasn't the kind of man to say, "Oh, well, lost another one. Next!" He'd barely been sleeping. He and Albert had spent more time together in the last week than most married couples do, trying desperately to work out the physics of what had happened. The two of them were obsessed with solving the problem.

So for Halli to basically say, "No, done with all that, felt like taking the day off"—no wonder Professor Whitfield had panicked.

But now he was quite a bit calmer. And ready to enter into a new phase of deciding how to deal with things.

"You have her class list," he confirmed with Halli.

"Yes. And I know where the school is. But I really think this is a mistake."

"I know you do," the professor answered. "But I don't know how else to handle it right now. You have to do your best."

"For how long?" Halli asked.

"According to your theory, that depends on Audie, doesn't it?"

It wasn't what Halli wanted to hear. But that didn't mean it wasn't the truth.

Ginny raised Halli to know the difference.

15

The wave catapulted Halli out of bed.

Then she heard Ginny scream.

Halli felt disoriented at first. It was dark in the little cabin of the boat, and she wasn't on the bed anymore. She and everything else that wasn't tied down had slammed into the left side of the cabin and now lay there in a heap.

"Halli! Halli!"

She scrambled toward the hatch above.

Another wave hit the boat, tilting it sickeningly onto its side. Halli waited for the boat to right itself, then she pushed open the hatch and quickly climbed onto the deck. She slammed the hatch behind her to keep the cabin from flooding.

Halli peered into the darkness. "Where are you?"

"Here!" Ginny shouted. "Hurry!"

Halli rushed to the side of the boat. Ginny dangled halfway into the water, clinging to a rope.

Halli started to pull on Ginny's arms, but her grandmother screamed.

"What's wrong?" Halli shouted.

"Broken!" Ginny shouted back. "Tie in! Another wave!"

Halli barely had time to snap the harness around her waist before another wave smashed into the boat. She skidded across the deck, scrabbling for anything she could hold on to.

When she looked over the side again, Ginny was all the way in the water. Halli reached out and grabbed the nearest thing she could, a fistful of her grandmother's hair. She pulled until Ginny came up sputtering.

"Come on!" Halli shouted, leaning out further to capture Ginny's arm. Ginny screamed. Halli kept pulling. The most important thing was getting Ginny safely back on the boat. They could deal with any injury later.

Finally Ginny lay sprawled on the deck, cradling her arm and howling with pain.

"Let me see," Halli said, trying to force Ginny onto her back. Ginny resisted. "Let me see!" Halli demanded.

Ginny gave in and let Halli turn her. But she still guarded her right arm, holding it protectively against her chest.

Halli began feeling along the arm for where the break was. When she couldn't find it, she tested the bones above. Finally Ginny flinched.

"It's your collar bone," Halli said.

Ginny cursed.

She was going to be useless from then on, and they both knew it.

And they were still days away from land. How many days depended on the wind, the currents, the weather, and how far Ginny and Halli could row each day. But now it would be just Halli at the oars.

A girl who, no matter how hardy and competent she was, was still only twelve years old.

Halli sat back on her heels and assessed their situation. It was nighttime. The sea was choppy—more than choppy, with big waves hitting the boat every few minutes—but at least she could see stars in a clear sky, which meant there wasn't the immediate threat of a storm. They were alone in the middle of the Atlantic. Just as they had been for the past 86 days. And this was just the latest in a long string of difficulties:

The shark that had stalked them for three days. Food that washed overboard. Storms that nearly capsized the boat. Broken oars. Lack of sleep. Ginny's bruised rib after a wave rammed one of the oars into it. The swelling in Halli's forearms whenever she rowed for more than three hours at a time. The cuts and sores that never seemed to heal in the wet, salty conditions. And now this.

Things happen, Ginny always taught Halli. *That's life. Now what are you going to do about it?*

There was no point in wishing things were different—they weren't. Halli had to get to work. She tightened the harness around Ginny's waist. If she hadn't been wearing it during her shift, she would have been lost to the waves before Halli even knew about it.

"I'm going to go get supplies," Halli told her. "I'll be right back."

She opened the hatch and climbed down into the cabin. The first aid kit still sat safely secured against the wall. Halli pulled it away, then rummaged in one of the cabinets beneath it for the long strips of cloth she'd need to sling Ginny's arm. Then Halli took her supplies above.

She handed Ginny a couple of pain pills and a thermos of purified water. She strapped a light across her own forehead so she could see the injury better. The area around Ginny's collar bone already looked bruised and inflamed. But at least no bones had broken through the skin.

"I think I cut my foot, too," Ginny said, holding it up for Halli to inspect. The bottom of it dripped blood. But not enough blood to pose a serious threat.

"Let me take care of your arm first," Halli said. Ginny had trained her in first aid. Already the girl had been called upon to use far more than either of them would have liked. But it was better to know than not know, Ginny always said—better than pretending nothing bad would ever happen. Bad things happened all the time. *You'll feel better if you know you what to do.*

Halli knew that even though it was Ginny's collar bone that was broken, the best way to take weight off it and reduce the pain was to sling the arm on the broken side. Once she finished that, she cleaned and bandaged Ginny's foot.

"How do you feel?" she asked her grandmother after it was all over.

"Like hell," Ginny said. She leaned back and closed her eyes. Then she reached over and patted Halli's leg. "Thank you. You did great."

Halli slumped down next to her grandmother and let out a long, weary breath. The adrenaline that had carried her through the crisis was starting to wear off, and now a deep exhaustion set in. She hadn't slept her full three hours while Ginny was supposed to be rowing, and she had the feeling she wouldn't be sleeping again any time soon.

"Let's talk," Ginny said. "We need a plan."

Halli simply nodded. Then neither of them spoke again for several long minutes.

Another wave battered the boat, and Halli instinctively grabbed onto Ginny's harness to make sure she stayed put.

That seemed to jar both of them out of their stupor.

"We could call for help," Ginny said.

"We could," Halli agreed. She'd already been thinking about that.

"It might take them days to get to us."

"I know," Halli said. It wasn't as if they were rowing across a lake where all the boats were reasonably grouped together. Halli knew the various teams were spread out over the ocean, all of them heading in the same general direction, but still hundreds of miles apart from each other. She and Ginny hadn't seen a single other person since starting out three months ago. The only reason they knew there were still other teams out there rowing was that they could follow their tracking information each day.

Last time Halli checked, the race's support boat was far north of them. It had been sent to rescue Team Gray, whose boat had started leaking after a particularly aggressive shark repeatedly rammed into it.

"Or you could keep rowing," Ginny said. "By yourself."

Halli closed her eyes again. "I could."

The two lapsed back into silence.

Finally Ginny said, "I know you could do it, Halli. You're a strong girl and you know how to navigate. But it's up to you."

Halli gazed across the wide expanse of ocean toward the sunrise just beginning to peek over the horizon. She had been looking at that same basic scenery—the ocean, the sky, the boat, her grandmother—forever now, it seemed. She had battled fear, exhaustion, pain, boredom, but she'd also felt moments of great joy. Of great pride and satisfaction in what she was accomplishing. So far these had been the most intense three months of her life.

"Do you really think I could?" Halli asked her grandmother.

"I wouldn't let you do it if I didn't think so," Ginny said. "I wouldn't risk either of our lives that way."

"But what about my arms?" Halli asked. "The way they swell up?"

"You'll have to take breaks," Ginny said. "Lots of them. And sleep every chance you can get. You can throw out the anchor to hold us in place every time you rest."

Halli thought about it for a while longer. She wasn't competitive—that wasn't the issue. She didn't care whether they came in fifth or fifteenth in the race. A few of the other teams—the ones with four rowers—had already crossed the finish line. She didn't care.

But she did care about completing the journey if they could. She knew Ginny had looked forward to rowing the Atlantic for a long time. She had waited for years until she thought Halli was old enough to go with her.

"All right," Halli said, her voice betraying how tired she really was. "Let's try."

"All right," Ginny agreed.

"But if you're in too much pain, or if you think you need to go to a doctor sooner—"

"I'll manage," Ginny said. She smiled at her granddaughter and patted her leg again.

Then she lost the smile and switched back to that tough tone Halli was used to. "Better get to it, then. This boat isn't going to row itself."

16

I t was Monday back in my world, and Halli showed up to my school covered in sweat.

"Overslept again, huh?" Winslow Henry said with a smirk.

"Excuse me?" Halli answered. She'd been just about to walk in to my first-period class—Algebra I—when this short, scrawny guy started talking to her.

"You're sweating again," Winslow said. The last time he'd seen me like that was a few weeks before, when I was still trying to deal with the time zone difference of meeting Halli in the Alps every night. On one of the mornings after, I accidentally slept through my first two classes and had to race to make it to school by the third. I showed up all sweaty and breathless. And since

Winslow is in both my first and third periods, he knew that I'd missed. And since Winslow is Winslow, he enjoyed giving me a hard time about it.

But Halli had plenty of time to get to school that morning. It's just that in her case, she chose to strap on my backpack and run all the way there instead of taking the bus or asking my mom for a ride.

Not that she felt any need to explain that to Winslow. But she did see the opportunity he presented. She followed him into class and decided to stick close. Maybe if she kept him talking, she could pick up a few hints about what she was supposed to do.

Most of the desks were already filled, but there were a few empty ones toward the back. Winslow sat in his usual spot, and Halli picked a desk across the aisle.

"Why are you sitting there?" Winslow asked.

Halli shrugged. "Felt like it. Where do you want me to sit?"

Winslow scoffed. "Like I care." But Halli saw his eyes dart to the desk behind him. Winslow is one of those people who needs things always to be the same, predictable. I know, because I'm usually one of those people, too.

Halli casually picked up my backpack and switched desks. She could see Winslow relax.

He and I have a strange relationship. Not exactly friends—in fact, not at all—but more like two people who recognize a fellow sufferer.

Some people's brains just don't accept math. I have really come to believe that. And obviously Winslow's and my brains are completely resistant. Which is fine, if you view algebra as a disease, which I do. Not fine if you need the math credits to get accepted into an elite college you've had your eye on for years, or even into a semi-elite college like the one Winslow's parents want him to go to. As a result, he and I have been like two crabby inmates who strike up an unlikely friendship, but never really like each other.

The bell rang, and the teacher began. And for about the first ten minutes, Halli was sort of interested. Interested in her surroundings, at least.

She gazed around the room at my fellow classmates. Took in the kind of clothes they wore, the way they did their hair here on my home planet, the kinds of personalities she could see, just by how people sat in their chairs. She could tell which people were afraid of being noticed and called on, and which ones hoped they would be.

Halli wasn't afraid of math. Not the way I am. It's just that she didn't think of it as "algebra" or "geometry" or any other formal discipline. She used it like she used anything else in her life: for practical purposes. She could calculate distances, plot out angles and trajectories—anything she might need for navigation.

So she sat in class the way I never do, unafraid, relaxed, just taking in everything around her.

And Ms. Gonzales obviously noticed. Maybe she assumed from Halli's confident posture that I knew the answer for once.

"Audie?" It took Halli a second to remember that meant her.

"Yes?"

Ms. Gonzales pointed to the formula on his white board. "The solution?"

"I don't know," Halli said pleasantly.

"Well, give it a try."

"I really can't," she said.

Ms. Gonzales wasn't used to that from me. Usually I'll torture myself through some problem and at least try to find the answer. But Ms. Gonzales knew she'd reached a dead end, and she wasn't going to keep badgering me, just to make me look stupid. She isn't a bad person, she just teaches a bad subject.

"Okay, how about you, Winslow?"

His voice came out squeaky and high. "Uh ... y equals ... six?"

"No, sorry," Ms. Gonzales said, then she gave up and called on some girl who'd been waving her hand in the air.

Winslow Henry kicked his foot backward against Halli's chair. Usually that's my signal to kick him in return.

Instead Halli leaned forward and whispered, "Is this how it is every day?"

Winslow half-turned in his seat and gave her a sour look. "Yeah, genius. What kind of a stupid question is that?"

Halli looked at the clock. According to the schedule Albert had sent her, she still had forty-four minutes left to sit there.

Her life was slipping away.

THREE DAYS AFTER SHE MADE THE DECISION TO KEEP rowing, Halli knew she'd made a mistake.

It wasn't the physical labor—as impossible as that was, she was doing it.

It was Ginny: she was getting worse.

"I think your foot's infected," Halli said once she removed the bandage to inspect it. The wound looked red and swollen, and the skin around it felt hot. The rest of Ginny felt too warm, too, like she had a fever.

"I'll be fine," Ginny said. "Get some sleep. Did you eat?"

Halli nodded, even though she hadn't eaten in hours. She'd been rowing harder and longer since that morning, when she first suspected Ginny might be sick.

Halli searched through the first aid kit for any kind of pills that might help. "Take these," she said, handing a few to Ginny.

"How much farther?" Ginny asked, swallowing them down with some water.

"Not far," Halli said. Which was far from the truth. Halli had spent the whole previous day rowing into a stiff wind. She barely made any progress.

"How many more days?" Ginny pressed.

"Just a few."

Ginny closed her eyes and leaned back onto the bed. "Good girl," she said softly. "Keep going."

She reached shore on day 92. Her arms looked like balloons. She could barely bend her wrists anymore. The skin on her palms looked ripped and raw. She was dehydrated, malnourished, badly sunburned from head to toe, and exhausted beyond all measure.

Ginny was a wreck, too.

And the history reporters were there to meet them.

"Virginia Markham! Halli Markham!" one of the reporters shouted, filming them through a camera that looked like square binoculars. Halli didn't know it at the time, but that reporter was named Bryan Stewart, and I was going to meet him later—just a few weeks ago now—at Halli's parents' private island, where he came to report on their board meeting. It was Bryan who, along with Jake and Sarah, ended up bursting into the room where Daniel and I were hiding while I tried to contact Halli again.

The world is a circular place. We all seem to come around to each other again.

"Halli Markham!" he shouted. "How do you feel?"

Halli didn't have words to spare. She let the race

workers at the dock help her and Ginny off the boat, then she stood on rubbery legs trying to get used to the feeling of stable, unmoving land.

"We're taking your grandmother to the clinic," one of the race people told Halli. "You should go, too."

Halli nodded. Then collapsed to her knees. She had used up absolutely every ounce of energy she had rowing them to shore those last few days. But she'd done it: completed something she knew Ginny wanted completed.

"Halli Markham," Bryan tried again, "anything you want to say to all the people out there?"

But Halli was already asleep on the rough wet wood of the dock.

THAT WAS THE GIRL WHO CURRENTLY SAT IN MY algebra class. World adventurer, world explorer, confined to a hard, uncomfortable desk in a rundown high school classroom, sentenced to listening to my teacher and my classmates discuss whether $x=y$ for nearly an hour.

I'm surprised she even lasted that long.

When the bell finally rang, Halli got up with the rest of the students and left class.

Then she kept on going. Down the hall, out through the double doors, out onto the campus.

She glanced around her, saw that no one was particularly watching. Why would they? I was nothing to most of those people.

Which was a good thing for Halli. She wasn't used to being anonymous, and she was starting to really appreciate the advantages of it.

She shouldered my pack and took off at a run.

17

Halli treated herself to a long and satisfying run.

The weather was perfect: sunny and a little bit cold. It was the kind of autumn morning when Halli loved being out in the wilderness, just hiking alone with her dog.

She missed Red. She knew he was alive—I'd told her so—and also knew that I would take as good care of him as I could.

What she didn't know was that the two of us were currently separated—that in the chaos of me being taken to the hospital, I'd lost track of him somehow and now I wasn't sure where he was. I had some vague memory of Daniel promising to take care of him, but I wasn't sure if that were really true, or just wishful thinking. It was probably best that Halli didn't know anything about it. With Ginny gone, that dog was her only real friend. And Halli felt as protective of him as Ginny used to feel about her.

It had been a week since Halli rowed the Team Red boat ashore. She wandered alone in the marketplace searching for some treat to bring back to Ginny, who was still confined to the clinic.

Halli stood at one of the stalls examining earrings made out of shells when she felt something soft brush against her bare foot. She looked down and saw a small yellow creature. She crouched to get a better look.

It was a puppy, maybe just six or seven weeks old, so small she could almost cup him between her hands. And so skinny she could see every one of his ribs. A thin rope hung around his neck, tying him to the base of the stall. Halli stroked the puppy's soft head. He gazed up at her with goopy, sad eyes.

"You like him?" the merchant asked.

"What's wrong with him?" Halli asked.

"Nothing wrong! Very young—like you! You like him? He likes you! You should buy."

Halli sat cross-legged on the ground. The puppy instantly crawled into her lap. He curled up in a little ball while Halli continued softly stroking his head. His little body trembled against her legs.

"You like him?" the man asked again. "You should buy."

Halli stared down at the tiny bundle. She understood Ginny's policy about animals—it was the same as her policy about anything in their lives: *If you have something, use it. If you don't use it, don't have it.*

Halli had already had to make a hard choice once about an animal she loved.

When Halli was little, she had a horse named Samson. She adored him. She spent hours every day riding him, brushing him, even lying on his wide back as he rested in his stall. But over time, as Halli grew older and she and Ginny began going on longer and longer expeditions, Samson had to be stabled where there were other horses and people to take care of them.

"Is that fair to Samson?" Ginny asked her young granddaughter. "He loves you, but you hardly see him. Don't you think he might want some other girl to be his friend now, and ride him every day and love him the way you do?"

Reluctantly, Halli gave him away. And she hadn't felt the urge ever to go through that again with any other animal.

But she'd never held such a small creature in her hands, an animal whose eyes seemed bigger than his body, eyes that were staring straight into hers now.

"How much?" Halli heard herself ask.

The man named his price. It sounded ridiculously high.

"I don't have that much," Halli said.

"You Halli Markham?" the man asked.

Halli nodded, hoping he would be like so many of the other islanders who had treated her so well over the past week, giving her free food and lots of little gifts.

But the man obviously saw an opportunity. "Halli Markham is famous. You want, you pay." He stuck to his price.

The dog was panting now, still looking at Halli with those deep brown eyes.

"I have the money in my room," she said. "I'll bring it right back." She started to untie the rope around the puppy's neck.

The man stopped her. "You leave him. You bring money first."

Halli could see there was no negotiating with the man. She gently set the puppy back on the dirt. "Don't give him to anyone else," she said.

The man laughed.

Halli took off at a run. The puppy yelped at first, then the yelps turned into a mournful howl the further she ran away.

"I'll be right back!" Halli shouted to the puppy, but his howl grew even more desperate.

She raced back to the inn where she was staying,

and into her small seaside room. She rummaged through her bag until she found the coin purse she'd hidden inside one of her socks. She counted out the money, poured it into a different sock, then raced back toward the marketplace and the stall at the end of the row.

The man laughed when he saw Halli tearing toward him. The puppy yowled with a voice so big it seemed impossible his little lungs could produce it.

"He say he want to be on Team Red!" the merchant laughed. Halli didn't think it was funny. She just wanted to get the puppy and herself away from that man as soon as possible.

She poured her coins into his open palm, then quickly untied the puppy. She scooped him into her arms, which immediately calmed him down.

"You be nice girl to that dog now," the man said.

Halli turned away in disgust. She carried away her prize, cradling him close against her chest.

"When's the last time you ate?" she whispered to the puppy. "Huh? Let's go get you some food and water. I'll wash out your eyes. I'll make you a nice soft bed. Then we'll go visit Ginny—she's going to love you. Everything's going to be all right, little Red." *Team Red.* "You're mine now."

The puppy licked Halli's chin. And that was it for both of them: true and everlasting love.

I only wish I could say I was doing a better job of taking care of him for her. But I had my own problems at the moment.

18

"Halli? Can you hear me?" The doctor shined a light in my eyes.

I moaned.

"Halli? Miss Markham?" she tried again.

It was too much trouble. Too much trouble to climb out of my fog, to stay awake, to open my eyes and deal with whatever was going on.

"I think she heard you," Jake said.

"Halli," Dr. Rios repeated more sternly this time. "You have to wake up now. I need to examine you. Look at me. Right now."

The woman was annoyingly persistent. Clearly she wasn't going away. I slowly pried my eyes open, just barely enough to squint. Even that hurt my head. The room was so bright the light almost felt noisy. I groaned and shut my eyes again.

"Halli?" Jake tried. "It's me. I'm right here." He sounded worried. Good. Served him right.

"Where's ... Daniel?" I asked. Three syllables that felt monumental to get out.

"No, it's me, Halli. It's Jake."

Yes, I know who you are. You're not the one that I want. You're the one who caused all this. You and your stupid jealousy over Daniel. Daniel's no threat to you—he won't even kiss me. Even though he knows it's me inside here, he can't bring himself to cheat on me with *me*. Not while I look like Halli. So go away. You've done enough.

But the most I could manage was, "Wah..."

"Water?" Dr. Rios guessed.

I gave her the slightest of nods. A nurse came around to the side of the bed and gently fit a straw between my lips. She told me to suck in and I tried, but it hurt too much. I gave up.

"You can hear me now, yes?" Dr. Rios asked. I still couldn't figure out her accent. Middle eastern or Mediterranean or something.

"Yes," I croaked in my gravelly voice.

"Do you know where you are?"

"Hospital."

"Very good. What city?"

"London."

"Excellent," Dr. Rios said. So far I'd mastered her quiz.

I had a question for her. "How ... long?"

"How long have you been here?" she said. "Three days."

Somehow that just sounded gross. Like I'd been stuck under a layer of mud for three days straight. Mud seeping into my eyes, my throat, my mind. I still couldn't think clearly.

And Halli's body just wanted to sleep.

"No, you need to stay awake now," Dr. Rios said, seeing my eyes start to close again. "I'm going to examine you. Mr. Demetrios, you can wait outside."

Jake squeezed my hand. "I'll be back, Halli. I won't leave you."

"Get ... Daniel," I tried again.

"Forget Daniel," Jake said. "I'm here."

Aarg. So frustrating. But obviously I was asking the wrong person.

I waited for Jake to leave. Then said the name again.

The doctor was busy shining her stupid light into my eyes.

I reached up and grabbed her wrist. "Daniel," I said as clearly as I could. "Please."

But all that effort was too much. Halli's body needed a nap. So it was back under the mud for me.

19

After escaping from my school, Halli ran for miles, hoping to clear her mind and come up with a better idea. This plan of Professor Whitfield's that she sit in my classes every day while life went on without her wasn't going to cut it. Just that short sample of it made Halli feel so restless, she thought she might jump out of my skin on her own, even before I came back to claim it. Halli was made for movement. School might as well have been a prison.

"What are you doing home?" Professor Whitfield asked when Halli was finally able to reach him. He had his own classes to teach. The two of them weren't supposed to talk until later that afternoon.

"It won't work," Halli said.

"Why? What happened?"

"Nothing happened," she said. "I went there, I pretended to be her, and I can see it isn't going to work. We have to think of something else. Right away."

"Halli..." The professor tried to talk some sense into her. Tried for fifteen minutes straight. But Halli's mind was made up.

"This isn't my life," she said. "I have other things to do."

"Like what?" the professor demanded. He had lost patience with her. She didn't seem to understand what needed to be done.

"I think I should come back there," Halli said.

"Back ... where?"

"To Colorado. To your college. I think it's the only smart move."

The professor wasn't expecting that. But he didn't immediately dismiss it.

"I've been thinking about it," Halli went on, determined to make her case. "As long as I'm here, we'll always have to be careful. Sneak around. Make sure Audie's mother doesn't know anything. But if I can somehow come live out there—"

"How, Halli?" the professor asked. "Audie is still in high school."

"Can't she ... leave? I don't know how it works."

At some point during the conversation, Albert had come into Professor Whitfield's office. He'd been sitting on the couch, listening in. Now he stood to make his face visible on the screen.

"Halli? Hold on a minute."

Albert booted up his laptop and started typing. He studied his screen for a while, then turned it so Professor Whitfield could see.

"What is it?" Halli asked.

"Just a minute," the professor said. He wrote a few numbers on a piece of paper. He looked at Albert's screen a few more times.

"What?" Halli said.

"Just a minute!" they both answered.

Finally Albert smiled.

"Okay, there's a possibility," Professor Whitfield said. He let Albert take his spot in front of the computer and explain it all to Halli.

"It's a good thing Audie's a geek," Albert said. "She's taken summer school the past three years. She already has enough credits to graduate. She didn't even need to take any of her senior year."

"So I can leave?" Halli asked.

"Well ... almost," Albert said.

There are things you do in your life that you think will only have consequences at the moment. Things you do your best at, not realizing that if you fail, some other person's life might hang in the balance.

I'd been trying for three and a half years to get past Algebra I. I had high hopes for finally doing it my senior year—okay, maybe not *high* hopes, but some hope at least—and I really was trying hard.

But now Halli was going to have to pay the price for my utter inability to pass that one stupid class.

Because the only thing standing between her and ever having to go back to high school?

Math.

20

"Just that one class," Halli repeated.

"Right," Albert said.

"So I have to sit there day after day just for that. No. I won't do it."

"Audie can't graduate without it," Albert said.

"And they won't admit you here if you don't have it," Professor Whitfield said. "I'm sorry, Halli. It's a requirement on both ends."

Halli took a break to lie back onto my bed. What she needed was another run or some kind of exercise. Her head was too jumbled. She needed to clear it.

She could hear Albert and Professor Whitfield discussing something in the background. She didn't care anymore. This whole thing was so ridiculous. She had absolutely zero interest in making sure I completed high school. But she did care very much about escaping to Colorado. It had seemed like the perfect plan.

For several reasons, including a few she wasn't ready to share with the professor just yet.

"Halli?" Professor Whitfield said.

She lifted her head up just enough to see the screen. "Yes?"

"Albert reminded me there is one more possibility."

She tried to muster some optimism. "All right, let's hear it."

"Do you think you could learn algebra?" Albert asked. "If you studied it on your own?"

"I don't know," she said, sitting up all the way now. "Why?"

"There's a kind of test you can take," Albert said. "It's called a CLEP test—College Level Examination Program. It's a way to get out of taking certain classes in college. I used it a lot in undergrad—got out of a couple of Humanities courses, Bio I, Calc I and II—"

"You realize I don't know what you're talking about."

"Oh, sorry," Albert said. "Bottom line is you study up on a subject, take a few practice exams, and then when you think you're ready, you take the real one. Multiple choice, ninety-minute test. And if you pass, you get credit for the course, just like you took it."

"But you said that's for college," Halli said.

"Yeah, but now they let home schoolers use them,

and some high schools accept the scores, too. From what I just read on Audie's school website, it looks like they do. So if you think you might be able to learn algebra on your own..."

A smile spread across Halli's face. Because she knew exactly how she was going to do it.

When Halli was nine, Ginny decided it was time for her to learn Russian. Not only to speak it—Halli had already learned various phrases during their travels—but to read it and write it, too.

Ginny treated it like a game. Every day she presented Halli with a new set of sentences featuring those strange letters from the Russian alphabet. None of them made any sense to Halli. But what did start to make sense were the patterns.

She learned to recognize certain symbols as they combined to make words: This set meant "Hello." This set meant "Goodbye." This set meant "Thank you."

Ginny's challenge every day was for Halli to translate those symbols as fast as she could, starting with the ones she'd learned the day before and the day before that. So Halli was always building, always improving. Ginny wouldn't let her go on to a new set until she'd mastered the old ones.

And just as Ginny suspected, once she turned it into a game like that—best of all, a speed game—Halli learned in rapid time. Words led to phrases, which led to sentences. Soon she could read a Russian newspaper with no difficulty at all.

Now it was Halli's turn to apply the method. To symbols as foreign to her as the Russian alphabet had once been.

She explained her strategy.

"You know, I've heard of that," Albert said. "Some teacher in Japan came up with a way to speed-teach math that sounds just like that."

"So you'll help me?" Halli asked.

"Of course," Professor Whitfield said. "What do you need?"

"Worksheets," Albert interrupted. "Lots and lots of them. You start with the basics, then you keep drilling them until you're ready for the next and then the next—"

"Good," Halli said. "Send me whatever I need. I'll start work right away."

If it sounded too easy, that was about to change. Because there was one more detail they had to take care of.

"You need permission," Professor Whitfield said.

"Permission for what?" Halli asked. She wasn't accustomed to asking anyone permission for anything.

"The school will have to agree to accept the test as credit. And they'll have to agree to let you—or Audie—graduate early."

Halli blew out a breath. "Fine. What do I have to do?"

Albert looked up the name of the three counselors at my school. "One of them can probably process the paperwork."

Halli wrote down their names and slipped the paper into a pocket.

"Anything else?"

"Well, there's Audie's mother," Albert pointed out.

"You'll need her permission, too," Professor Whitfield agreed.

Halli was growing more irritated by the minute. She had been completely independent for the past year of her life. And before that, Ginny treated her like an adult long before anyone else might have. Halli wasn't used to a life like mine, where you constantly have to ask and negotiate for what you want. Halli was used to doing and having and getting.

"Send me the worksheets," she told Albert before clicking off the call. Then she made herself a quick snack of peanut butter and banana, refilled her water bottle, and took off at a run, heading back toward my school.

Where she fully intended to get exactly she wanted.

21

"You'll regret it," Mrs. Brussell, the school counselor, said. "You'll miss your friends. You shouldn't be in such a hurry, Audie. This time in your life is precious."

Halli listened politely, then repeated her request. "I'd like to start the process now. What do I need to do?"

Mrs. Brussell tried one more thing.

"Audie, I think we both know from your grades that the chances of you passing an algebra test on your own are ... not good."

"That will be up to me to manage," Halli said, trying to keep the coldness out of her voice. She wondered how I could stand having people try to push me around all the time, telling me what I could and couldn't do.

What I was capable of. It made Halli want to grind my teeth.

But she forced herself to be civil. "Now," she said, giving Mrs. Brussell her standard fake smile, "you said you have a form for my mother to sign?"

Mrs. Brussell was no match for the will and determination of Halli Markham. But Halli knew my mother would be a harder challenge.

She spent the rest of the afternoon thinking about it. Trying out certain ways of phrasing it, of arguing her point. She imagined all my mother's objections, and tried to think of responses to all of them. But she knew that no matter how logical she was, this would still be difficult. The problem was, she didn't really know my mother.

If it had been Halli's mother, Halli wouldn't have even bothered asking for her permission. She would have done what she wanted and ignored anything either of her parents wanted.

But in my world, Halli was dependent. She hated that. But the fact was, until she could earn her own money somehow and move somewhere where she could live on her own, she had to take my mother into consideration. She couldn't burn that bridge. Not yet.

And I don't mean that she didn't like my mother. She just didn't know her. My mom seemed really pleasant, really nice, but Halli had no feelings toward her. It was as if my mom were just some roommate living in the same house. A roommate who bought all the groceries and paid all the bills.

Halli knew that the sooner she could move to Colorado, the sooner she could begin her independent life. It wasn't just about getting out from under my mom's watchful eye, the way she'd told the professor. It was really about Halli's plan for how she was going to make some money.

Because in her various hours spent searching the Internet, she'd been doing a different kind of math than algebra: calculating what it would cost to travel to all the places she wanted to visit, like India and Iceland and the Alps, and how much it would cost to find lodging there. So far she'd mapped out a series of trips that would cost her about $4,500. She wasn't sure how long it would take her to earn that much money, but she knew the sooner she got started on the project, the better.

There was that other source of funds, of course, if she chose to use it: the money in my savings account. But she didn't choose to use it. What she wanted was to earn her own money as quickly as possible.

And that's where another part of her plan came in. The part she hadn't shared with the professor and Albert yet.

Halli's skills lay in a very specific area: outdoor exploration and adventure. She might not be good at working in a restaurant or an office, or trying to make change at a fast food place, but she did know how to tie a knot that would allow someone to ascend a rope up out of a crevasse. And she could splint a broken leg with just sticks and a few items of clothing. She could navigate her way across mountains and deserts and oceans. She could speak dozens of languages. She could row, paddle, ski, climb, run, hike, backpack, kayak, sail. She could do all sorts of things that she knew, from her Internet research, people were willing to pay for. People wanted guides. People wanted instructors. Halli had a lot to offer, under the right circumstances.

But she wasn't going to be able to set up that kind of life in Tucson. Not because there weren't outdoor opportunities, but because she'd never be able to hide it from my mother—at least not for long.

How was she supposed to explain herself? "I know you think all I've done the past several years is stay in my bedroom and study physics, but really I've secretly been preparing myself to become a mountain guide. I'm going to go take some clients up to the top of Mount Wrightson today. Don't worry. We'll be fine."

Right.

But Colorado—that was a different story. Halli knew she could set up a new life there. Pretend she was going to college at Mountain State, but then start offering her services right away to the more than twenty guiding companies she'd found in the area. With her various skills, covering activities in every single season, she'd be able to work all year long. And maybe in that year, she could earn more than enough to start traveling.

The other useful thing about Colorado was that Halli knew from studying the maps that the mountains and rivers were exactly like the ones in the Colorado she'd spent so much time in back in her own universe. Some of the places had been given different names, but the maps proved to Halli she knew the terrain. She had been all over that wilderness for years.

Ginny owned a house in a town called River Grove, Colorado—the house where I'd first woken up in Halli's body a little more than a week ago—and Ginny and Halli stayed there for large parts of the year. They used it as their base, but then took off whenever they wanted to go camping or backpacking, hiking or skiing. Halli felt confident she would have no trouble navigating her way around. In fact, Colorado was exactly the perfect place for her to begin.

There were several steps to the whole plan, but Halli was ready to take them.

1. Get out of school.

2. Get to Colorado.

3. Get a job.

4. Get lost. Go out into the world and remake Audie Masters's life into something more fitting for Halli Markham. Something Halli could understand.

And what if, in the midst of all this, the real Audie

Masters showed up again? Great. Terrific. Halli would be happy to turn over the keys to this body again—as long as she had another one she could inhabit.

Halli hadn't forgotten a single word of the conversation between Professor Whitfield and me. The one about her being dead. About her body being gone. The professor might want Halli to do whatever she could to help find me and bring me home, but Halli, in her own secret mind, needed assurances. If she didn't have a live version of herself to take over, then she wasn't budging out of my body or out of my life.

The professor didn't know that. Albert didn't know that. I certainly didn't. But any of us should have guessed. Halli was a survivor—*is* a survivor. A future as a dead girl wasn't the future she was pursuing.

And if it turned out she had to stay as Audie Masters, then Audie Masters would soon be leading a spectacularly different life.

22

When my mom came home that night, Halli was ready for her. In a way I never would have been.

I've never been a particularly good liar. To be good at it, I think you have to have a certain amount of fearlessness. You need to really commit to your lie, no matter what someone throws at you.

Granted, I'd been able to hide from my mother the fact that I'd been visiting a parallel universe every night. And yes, I also managed to sneak off to Colorado without her knowing, so I could spend the weekend undergoing tests with Professor Whitfield.

But this was a different kind of lie. It required face-to- face conversation, and Halli couldn't waver for one second. But she was up for it.

"Mmm, what's that smell?" my mom asked when she walked in. Halli met her in the kitchen.

"Roasted vegetables," Halli said, pulling open the oven to show my mom. "Potatoes, leeks, garlic, carrots, zucchini..."

"Audie, that looks delicious! Where did you learn to—"

"Thanks," Halli said, cutting her off. "It still has to cook a while longer. I was hoping you and I could talk about something in the meantime. Something important."

My mother looked worried. "Of course, honey, what is it?" She sat down at the kitchen table.

Halli sat, too. She took a deep breath, like what she was about to say was hard for her.

"I did a lot of thinking last week," she began. "And I think you're right about Columbia University—I've been pushing myself too hard."

"Good, honey. I'm glad you understand that."

"But it's more than that," Halli went on. "I thought about a lot of things—school, my future, what I want to do with my life. And I came to a decision."

Halli got up. "Wait a minute. I need to show you something."

She went to my bedroom and came back with a folder of papers. She handed it to my mother.

"What's this?"

"I talked to someone at the school today," Halli said.

"I found out I have enough credits to graduate right now—I had enough after this summer. Now all I have to do is take a test, and I can graduate. I want to do that. I want to leave. Right away. But I need your permission first."

My mom stared at Halli in shock. "But ... I don't understand. Why would you want to leave? Did something happen?"

"No, nothing happened," Halli said. "I just want to move on with my life. There's nothing for me here anymore. I want to go someplace else."

Halli had laid it out so calmly, so rationally, she assumed my mother would see the sense of it. But that's because she didn't understand the kind of relationship my mom and I have. She wasn't counting on my mother suddenly bursting into tears.

"Audie, what is going on with you?" My mom's face scrunched up in that way I can't bear to see. She doesn't cry that often, but when she does, it's like her whole face falls apart. Every ounce of grief is just there for you to see.

Halli adjusted her strategy. Obviously my mom was going to need more than a simple, logical argument. Fine—she could do more.

Halli reached out and patted my mother's hand. But she wasn't backing down—she was going to get that permission form signed, one way or the other.

"You've changed," my mother cried. "I feel like we

barely talk anymore. There's something wrong. What happened? Tell me, sweetie, please. Is it because of Will?"

"Will? Of course not. Why would it be because of him?"

Um, maybe because I'd poured my heart out to my mother not that long ago, confessing that I'd secretly been in love with Will for a long time, and that he'd broken my heart for the last time by showing me a ring he bought for Gemma. I was already trying to get over him at the time, but that did it. I knew it was hopeless—I'd never had a chance with him, and never would.

"Something has to have happened," my mom said. She reached for a napkin and blew her nose. It seemed like the worst of the crying was over, but her face still looked wracked with emotion. "You don't just decide something like this out of the blue. Please, honey, tell me. Whatever it is, you know I'm on your side."

Halli paused. She chose her words carefully.

"Haven't you ever been in a situation where you woke up one day and realized the road you were walking down was the wrong one?"

My mother sniffled. "Yes, I suppose so."

"That's what happened to me," Halli said. "I've been working so hard, driving myself forward, and it wasn't until last week that I stopped to ask myself whether I still wanted the things I thought I did."

"So ... Columbia?" my mother asked.

"I don't want that anymore."

This must have been both a shock and a relief to my mother. She'd been telling me over and over not to put all my hopes on that one university—to apply other places, to even think about going to the university in our town and still live at home. But it probably never occurred to her I might give up the dream of Columbia entirely.

"What *do* you want?" my mother asked.

"I want to move to Colorado," Halli said. "I want to go to Professor Whitfield's college."

My mother's mood instantly darkened. She wasn't a fan of Professor Whitfield's. In fact, she'd been suspicious of him for a while.

"So *that's* what this is about?" she said. "Did Professor Whitfield talk you into this? Leaving school, forgetting about Columbia—"

"Not at all," Halli said. "I'm the one who asked him."

"So you've already talked to him about this?" she asked, her voice getting wobbly again. "Before talking to me?"

"I wanted to make sure I could go there," Halli said. She was just making it up as she went along now, trying to say what she thought my mother wanted to hear. "He said he can get me a scholarship. It'll pay for everything."

And that much was kind of true. Sort of. Professor Whitfield had said he could probably get Halli—or rather, me—a scholarship through the physics department, and it would pay for things like tuition and books. But only the bare essentials. Halli would still have to find somewhere to live, and some way to afford it, so there were still a lot of details to work out.

But she'd finally hit on something my mother was interested in. Paying for college has always been a major issue in our house. And now as far as my mom was concerned I was telling her I'd solved that problem —not only by giving up my dream of Columbia, but also by finding a school that would pay for me to go there. Maybe going to Colorado wasn't such a bad idea after all.

"But honey, you could stay here," my mother tried again. "Didn't your teacher say the University of Arizona has an excellent physics program?"

"I want to study with Professor Whitfield," Halli said. "As soon as I can. He said he could start the process as soon as I graduate. I don't want to waste any more time in high school. I want to move on with my life."

Halli made a persuasive case. My mother probably felt that. But she wasn't ready to give up on me yet.

"You said you have to take some test?"

"Algebra," Halli said. "And then I'm done."

All the tension drained from my mother's face. Her shoulders relaxed again. She didn't exactly smile, but if it had been me instead of Halli sitting across from her, I would have seen that she wanted to.

"You have to take an algebra test," my mom repeated. "And then you can graduate."

"Yes."

My mother cleared her throat. She opened up the folder Halli had given her. "So the only things you need to graduate are finishing that test, and getting my permission, right?"

"Right."

"I'll tell you what," my mother said. "As soon as you pass your test, then I'll sign these forms. Okay?"

That seemed fair to Halli. She nodded.

"And until then," my mom went on, "you'll go to school. All of your classes. So if you can't pass this test until, let's say, some time next year, you'll still stay in school until you can graduate. Agreed?"

"Agreed," Halli said. She wasn't expecting it to be so easy in the end. She, too, had to suppress a smile.

My mother closed the file. "It's settled then. I'm going to go change, and then I'd love to have some of that delicious dinner you made. Okay, honey?"

She stood up, leaned over, and gave Halli a hug. Halli took it. It seemed the least she could do after a successful negotiation.

"I'm glad we could have this talk," my mom said. "I was wondering what was on your mind. Please don't ever keep things from me. You know I love you, and whatever it is, we can work it out."

"All right," Halli told her.

"Oh, and if you really want to attend Professor Whitfield's college," my mom added, "I think you and I should visit there together. I think it's time I met this man who seems to have so much influence over you, don't you think?"

Halli had zero interest in having my mother tag along whenever Halli finally made it back to Colorado. But she smiled nevertheless. "Sure." She could figure a way out of it when the time came.

"I love you, honey."

Halli smiled. "Me, too."

My mom headed off toward her bedroom. Free to be herself again, Halli frowned.

Dealing with people—someone's parent, in particular—was such a waste of time. Halli needed her freedom. As soon as possible.

But now it was up to her.

She took the vegetables out of the oven, then went to my room. And started looking over the first of the algebra problems Albert sent to her.

Doing something feels better than doing nothing, Ginny liked to say. *Makes you feel like you have some control. Even when you don't.*

It was true, tackling the worksheets did make Halli feel better.

I could have used some of that feeling myself at the moment. I wasn't in charge of even the smallest part of my life. I couldn't even order Halli's eyelids to stay open. Or focus on a thought for more than a few seconds at a time. What would Ginny have said about that?

Things happen. There's nothing special about the body. Get to it, then. This body isn't going to row itself...

"Halli?"

A soft, warm hand squeezing mine. As comforting and delicate as a pillow against my palm.

"Halli dear? Can you hear me?"

I forced my crusty eyes open. And gazed up into the clear blue eyes of a woman I once thought I could trust.

"Mrs. ... Scott?"

The elderly woman smiled back at me. With the kind of tenderness in her expression that a grandmother might have for her grandchild. "Oh, Halli dear. How precious you are. We're all so thankful you're alive. But we don't have much time, I'm afraid. So I'll speak quickly."

I definitely needed to wake up for this.

23

I stared at Mrs. Scott in amazement.

"What are..." But I couldn't complete the sentence before I started coughing. My voice felt and sounded like sand being scraped over concrete. Like I hadn't spoken in days.

Mrs. Scott reached for the cup of water beside my bed and helped me lean forward while I took a few sips. Then she gently laid me back down again.

I still couldn't believe she was there.

"You're wondering why I disappeared," she said.

I nodded.

I'd first met Mrs. Scott at that board meeting Halli's parents arranged. At first I thought she was my ally—Halli's ally—and that I could trust her to give me good advice. When I realized she was from London, I even asked her if I could come stay with her once I'd concocted the scheme to travel there to find Daniel.

We'd made plans for me to leave with her the following morning. But when I arrived at dinner that night, she was already gone. Without a word, just gone.

Which made me think Jake had been right about her: that despite what she said about admiring Ginny Markham, in fact she and Ginny had been bitter enemies. Which meant she also lied about wanting to help Halli.

"I came to apologize," Mrs. Scott said. "To explain, really. I couldn't bear there being any misunderstanding."

"You ... left..." I managed.

"Yes. Quite against my will," Mrs. Scott said. "One moment I was dressing for dinner, and the next I was being escorted to the dock and then promptly rushed onto a plane and flown back here in the middle of the night."

I'm sure I looked confused.

"Why, you ask?" she said. I nodded. "Because your parents felt threatened, I imagine. That young man—Jake, I believe—is undoubtedly contacting them right now to report that I'm here. I'm certain they don't want me to see you."

"Why?" I asked before lapsing into another coughing fit.

"Because, my dear, they don't want you to know anything about what they're doing."

Before I could ask any more, the door to my room swung open, and one of the nurses came in. "You're awake! I'll tell the doctor." She pressed a button on her collar.

Mrs. Scott and I both stopped talking.

The nurse fussed over me for a few minutes, freshening my water, straightening my bedding, checking the tubes connected to my arm. Mrs. Scott sat beside me the whole time, still holding my hand.

"Poor lamb," she said at one point. "If only you'd come home with me."

The prospect of that made me suddenly tear up. I didn't want to be in that hospital. How I would have loved being in some happy, comfortable home with this homey, comfortable woman.

Mrs. Scott patted my hand. "You're welcome any time, Halli dear. As soon as you're well enough to leave, please do come stay with me. I would be relieved to take care of you."

I nodded. And gulped back the pain in my throat. It's a bad idea to try not to cry at the same time you have no saliva in your mouth. It creates this whole backlog of dry meeting wet, and makes you feel like you're holding back a tidal wave with every miserable swallow.

The door to my room opened again, and in walked Jake.

"Mrs. Scott," he said politely, "I'm afraid I have to ask you to leave."

"Why?" I croaked out. I clutched Mrs. Scott's hand all the harder.

"You're too weak," Jake told me. "You shouldn't have any visitors at all. Your parents specifically ordered that."

"I don't care what my—" but then the coughing took me over. And proving Jake's point, I kept on coughing so hard the nurse had to shoo them both out so she could attend to me. She pressed the button on her collar again, murmured, "Urgent," and supported my back while my whole chest rattled with the coughs. By the time the fit was over, Mrs. Scott was gone.

And so was I. Exhausted by the effort, Halli's body slipped back under the waves again.

24

"What are you doing?" Lydia asked.

It was Tuesday back in my world, three days and several time zones behind the universe where I was currently staying, and it was Halli's first full day of school. When the bell rang for what she knew was my lunchtime, she didn't head for the cafeteria, the way I always did, but instead found a quiet spot on the grass to eat her peanut butter sandwich and keep going through the algebra worksheets Albert had sent her.

Halli looked up and shielded my eyes from the sun. "Heya!" she greeted Lydia. "Have a seat."

Lydia looked around. This was highly irregular. We always sat at the same table inside and always ate the exact same things every day: yogurt, an apple, and a miniature candy cane for Lydia, a bag of chips or some other junk food for me.

"It's beautiful out here, isn't it?" Halli said. She was wearing a pair of my shorts and a sweatshirt over the T-shirt she'd run in to school. She looked very sporty. She sat with my legs stretched out, trying to give my poor pasty limbs a chance at the sun.

"What's all that?" Lydia asked, pointing to the worksheets.

"Algebra."

"Hm. So I heard."

Halli cleared them away to make room. "Sit down. Are you teaching tonight?"

"Um, no. Not until Thursday afternoon." Lydia still seemed skeptical, but she took one more look around, then tucked her skirt under her and sat on the grass.

"Could I come as your guest again?" Halli asked.

"Sure, if you want."

Lydia had mentioned that all the yoga teachers got free guest passes. Halli knew she had to be very cost-conscious until she had money of her own.

"I still don't understand what's changed your mind," Lydia said. "I've been begging you for what, two years?"

"And you were right for two years," Halli said. "I should have listened to you before."

It was such a disarming thing to say, Lydia couldn't argue anymore. Which was exactly Halli's strategy.

She'd found from experience that if you agree with people right away, it takes all the fire out of them.

Halli leaned back on my elbows and tipped my face to the sun. "It's so gorgeous out today. I wish we never had to go back inside."

"Hm," Lydia answered. She studied me over the top of her yogurt container and ate a few spoonfuls before she spoke.

"Your mom called my mom last night, you know."

"Hm," Halli answered back. She kept my eyes closed and soaked up the warmth.

"She was crying."

Halli popped open one eye. Then she closed it again. She waited for Lydia to say more.

"Why didn't you tell me?" Lydia asked. "We spent all day together on Sunday."

"I know," Halli said. "But I wasn't sure yet. I didn't know until yesterday."

"And then ... what? You just decided out of the blue to ditch all your plans about Columbia and New York, and run off to Colorado instead? And not even wait until graduation? What's going on, Audie?"

Halli sighed. She sat up and wrapped my arms around my knees.

"It's just time," she said. "I need a change. A big change."

"Since when?" Lydia asked. "Why?"

Halli crafted her words carefully. "You know what

you said to that woman in your class the other day? About how she shouldn't get frustrated that she couldn't do all the poses, because one day, if she kept practicing, *pop*—her body would change?"

"Yeah, so?"

"So that's how it was with me. *Pop*. I've been thinking about it for a long time, and then suddenly yesterday I knew."

"I still don't understand," Lydia said. "You've been obsessed with Columbia and the Amazing Professor Hawkins since what—junior high?"

Halli shrugged. "I don't know what else to say."

Lydia ate in silence for a few moments. She unwrapped her candy cane and sucked on that. Then she pointed out the obvious.

"I heard you have to pass an algebra test."

"That's right."

"But you can't do algebra."

"We'll see."

Lydia laughed. "'We'll see'? Audie, that's like saying you might be able to breathe underwater."

"I have a plan," Halli said.

Lydia rolled her eyes. "Okay."

The bell rang. Lunch was over. Physics was next.

She wasn't worried about it. Not the way I would have been if I had never taken it before. Halli wasn't worried about any of my classes. She had already spent the morning confidently telling teachers "I don't know" whenever they bothered to call on her. She even kept a straight face in World History when Ms. Travers asked her some question about the Vietnam War—a war Halli had never heard of. There hadn't been any wars in her world since the last one in the 1940s.

So she'd handle Physics just the same, with as many "I don't knows" as it took to get her through the time. She didn't care if Mr. Dobosh looked at her funny, or if any of the students did, because none of them meant anything to her life. The only class that sounded even somewhat promising was my last one, Algebra Support, since it sounded like it could at least help her in her quest to pass the test and get out of there as soon as possible.

"Let's eat inside tomorrow," Lydia said. "It's too itchy out here."

"Depends on the weather," Halli said. "If it's like this, I have to stay outside."

Lydia considered her best friend, this girl who rarely left her bedroom unless she had to go to school or to work or occasionally over to dinner at Lydia's house. I've never in my life shown any interest in grass or trees or heaven forbid, sunshine. And then there was the whole yoga thing.

"I don't understand you," Lydia said. "I think something's going on."

Halli smiled. She stood up and brushed off my legs. "See you later." She'd already studied the map of our campus, and knew where the science classrooms were. She started heading west.

"Wait," Lydia said. "I'm ... I'm going shopping tonight. For shoes to wear to the ball. Do you want to come?"

Halli couldn't know this, but Lydia never asked me to go shopping with her. I've always had such a bad attitude toward it, mainly because I never have as much money to spend as she does. Her job teaching yoga pays a lot better than my job working for our mothers. Plus I've never cared about clothes nearly as much as she does. So Lydia learned a long time ago she'd have more fun shopping alone.

But something about Halli must have intrigued her enough to risk spending a few hours with her at the mall. Maybe Lydia wanted to test how much I'd really changed.

Halli didn't care about clothes, either. Her closet in Colorado told me that much. All she had in there were one skirt, one dress, two nice shirts, and the rest were all jeans, shorts, sweaters, and T-shirts. And not too many of those, either. Her closet was the barest, cleanest one I've ever seen.

She also kept only a few pairs of shoes: one pair of hiking boots, one pair of sneakers, one pair of sandals. No wonder one of her first tasks was to bag up all the various moldy, mismatched, too-small and too-scuffed-up shoes of mine. I never noticed them anymore, but the pile of them littering my closet floor must have driven Halli nuts.

As she mentally scanned the shoes she'd bagged up and moved into our storage shed in the back yard, Halli couldn't really remember me having any shoes nice enough to wear to some fancy event. So shoe shopping might not be such a bad idea.

Besides, Halli recognized Lydia's value as a kind of tour guide to my world. If Lydia were willing to take her out some place Halli might not otherwise go, and let Halli observe a portion of my civilization beyond my house and my school and whatever Professor Whitfield and Albert tried to teach her from afar, she knew it was in her best interest to say yes.

Although she still needed to be practical.

"How much?" Halli asked. "For a pair of shoes?"

Lydia rolled her eyes. So I hadn't changed at all—I was still always freaked out about money.

But Halli wasn't having any of that attitude. Ginny always told her that you teach people how to treat you. So Halli called Lydia on it right away.

"Don't be mean," she said pleasantly, but directly. "I'm asking because I need to know. How much money will a pair of shoes cost?"

"Oh ... I wasn't trying to be mean..." Lydia wasn't used to me standing up for myself. She'd seen Halli in action with Gemma, but I guess she hadn't expected it to happen to her. "You know ... maybe twenty dollars for a cheap pair. We can look for stuff on sale if you want."

"All right," Halli said. "That sounds good." She knew I had about twenty-seven dollars and some change in my purse at home. She didn't want to touch my savings account, but she didn't mind spending my cash. She could replenish it as soon as she found work.

"So ... do you want to go straight from school, or later tonight?" Lydia asked. She was unusually solicitous. Usually she just tells me what we're doing, no questions asked.

"We can go after school," Halli said. "I just need to be home in time to cook dinner."

"You're ... cooking now, too?" Lydia said. She looked like she wanted to laugh, but suppressed it. She probably didn't want Halli calling her out on it again. Instead she just asked, "Since when?"

Halli smiled. "Like I said, lots of changes."

25

True to her word, Lydia took Halli to the cheapest shoe store in the mall, and found her a great sale: buy one pair for $14, get the second pair half off. So Halli bought some black flats to go with her dress for the ball, and a new pair of sneakers that she wore out of the store.

Lydia wasn't thrilled with the selection there. She wanted higher heels, a wider toe box, pale green if she could find it. Lydia always knows what she wants.

"Let's try a couple more places," she suggested, checking her watch. "I'll still get you home before dinner."

Halli didn't mind spending more time tagging along. She'd already gained valuable information by watching Lydia extract cash from an ATM, and she'd secretly been able to observe all kinds of different people: what they wore, how they behaved, what they talked about whenever she was close enough to eavesdrop.

So far she hadn't found a single person like her.

It's not like she and Ginny were considered ordinary even in Halli's own universe. They were famous for a reason. But Halli had hoped she might meet at least one person from my life who was interested in the same things she was. So far the closest she'd come was Lydia's obsession with yoga.

But then, on their way toward Lydia's favorite bohemian-style clothing store, they passed a window display that set Halli's heart racing. The sign in the window said *Get Out More*, and the mannequins were dressed like the kind of people Halli wanted to know.

"You go ahead," she told Lydia. "I'll be in here." Then without waiting for an answer, Halli opened the doors and entered a two-story palace of play.

Bicycles. Skis. Canoes. Kayaks. Tents. Sleeping Bags. Backpacks. And that was just on the first floor.

"Hi, can we help you today?" a man in khaki shorts and a khaki shirt asked her.

Halli nodded and kept walking.

There was an announcement board at the base of the staircase, listing all the classes offered in the store that month: *Rock Climbing Basics. Hiking Basics. Backcountry Cooking Basics. Outdoor First Aid. Navigation*

Basics. How Not to Get Lost, and Be Found When You Are.
At least a dozen topics.

Halli scanned the list. She could teach each and every course on that board.

"Looking for anything in particular?" the helpful man asked.

"Do people get paid to teach these classes?"

"It depends," he said. "Some of them are in-house, taught by our staff, some are by experts."

"How much do they get paid?" Halli asked.

I've never been good at asking people questions like that, but it didn't seem to bother Halli. Or the salesperson she was talking to.

"I'm not sure," the man said. "You can talk to our community coordinator."

"Now?" Halli asked.

"No, he won't be in until the morning. I can write down his name for you."

"That would be good," Halli said. She had no intention of working in that store, but she wanted all the information she could get about how much money she might make teaching what she knew.

She accepted the slip of paper with the coordinator's name, then turned and ascended the stairs.

The second floor was packed with clothing of every kind: pants, shirts, jackets, hats, sweaters, socks, scarves, gloves. Clothes for skiing, hiking, running, biking, clothes for the cold, for the rain, clothes on the sale rack from the summer that was gone. Halli took her time weaving through the collections, running her hands along the fabrics, stopping here and there to take a closer look.

And the whole time she could feel the tension leaving her body—my body. Could feel the secret smile on my face. For the first time since waking up in my world, she felt comfortable and at ease. She didn't have to be on alert, ready for the next thing that might come at her. She could relax. She was home.

At least for this moment.

Off in the distance she could see a section devoted exclusively to boots. And since Ginny had always taught her to build her expedition gear from the feet up, Halli knew she'd have to start there first.

"Can I help you find something?" another friendly salesperson asked.

Halli shook her head. She didn't feel the need to speak. This was a meditation for her now, a quiet time of solitude, just her and the life she used to know.

She browsed through the boots, picking them up, studying their designs, their materials, and comparing them to what she knew. Some of these would do very well for her, she thought. And that was a very encouraging idea.

What wasn't so encouraging was the price tag: around $200 for a good pair. She didn't know how long it would take to earn that.

Of course, she already had a long list of expenses: travel, lodging, food, supplies. She always knew clothing would have to be included. I might have enough in my closet to get her through a typical day of my own life, but not through a typical day of hers. Halli knew that at some point she'd need to return to a store just like this and start rebuilding her wardrobe from scratch.

"There you are," Lydia said a while later. She sounded a little annoyed. "I've been looking all over for you. What are you doing just sitting up here?"

In the same way some people go to art galleries and sit on the benches and stare at the paintings, Halli had planted herself in one of the chairs in front of the boot display, and sat there contemplating her life.

Making plans. Always plans.

But it was time for action again. "Ready?" Halli said, slapping my thighs and standing up. "Let's go." She led Lydia back down the staircase.

"You weren't seriously thinking about buying any of those, were you?" Lydia asked. "I mean, it's not really you."

"Some day," Halli said.

"Why? Is this about Colorado?" Lydia asked. "Are you really going to go?"

"Yes."

The salesman who'd written down the name for

Halli saw her returning to the first floor. "He'll be in around nine," he reminded her. "Give him a call then."

"Thanks," Halli said, then she continued out through the door.

"Who'll be in around nine?" Lydia asked.

Halli smiled. "You have a lot of questions."

"It's because I don't understand what's going on with you lately," Lydia said. "It's like you're a whole other person. Cooking, doing yoga, studying algebra—on *purpose*..."

"People change," was all Halli said.

"You don't," Lydia answered.

Halli patted her on the back. "I do now."

26

My mom was still at work when Halli got home. She quickly chopped up some vegetables, got a stew started, then went into my room to get to work.

There was a message on my laptop from Professor Whitfield. Halli returned the call.

"Any sign of her yet?" he asked.

"None," she said.

The professor looked bad. Like he hadn't been sleeping very well. His beard looked a little too wild and bushy. His hair wasn't much neater.

Albert stuck his face in front of the screen. "Hi, Halli. How are those worksheets working out?"

"Great," she said. "Keep sending them. I really appreciate it."

Albert retreated again, leaving just the professor in front of Halli. He rubbed his eyes. He really looked tired.

"I've been doing some calculations," he said. "Everything I can think of. I reviewed all the readouts from when Audie was here. I just can't get a handle on this. I don't know what else to do."

"I know it's hard to accept," Halli said, "but I don't think we can do anything. Not until Audie contacts me again. You need some sleep. You look awful."

Professor Whitfield shook his head. "When the worst thing that has ever happened in your career has happened, sleep isn't really an option."

"Professor," Halli said sternly, "you need to face reality. Audie may never come back. Or she might—we don't know. But until we do know, we have to move forward. The longer I'm here, the more likely someone is going to wonder whether something's wrong. Audie's friend Lydia asked me a lot of questions today. So did Audie's mother last night. I'm not sure how much longer I can fool people. So let's focus on getting me out of here as soon as possible."

Professor Whitfield ran a hand across his beard. "Yes, you're right. Albert and I talked about it last night. We think it would be very useful for you to bring Audie's body back here so we can run more tests on it. I don't know what we'll find, but it seems worth a try."

"Exactly," Halli said. "Good idea. Although I have to

warn you, Audie's mother wants to meet you. So she might have to come along, at least for a few days."

This was not good news to the professor. He nodded grimly.

Albert stuck his face in front of the screen again. "Then if we're trying to expedite things, maybe I should send you even more worksheets than I was planning. You could even try a practice test this weekend, if you feel up to it. Just to see where we are."

"Sounds good," Halli said. "Why not?"

"You know," the professor said, "maybe Audie's mother wanting to come visit isn't a bad thing after all. It would give you an excuse to come out here right away, rather than wait until you can graduate. We'll treat it like any pre-college visit. We can get someone to show Audie's mom around campus while you and Albert and I work in the lab."

"I like that," Halli said. "When can we do it?"

"As soon as next week, I'd imagine," Professor Whitfield said. "Let me see what travel arrangements I can make."

"And you'd better make sure Audie's mom can come then," Albert said. "Remember, Audie said she travels a lot."

"Not often enough," Halli muttered. She would have loved to have the house to herself, instead of my mother hanging around every night and all weekend.

"I'll work on it on my end," the professor said. "You just keep studying algebra."

"I will, but..." Halli peered at the face on her screen. "Professor, there's something I learned on expeditions. It doesn't matter if you're the healthiest person on your team, because you can only go as fast and as far as the weakest member. So it always pays to make sure everyone else is well-rested, properly hydrated, well-fed—you get the picture."

Professor Whitfield raised an eyebrow. "Yes..."

"So that's why I'm telling you, you have to get some sleep. Start taking better care of yourself. People make mistakes when they're tired. I don't want you to make any mistakes."

"You mean any *more* mistakes," he said. Halli could hear the defeat in his voice.

"Look," she said, "things happen." She could imagine Ginny's voice in her head, filling in the rest: *That's life. Now what are you going to do about it?* Halli had been where the professor was so many times in her life, forlorn because of some unexpected crisis—a crisis she knew *she* had caused—that Halli was sure meant she and Ginny would fail.

But there was no point in giving in to self-pity. It just interfered with coming up with solutions to solve whatever problem they faced.

"I have to study now," Halli said. "Send me more worksheets. I'll study all night if I have to.

"But not you, Professor," she added. "Go to bed early. You're no good to me like this. I mean it."

Professor Whitfield blinked. Audie Masters had never talked to him that way. If there were ever any doubt that it wasn't me behind that face he was looking at, Halli had just dispelled it.

But the professor knew what was true. And he knew Halli was right.

"I'll do my best," he said.

"Me, too," Halli answered. Then she clicked off the call.

And lay back on my bed for a while, staring up at the ceiling, thinking about the first time she felt exactly the way the professor did.

27

Halli was seven when Ginny took her on her first trek to the North Pole. I actually saw some of the footage of that when Sarah showed it to me one day when we were together up in the Alps: a miniature hologram of Ginny and Halli leaning into the fierce wind, both of them on skis, harnesses around their waists so they could each pull a sled heaped with their supplies.

I remember watching that and feeling so ... inadequate. Like I'd never done anything interesting with my life, even in seventeen years, let alone in my first seven.

But what Daniel said about it afterward made sense: that I didn't grow up with someone like Ginny. I didn't grow up with any of Halli's early experiences. It wasn't fair for me to compare myself to her, any more than it would be fair for her to feel inadequate because she didn't understand physics. We all have our skills.

And one of Halli's is definitely survival. Ginny made sure of that.

It was mid-April, and the two of them had already been traveling across the sea ice for 22 days straight. They'd brought enough food to last for a month, even though Ginny hoped they would finish their route sooner than that.

But they'd run into problems: wind storms, shifting ice, and worst of all, the polar bears.

"You have to always keep watch," Ginny warned Halli. "Polar bears are silent and they're smart. They'll sneak up behind you, and you won't even know it until they attack."

That would have been enough for me to hear. I would have been all, "Hey, thanks, Grandma, but I think I'll stay home instead."

That kind of thought never even occurred to Halli.

Instead she followed Ginny's example: ski with the right leg, ski with the left, pause and look around; ski right, ski left, pause and look around. It obviously added hours to their work every day, but it was better than suddenly feeling the jaws of death clamped around their necks.

They met their first polar bear on the third day: a large, hungry male running toward them with that strange pigeon-toed gait they have, his beady black eyes trained on the two humans he viewed as dinner.

"Move your sled," Ginny ordered. "Now."

The two of them quickly pivoted their sleds sideways on the ice, then stood in between them. They wanted to make it look like they were big animals—like the sleds were part of their bodies. Then Ginny handed the flare gun to Halli and kept the pulse rifle for herself.

"Shoot him a warning," Ginny said.

Halli swallowed hard, then aimed the flare gun. Ginny had taught her how to use it and then made her practice, but this was different—this was real. Halli's hand shook as she fired the flare out in front of the bear.

It landed far in front of him. He ignored it and continued running.

"Get behind me," Ginny snapped. She braced the pulse rifle against her shoulder and squeezed the trigger. Halli clamped her hands over her ears. The vibration from the rifle hurt: a loud, piercing, penetrating kind of sound that she could feel all the way through to her bones.

The bear felt it, too. He twisted his head to the side as his feet slid to a stop. He shook his head, obviously trying to rid himself of the sound. But Ginny pulled the trigger again, sending a whole second wave of it, even stronger than the first.

The bear roared, then turned away. He loped off

into the distance, then turned back to look at them again.

Ginny and Halli waited.

The bear seemed uncertain. He took a few steps toward them, then a few more.

"Shoot another flare," Ginny said.

Halli used both hands this time, hoping to hold the pistol steady. She aimed and shot. Once more the flare landed short.

"Again," Ginny said, keeping the rifle braced against her shoulder.

Halli shot again, and this time the flare fell almost in front of the bear.

He roared, but didn't move.

Ginny kept the rifle ready.

The three of them stood that way for another several minutes. Then finally the bear turned and headed off in another direction.

"Will he come back?" Halli asked.

"He might," Ginny said. "Let's keep going."

The two of them started forward again, but Ginny kept the rifle in her hand. Halli still carried the flare gun.

An hour later, just as Halli was wondering whether she could stow the heavy pistol and not have to carry it anymore, she saw movement to her left.

Ginny whipped around and shot. The vibration hit the bear hard. He roared in pain and shook his head as he backed away. Ginny sent three more waves toward him until finally he took off at a run.

Ginny cursed.

She looked up at the darkening sky. A wind storm was coming, kicking up the loose snow all around. In another minute, they wouldn't be able to see more than a few feet in front of them.

"Anchor your sled," Ginny said. "Hurry."

Halli fumbled to pull the ice screws out of her sled bag. The thick gloves she wore kept her fingers warm, but they also made it hard for her to work the zipper. Ginny had already anchored two sides of her sled before Halli started on her first. She twisted the screw into the ice and was just moving to do the next when the wind hit.

Halli shouted as her feet shot out from beneath her. Ginny threw herself on top of the sled to keep it from flying up and hitting Halli in the head. Halli scrambled over to add her own weight, but Ginny pushed her away.

"Stay down!" she shouted. "Hold on!"

Halli crouched on the ice and gripped Ginny's leg to keep from sliding away. The wind felt like a tornado, swirling all around them, beating them from the sides, the top, and slipping underneath to try to drag them off their feet.

Then finally—maybe ten minutes later, maybe more —it began to subside. And Ginny immediately let go of

Halli's sled and raced back to her own. She unzipped the side of her bag and reached inside for the pulse rifle that she'd quickly stowed before the wind hit. Then she pivoted in every direction, checking for the bear.

Halli's breath came hard. There were too many things to be afraid of all at the same time. But seeing Ginny keep guard against the bear made Halli start to feel calmer, somehow. Like Ginny was in control again. Even though it might be crazy to think any human could be in control in a place like that.

"Hungry?" Ginny called through the lessening wind.

Halli had to think about it before she answered. But the truth was, she was. They hadn't eaten for hours. And the stress had used up whatever reserves Halli's young body might hold.

"We need to eat," Ginny said. "Heat some water. I'll keep watch."

Halli wondered later if it had just been a tactic of her grandmother's to get her to focus on something besides her fear. Whether Ginny planned it that way or not, it worked. Halli had to throw all her concentration into putting together the solar-powered stove, chipping enough ice from the ground to fill the pot, then monitoring the heat to make sure she kept it high enough to melt the ice into water.

"I'd like some soup," Ginny told her. So Halli pulled out one of the food bags, found the packages of dried soups, and added one to the pot. Five minutes later, she poured split pea soup into an insulated mug and handed it to Ginny.

"You keep watch," Ginny said, handing her the rifle.

Halli stared up at her wide-eyed.

"You can do it," Ginny said. "I know you can."

Halli nodded and took the gun. And hoped that her grandmother would drink her soup in record time.

"Go ahead and eat," Ginny finally said, taking the rifle from Halli's frozen grip. Halli still looked to her right, to her left, and behind her, the way she'd been doing obsessively for the past few minutes while Ginny left her in charge.

"We'll be fine," Ginny said. "Eat."

Halli reheated the rest of the soup and poured it into her own mug. Then she sat on her skis to give her a little more insulation from the ice, and hungrily slurped it down.

"Let's talk about the ice screws," Ginny said, still scanning the horizon for the bear. "What can you do to be faster next time?"

Next time. Halli knew that was code for "you messed up," but Ginny never put it that way. She never scolded Halli for her mistakes. Instead she made Halli analyze what went wrong, and decide how she could do things better next time.

"My gloves," Halli said.

"What about them?"

"I should have taken them off."

"Never take them off," Ginny said, looking right, left, and behind her again. "You'll get frostbite, they'll swell, they'll be useless. What else could you do?"

"Practice?" Halli suggested.

"I think practice would be good," Ginny agreed.

So right then, with Ginny looking on, Halli put herself through a drill of unzipping her sled bag, pretending to reach in for the ice screws, then turning and beginning to anchor the sled.

"What did you forget?" Ginny asked.

Halli looked around. And saw that she'd left the sled bag unzipped. She quickly fixed it.

"Good," Ginny said. "That's very important. We don't ever want anything to blow away."

Halli spent the next half hour practicing retrieving the screws and twisting them into the ice. Finally Ginny told her that was enough for the time being.

"Ready to go again?" she asked.

The blowing snow had finally settled once more. They could see far out in front of them.

Halli undid the ice screws and stored them in the bag. Ginny did the same. Then the two of them reattached their sleds to their waist harnesses and began skiing again. Ski, ski, look. Ski, ski, look. But the bear never returned that day.

Two days later, there were different bears: a mother and her two cubs.

Four days after that, another male. And by the

twenty-second day, they'd faced and repelled a total of seven bears. It might have seemed routine by then, if not for the fact that each bear posed exactly the same danger of attacking them before they could defend themselves. And even though the pulse rifle meant pain, any one of the bears might still decide the pain was worth it in exchange for a meal.

They had just finished a long stand-off with a lone female bear when Halli heard a familiar sound.

"Anchor!" Ginny shouted.

A wave of black cloud raced toward them, much faster than any Halli had seen before. And even though she'd learned to retrieve her ice screws quickly now after so many repetitions, this time she wasn't fast enough. She only had two sides screwed in before the wall of wind hit.

Her sled whipped into the air, tethered by the two straps. Ginny fought to anchor the fourth side of her own sled, and didn't manage to catch Halli's in time.

The sled bucked through the air. Ginny yanked Halli away so the runners wouldn't hit her. But as the two of them watched, suddenly supplies started flying out of Halli's sled bag: clothes, gear, and worst of all, food.

She hadn't zipped it closed. Halli knew it right away. She'd been in such a hurry —

She reached out to grab what she could, but Ginny pulled her away. "Too dangerous!" she shouted, and

Halli knew she was right. The sled bounced and whipped and twisted on its tethers, spewing contents everywhere. Then the wind hurled the sled itself away as Halli watched in horror.

Half of their remaining food had been on that sled.

As soon as the wind burst ended, Ginny searched the immediate area, but there was no doubt the sled was gone.

"I'm so sorry!" Halli cried. "I should have been faster! I should have seen the storm. I'm so sorry! I know it's all my fault—"

"It's not your fault, and there's no use going over it again," Ginny told her. "It happened. Now we have to decide what to do."

"But I should have closed the zipper!" Halli said. "I know that was the most important part!"

Ginny gripped her by both arms. "Halli. Stop. This is what happened. It's over—move on. Now what are you going to do next?"

Halli could feel tears start to well up in her eyes. She knew she'd let Ginny down. That she'd endangered both of them. That she hadn't been quick enough or smart enough to do what she was supposed to.

Ginny must have seen how distraught Halli was.

"Want to hear a secret?" Ginny asked.

Halli swallowed hard and nodded.

"The first time I came out here, I wanted to cry all

the time," Ginny said. "About the bears, the cold, how hard it was—everything."

"Really?"

"Really," Ginny said. "But do you know what happened when I did cry?"

Halli shook her head.

"My tears froze. They iced my eyelashes together. Then I couldn't see until I pried them apart, and then I was afraid I wouldn't see the bears—it was a disaster. So I just decided I could never cry out here. I'd save all of it for when I got home."

"And then did you?" Halli asked.

"No, by then I forgot," Ginny said. "But if you want, I'll remind you. I'll say, 'Halli, don't forget you wanted to cry that one day. Go ahead now if you want.'"

Halli gave her a tentative smile. "I'm really sorry."

"I know you are, but it could have been my sled," Ginny said. "And then we wouldn't have the tent or the delicious cashews or anything else I was carrying. It's why we split up the gear and the food—just in case something like this happens. Because bad things can always happen, Halli. Always. If you understand that, you'll learn to just keep going, the way I do."

Ginny slapped her thick gloves against the thighs of her thick pants. "So let's keep going, shall we? You keep a lookout for any bears, and I'll pull my sled. We need to keep going as long as we can tonight. The sooner we get to the pickup point, the sooner we'll get to eat all the rest of our food and have a little party, all right?"

Halli nodded.

Ginny gave her granddaughter a quick hug. "Things happen, right?"

"Right."

"And what do we do?"

"Keep going," Halli said. "And decide what we're going to do next."

"That's my girl," Ginny said.

That night when they finally rested in the tent, Halli wearing Ginny's oversized jacket since she didn't have any extra clothes of her own anymore to wrap around herself, Halli typed out her daily report so that everyone following them could know what happened.

She'd been writing reports from the field for the past two years, ever since Ginny suggested she write her first one when Halli was five. That one had been short and simple: *"So much rain we all most drownd."*

This time her report was nearly as short: *"Today my sled blew away. Saw one bear."*

"That's all you want to say?" Ginny asked after reading it.

Halli shrugged. She didn't really feel like writing anything at all. She wished she could forget the whole day.

"Want to hear what I wrote?" Ginny asked.

Halli nodded.

"Fierce wind storm took us by surprise and swept away Halli's sled. Lost all her gear and half our remaining food. But safe after another bear encounter: another female, not as aggressive as the one with cubs. Only needed the flares to scare her away. Halli and I in good spirits despite our meager dinner of nuts and warm water. Will squeeze into one sleeping bag for remainder of trip. Tent safe, so all is well."

"You always say it better," Halli said.

"Think about it," Ginny answered. "Think about all the people out there—the ones reading what you write every night. People like to feel brave. They like to feel they could do daring things if they tried. But not everybody has the time or the freedom you and I do. So people like to come along on our journeys. And it's up to us to give them details so they feel like they're a part of it. Do you understand?"

"Yes, I suppose."

"So when you write something," Ginny said, "think about all those little girls and boys sitting in their warm, cozy homes, wondering what dangers and excitement Halli Markham faced today."

"But today wasn't a good day," Halli said.

"What do you mean?" Ginny said. "We're here, aren't we? We're together, we're safe. So it must have been a very good day. We survived our challenges. You shot that second flare right in front of the bear's feet—that's why she ran away. And you managed to screw in two of your anchors before that wind hit—

do you think most people could have done even that much?"

Halli knew her grandmother was trying to make her feel better. And it was almost starting to work.

"Try again," Ginny said. "Don't be afraid to tell people both the good and the bad parts. They like the bad parts. They like to know you got through them. It makes them feel like maybe they can do hard things, too."

So Halli started over.

"GOOD. Saw one bear. She looked at us for a long time, but didn't come close. BAD. Wind storm took my sled. GOOD. I can ski faster now because I don't have to pull it any more. BAD. All the crackers and candy were on my sled."

She showed it to Ginny, who smiled and nodded. Then Ginny transmitted both reports out into the world.

A little while later, as Halli and Ginny huddled together inside the one remaining sleeping bag, Halli yawned and asked if it was true.

"Do you really think people care what happened to us today?"

"I'm sure of it," Ginny answered.

"Why?"

"Why do you like all the stories I tell you about famous explorers?" Ginny asked. "Why do you read all their books?"

"I don't know," Halli said. "They're exciting. I like to know what happens next."

"You like to know that they survived," Ginny said.

"Yes," Halli said. "I always want that."

"Well, think of it," Ginny said. "There are a million strangers out there in the world tonight who wanted to know that you survived another day out here. And now they do. So they can have their hot cocoa and put on their warm pajamas and go to bed."

Hot cocoa. Something else that had been on Halli's sled. Gone now.

But Ginny didn't leave any time for self-pity. No point in that. She was on to her next question. "So what is our brave adventurer Halli Markham going to do next?"

Halli thought about it for a moment. Then gave the kind of answer she knew Ginny herself would give.

"Get enough sleep tonight so I can ski as far as possible tomorrow."

"That's my girl," Ginny said.

28

"Miss Markham? Can you hear me?" a nurse asked.

I peeked open one eye to make sure she was the only one in there. Maybe it was just a nightmare, but I could have sworn I heard Halli's mother's voice. Even if I were feeling a hundred percent healthy, that woman would be the last person I wanted to see.

But the nurse and I were alone. I went ahead and opened my eyes.

"There you are!" she said. "How are you feeling?" She had a beautiful voice, with a soft, lilting accent that sounded like she might be from the Caribbean or somewhere like that. It felt very soothing to my ears.

I licked my chapped lips.

"Water?" the nurse asked.

I nodded.

She helped me with the straw, then held the cup while I drew in fresh clean water. It felt so good on my tongue and my lips. Like rain on a pile of sand.

"Please," I rasped, "can you help me?"

"Certainly, Miss Markham. Shall I call the doctor?"

She was reaching for some button on her collar when I stopped her.

"No. I need someone. His name is Daniel. Do you know who he is? Has he been here?"

"Yes..."

Good. I didn't think I'd imagined his voice before, but my brain was so muddled, I couldn't say for sure.

"Can you find him for me?" I asked. "Please? It's very important that I talk to him."

Out of everyone in that world, only he and his parents knew the truth about me: that I wasn't sick, wasn't damaged in some way, but had merely switched universes and taken over Halli Markham's body. That's all.

I fell into another coughing fit. The nurse gave me more water, then waited until I could breathe normally again before she broke the bad news.

"I'm sorry, Miss Markham, but that young man you spoke of is forbidden."

"Forbidden? What are you talking about?" I tried to sit up. Easier said than done. I'd been lying in that bed for days, and Halli's body felt uncommonly weak.

I collapsed back against the pillow. "Why is he forbidden?"

"Dr. Rios's orders," the nurse said.

"Why?" I tried again.

The nurse looked around, then leaned forward to whisper. "Your mother arrived in the night. She made all sorts of rules. She said you are allowed no visitors unless she approves. And Mr. Everett especially is forbidden."

"But why? Do you know?"

The nurse looked over her shoulder again. "I believe it is because of that other young man."

"Jake?"

"Yes. Very jealous. They do not get along whatsoever. *He* is allowed. I can bring him to you, if you wish."

"No, thank you," I answered bitterly. If he was the one who talked my mother into having Daniel banned, I had nothing to say to Jake Demetrios.

Another nurse stuck her head into my room. "Bertrise? Are you almost finished? I could use some help in 308."

"Yes, yes, coming soon," Bertrise said. She waited until we were alone again, then leaned forward to gossip some more.

"I shouldn't say, Miss Markham, but your mother is..." Bertrise clicked her tongue and pressed her hand against her temple like she had a splitting headache.

"She's difficult," I said. "I know."

"But she's your mama, I know, but to wait four days before coming to see her only daughter? Who is sick in hospital?" Bertrise clicked her tongue again. "It isn't my business…"

Maybe not, but I was grateful for the information. So I'd been out of it for four days. Tuesday, Wednesday, Thursday, Friday —

"Is today Friday?" I asked.

"Saturday morning," Bertrise said. "A beautiful day outside."

I sighed. How I would have loved to be somewhere out there instead of somewhere in here.

"When can I leave?"

"Only the doctor knows," Bertrise said.

"But there's nothing wrong with me," I said.

"We must be careful."

"I'm fine."

What wasn't fine was being isolated. I needed to contact Daniel right away. And not be subjected to Halli's mother, if I could help it. I agreed with the nurse —it was interesting that Halli's mother waited four full days before flying over here to check on me. Of course I would have been happier if she hadn't come at all.

"Is there anything else I can do for you?" Bertrise asked.

"Maybe," I said. "Let me think about it for a while. Can you maybe come back?"

"Of course. I'll only be down the hall." She pressed a

button on her collar. "Dr. Rios? Miss Markham is awake."

"No, I'm not ready—"

But it was too late. Besides, if I wanted to get out of that bed and out of the hospital, it was probably to my benefit for the doctor to notice I was conscious.

Bertrise smiled and patted my hand.

"There now, the doctor will be here soon. Try to rest. You mustn't get too excited."

I slumped back against the bed. Mustn't get too excited. No, just must be held against my will in some hospital in a foreign land in a foreign universe and prevented from talking to the only person who might be able to help me escape.

Mustn't get excited.

29

"Hey, Aud. Wait up."

It was Wednesday morning, and Will jogged down the hall to catch Halli before she went into first period.

"Haven't seen you around," he said.

"I've been here," she said. "Unfortunately."

He handed her the smartphone. "Here. It's ready. Let me know if you need any help setting it up."

"Thank you." She smiled at him—a genuine smile. "I really appreciate that." Then she started to turn away.

"Hey, I was thinking," Will said. "I told my mom I'd do a software upgrade at the office this week. I thought I might go in this afternoon. You want a ride?"

"Oh. All right, sure."

Halli had forgotten all about my job as bookkeeper until my mom brought it up the night before.

"I'm so glad you're coming in tomorrow," she'd said. "I need you to update the donor list, and there's a stack of bills. It's good you're not sick very often. Just one week off, and we're so far behind."

Halli had never done any bookkeeping in her life. Ginny always managed the finances. In the year since Ginny died, Halli hadn't really worried about her money—she knew there was plenty. All of Ginny's properties were completely paid for, and any expenses Halli had—food, gear, travel—were deducted from Ginny's various bank accounts. Halli knew she'd have to sit down at some point and really look at everything she inherited, but she hadn't been able to bring herself to do it yet. She generally avoided things that reminded her of her grandmother's death.

"I'm parked in the front lot," Will told her. "I'll see you there after school."

"All right," Halli said. "I'll be there."

Out of the corner of her eye, she saw a blonde head coming toward them. Halli didn't know it, but it was just like the last time Will offered me a ride to work— Gemma just couldn't resist coming over and butting in.

"Oh, good," Halli said with an obviously fake smile. "Gemma."

"Audie," Gemma answered briskly. She usually likes to draw my name out—*Auuuudie*. I think she enjoys showing off how British it sounds coming from her mouth. But apparently she wasn't in the mood for showing off that morning. Or maybe Halli's behavior a few nights before had left her a little nervous.

"I couldn't help overhearing," Gemma said to Will.

"Because you were listening," Halli pointed out.

Gemma's eyes darted toward Halli before focusing on Will again. "Remember you said you would help us today. Mummy is up to her forehead in last-minute details—"

"Can't," Will said. "Gotta work."

Gemma's mouth got small. Her eyes did, too. But then she shook out her hair, like it was a way of pushing a reset button and starting all over again.

"William." She smiled in her feline way and draped her manicured hand across the back of Will's neck. "I need you. Mummy needs you. You said last night you would help. There's still so much to do, and Mummy *does* want the ball to be perfect."

"You'll have to tell her I can't," Will said. "Not today." Halli saw him move away from Gemma ever so slightly. But Gemma was a pro. She stayed with him, and even gripped his neck a little more tightly.

"Will," she purred, "please?"

Will reached back and dislodged her hand and brought it down to his side. He held on to it and kept it there.

"Look, Gemma, I already promised my own mom.

Yours will have to wait. Tell her I'll come over tomorrow."

"But tomorrow is so late!" Gemma made a pouty face, but Will ignored it. He turned back to Halli.

"So I'll see you later," he said.

"Sure," Halli said, suppressing a laugh. "See you."

She pretended to head toward the classroom, but just for the fun of it turned back a moment later to watch the two of them go.

Gemma tugged Will down the hallway and murmured something in his ear. She rested her head on his shoulder. Will wrapped his arm around her waist.

But then he looked back at Halli. And seemed embarrassed to find her watching. He gave her a slight wave. Halli smiled and waved back, then turned to go to class.

Her impression of him from the other night certainly hadn't improved. He continued to let some overpampered girl order him around. It was pathetic.

Halli's taste in guys ran much more to the manly. I've witnessed it myself: Karl the muscular German pilot. The guy she met when we were together in the Alps—the one she'd been climbing with when the avalanche...

Karl was dead now. I saw it happen. He was the first one the avalanche took. It's why I flung myself out of my own universe into theirs to keep the same thing from happening to Halli.

Will Stamos-Valadez was no Karl the German pilot. Will was just a boy. Halli knew I liked him, but she couldn't understand why.

It's like she said to Will about Gemma: *You can do better.*

30

Halli had just finished a speed round of the current worksheets when the bell rang in Algebra Support. She gathered up her materials and headed out the door.

She followed the wave of people outside, and took a guess at which parking lot Will had been talking about. Since she didn't know what his car looked like, she waited under the lone tree out there until she saw Will coming around a corner. Then she walked over to join him.

Will seemed to be in a hurry. He unlocked the car doors and slipped behind the wheel.

"Gemma's looking for me again. Let's go."

Sure enough, a few seconds later his phone vibrated. Will pulled it out of his pocket and checked the display.

Halli could see it said *Gemma*.

Will put the phone back in his pocket without answering.

Halli smiled to herself and looked out the passenger window.

She waited until they were out of the parking lot, onto the main road, before she twisted in her seat and fixed her gaze on Will. She was curious about something, and when she was curious, she asked.

"Do you like her?"

"Who?"

"Gemma."

"Of course I like her," Will said. "We've been going out for almost a year."

"I'm not asking if you liked her historically," Halli said. "I'm wondering if you like her right now. Because it doesn't seem like you do."

Will glanced over at her. "Audie, what's gotten into you lately?"

"Avoiding the question," Halli said. "That's fine. You don't have to answer."

She faced front again and relaxed against her seat.

"Why are you so interested all of the sudden?" Will asked. "Now and last Sunday night. What's going on?"

"Nothing is going on," Halli said pleasantly. "I was just making conversation."

"I don't want to talk about this," Will said.

"I can see that."

Neither of them said anything for a few blocks.

At the stoplight, Will turned to her. "Why did you say that the other night? That I 'seem' like a nice guy. What's that supposed to mean?"

"Exactly what I said. You do seem nice."

"But we've known each other all our lives. Why would you say it like that?"

"I don't know," Halli said. "Don't you ever think I seem like a nice girl?"

"Well ... yeah. Of course. Not so much right now," he added with a touch of sarcasm, "but yeah, generally, of course you're a nice girl. You know I think that."

"So that's what I meant," Halli said.

The light turned green. Will went back to driving in silence.

And here Halli was in strange territory. Because she knew how I felt about Will, but I also told her he's never shown even the least bit of interest in me. We've always been just friends. Halli was curious about that, too. And since she had no personal stake in the game, why not ask?

"So if you've always thought I was nice," she said, "then why not me?"

"Why not you ... what?"

"Why are you with someone like Gemma, when you could be with someone like me?"

Will's foot must have slipped off the gas pedal, because the car jerked a little before he regained control. From then on he concentrated very hard on the road. Safer to look there, I'd imagine, than at me.

"I mean, Audie ... you know I like you, of course."

"Of course," Halli said. "But I've never understood why, when somebody has someone perfectly good right in front of him, he keeps on looking around to find somebody else. It doesn't make sense. Why wouldn't you appreciate the people that life brings you, and then see where that leads? And if it ends, you wait and see who comes along next." Halli shrugged. "That's how I've always viewed it."

Now Will did look over. "How you've always ... Audie, when have you ever done any of that? As far as I know, you've never had a relationship in your life. My sister goes out with guys all the time—you just sit in your room studying physics."

Halli shrugged. "Maybe I'm shy. Maybe I need someone else to take the initiative." She saw exactly that happen with my relationship with Daniel. It wasn't until he made the first move that I could even admit how much I liked him.

"And you're still avoiding the question," she pointed out.

"What is the question?" Will answered irritably. "Why am I going out with Gemma? Because I like her. She's a good person. She's fun."

"Good," Halli said. "Then that explains everything."

Will fumed in silence for a moment.

"Why am I even bothering to explain any of this to you?" he said. "It's not like it's any of your business."

"You're right," Halli said. "Absolutely. We can talk about something else." She gazed out the window and hummed to herself. Will didn't say anything at all.

When they got to the office, he pulled into a parking space and shut off his car. Then he twisted in his seat to face Halli.

"Now it's my turn," he said. "I wasn't going to bring this up, but since we're speaking freely … what's all this about you trying to quit school early? And now you're not interested in Columbia anymore?"

"What do you want to know?"

"What I want to know," Will said, "is what's going on with you lately? Because I really don't understand."

"I can see that," Halli said calmly.

"Did something happen?" Will said. "Something I don't know about?"

Halli laughed. "It depends on how well you think you know me. Don't you think it's possible I have all sorts of secrets you know nothing about?"

"Audie…" Will groaned in frustration. "Never mind. What are we even talking about? I don't understand this whole conversation."

"Well," Halli said, "at first we were talking about the fact that you don't seem to mind getting pushed around by some spoiled girl you don't even like—"

"I do like her," Will said. "I told you. And she doesn't push me around."

"And then we were talking about whether I'm nice, and you're nice, and why people make the choices they do. I was curious what you thought about all that."

"What do *you* think about all of it?" Will challenged her. "You seem to have an opinion."

"I do," Halli said, "but you won't like it."

"Try me," Will answered.

Halli smiled. "I think you're weak."

Will's mouth dropped open. Never in a million trillion years would I have said something like that to him. Of all the things he might have expected, that certainly wasn't it.

"Weak," he repeated.

"Not physically weak." She reached out and squeezed his bicep. "Not bad. But I hate to see a guy being led around like a puppy by someone who doesn't deserve him."

Halli opened the car door. "Shall we go in?"

Will just stared at her.

"Audie, what is going on with you?"

"I don't know," Halli said. "Do you like it?"

31

The tension between the two of them must have been palpable, because when they walked into the office my mom and Elena exchanged a glance.

"Everything okay, kids?" Elena asked.

"Sure," Halli said cheerfully.

"Fine," Will muttered.

There were only two empty desks, so Halli waited until Will sat at one of them. She took the other.

My mom wasn't kidding about the amount of work that had piled up. There were bills, letters, and a nice, friendly stack of returned donor cards that had come with either checks or credit card numbers. That was always my favorite pile to see. It meant my mom might be able to pay herself her salary that month, which meant we could afford our own bills at home.

Halli flipped through the papers. She stared at the computer screen to see if she could figure out how she was going to fake this. But after about ten minutes, she knew what she had to do.

She waited until my mom got off her phone call.

"Can I talk to you?" Halli said.

My mother cracked her neck from side to side. "Let's go to the kitchen. I could use some coffee." She stood up and arched her back. "Oof. I think I've been sitting here too long."

Halli couldn't resist. She'd fixed Ginny this way hundreds of times.

"Hold still."

She stood behind my mom and used one hand to brace the side of her waist, while she dug a fist into my mom's low back. My mother moaned—loudly. Which only caused Halli to dig in deeper. Then she moved over and did the same to the other side.

"Oh, Audie, I don't think so—oww! Yes, right there!"

Halli stayed where she was until the groans subsided, then she moved upward to the rest of my mom's back. Eventually she made it all way to her shoulders.

"No, don't!" my mom yelped. "No, that hurts too much. Oh, okay, right there. Yeah, right *there*." Halli dug in deeper.

Finally my mom told her, "If you keep doing that,

I'm going to fall asleep. But thank you, honey. That feels so much better."

She straightened up and rolled her shoulders and stretched her back again. "Uh. I needed that. Thank you."

"Coffee?" Halli said.

"Perfect," my mom answered.

The two of them walked into the tiny kitchen. A pot of coffee sat in there, half full.

My mom was about to pour herself a cup, when Halli stopped her and gave the pot a sniff.

"No," Halli said. "We're better than this."

As always, she had her standards.

She poured out the dregs of the old pot, then brewed up some new. While they waited, she told my mom what was on her mind.

"This isn't going to work anymore," Halli said.

My mom seemed genuinely confused. "What isn't going to work?" Maybe she thought they were still talking about the coffee.

"Me working here," Halli said.

My mother just looked at her.

"It's time," Halli said. "I'll be leaving soon, so you'll need to replace me anyway. A few weeks shouldn't make a difference. And I need all my time to study. So I can't work here anymore."

My mom stared at Halli for another second more, and then the tears started to flow.

"Please don't cry," Halli said. "You can't keep getting upset about all of this. You need to understand that things are changing. We both need to adapt to that."

My mother covered her face with her hand and sobbed quietly behind it. But not so quietly that Elena and Will couldn't hear it. Both of them looked up.

Will caught Halli's eye and scowled. She gave him a guiltless gaze back.

Elena got up from her desk and came into the kitchen. She hugged my mom around the shoulders.

"What's going on?"

"Now she wants to quit working here, too," my mom cried. "I don't understand what's going on."

"Why do you want to quit?" Elena asked.

"It's time," Halli said. "I'm going to be leaving anyway."

"But can't you wait?" Elena asked. "My understanding is you still have to pass some test…?"

"I'll pass it," Halli said. "Then I want to leave."

Elena and my mom looked at each other.

"Well, can't you wait?" Elena asked. "Do your work here until it's time to leave?"

"I wouldn't be good at it anymore," Halli said. "I don't know how to explain it."

My mother continued crying. Elena tried to calm her down.

"So, when do you want to quit?" Elena asked.

"Today," Halli said. "Right now."

Now Elena was mad. She's been like a second mother to me all my life, so she probably felt she was entitled.

"Audie Masters, what is going on? Why are you doing this?"

Halli sighed. She stepped from the kitchen back into the office. Will was listening anyway, so she might as well make a general announcement.

"Look," she said. "I feel I need to say something here. I'm not trying to hurt anyone's feelings, or make life hard for any of you. But I have my own things to do now."

"What things?" Will and his mother said in unison.

"I'm tired of high school. I don't need to be there anymore. I want to get on with my life."

"What happened to Columbia?" Elena asked. "Your mom said you don't want to go there anymore."

"I don't," Halli said. "My mother was right—it's too much pressure. I'll do better at a small college like Mountain State. They said they'll take me as soon as I graduate. So I want to graduate as soon as possible.

"But you need to understand something," Halli said to all of them. "I'm not mad at any of you. We're not in a fight. We don't need to be angry with each other. Seasons end. And this season has ended for me. I want to try something new."

"I'm your mother," my mom said. "Does that season end?"

"No, of course not," Halli answered. "But I'll be eighteen in a few months, and I have some of my own ideas about how I want to spend my life. I'm not doing this to punish you. You're a good mother—anyone can see that."

My mom sniffled and ran her sleeve under her eyes.

Halli did feel sympathy for her. She knew it must be very hard to deal with a daughter who suddenly wasn't herself anymore.

But Halli also knew she wouldn't be able to fix this by staying around. She couldn't make it easier by pretending to be me. The longer she did that, the more likely it was that my mom or anyone else might start noticing things were wrong: I didn't know physics anymore. I didn't know how to do the bookkeeping. I suddenly didn't know so many things I've known all my life. How would it help the situation if people started wondering whether I'd had some sort of mental breakdown and couldn't remember things anymore?

No, it was better to be ruthless about it, make a clean break. Hard for people in the short-term, but better for everyone overall.

"This isn't about any of you," Halli said, gazing directly at Will. He met her eyes and stared back. "The sooner I can help you understand that, the better."

Will shook his head and looked away. Halli knew there was nothing else she could say.

She reached down under my desk to retrieve my backpack.

"I'll see you at home later," she told my mom. "I'll make us some vegetable soup tonight—you'll like that. And if your back still hurts, I'll give you another massage. But I have to go study now. I'll see you all later."

And with that, she walked out the door.

Leaving my mom, Elena, and Will to discuss what on earth had just happened.

32

Halli enjoyed her run home from the office. So much to replay in her head, so much to think about for the future.

She changed into sweatpants and a fresh T-shirt, then spent about half an hour chopping up vegetables to make a soup—potatoes, turnips, parsnips, carrots, a lot of those greens my mom couldn't figure out why she needed. Halli waited until it was all gently bubbling before she finally called the professor and told him what had happened.

The professor sighed. It was starting to be his main reaction to Halli's reports. But he took the matter in stride.

"You were probably right to quit," he said. "It's

unfortunate, but these things are going to happen. What did her mother say?"

"Not happy," Halli answered. She didn't bother going into the long version.

"Still no sign of Audie?" the professor asked.

"I would have told you."

"Yes, I know."

Halli peered into the computer screen. "You look better today. Did you sleep?"

"I did," he admitted. "You were right, what you said before. I need to stay sharp, for all our sakes. Thank you for badgering me."

Halli shrugged. "It's what Ginny taught me. She was always right about things like that. Hold on. I need to ask you something."

She fished out of my backpack the smartphone Will had given her. She had no doubt he wouldn't feel so generous toward her now, after everything that happened that afternoon. And she didn't feel guilty about that. Instead she felt grateful that the whole transaction had come up while the two of them were still getting along.

Halli was always grateful to find herself in the right place at the right time. Especially since she'd also experienced plenty of the opposite.

"What do I do with this?" she asked Professor Whitfield, showing him the phone. "How do I make it work?"

He explained to her how to transfer my phone number to the new phone. And he also explained that there'd be an extra monthly cost.

"Oh. All right. I'll wait."

She was tired of waiting. She wanted to start making her own money—now. It was time to discuss some of her options with the professor.

"I've done some research," she said. "It looks like there are several guiding companies near your college, and more in the surrounding areas. Do you know any of them?"

"Some," he said. "Mountain State has an outdoor education program. A lot of our students go on to become guides, so the companies recruit on campus. I've met a lot of the owners."

"Perfect," Halli said. It was more than she'd hoped for. "Then you can help me find work. I can guide skiing, climbing, hiking, kayaking—"

"Whoa, whoa," the professor answered, laughing. "It sounds like you're trying to make a full-time job out of it. Don't forget about school."

Halli stared at him blankly. "I won't be going to school."

"Yes," the professor said, "to college. Remember, I'm offering you a scholarship. Of course it's for Audie, really, but you'll have to pretend to be her until she can come back."

"No..." Halli started over. The professor obviously

wasn't getting it. "I'm taking this math test so I can stop going to school forever. I don't belong there—at Audie's school or yours. I belong outside. As soon as I leave here, I want to find work."

But Professor Whitfield seemed to think it was Halli who didn't understand. "The only way I can pay for you to come here," he said, "is if you enroll as a physics student. Just as Audie would. You'll have to sign up for classes. And you'll have to attend—but only until we find Audie again," he hurried to add.

Halli closed her eyes. If this was the professor's plan, it wasn't going to work. She needed freedom—not another new set of rules. And certainly not a new set of classes where she'd be expected to understand physics and any other subjects I was interested in.

"We can help you," Albert piped in from behind the professor. "It'll be like algebra. I can tutor you on the side."

I don't want that. Any of that. But Halli simply nodded. Arguing with them wasn't going to get her where she wanted, which was out of Tucson, into Colorado. She needed Professor Whitfield's college, and she needed his money. For now.

"You're right," she said. "I didn't understand before. Now I do."

"It'll be fine," Professor Whitfield said. "And it won't be forever. Audie *will* come back."

"Of course she will," Halli said. She gave him a

confident nod. "I have to go study now. Albert, please send me more worksheets."

"Will do," he called toward the screen.

"Everything all right?" the professor asked Halli. He must have seen something on her face.

"Mm-hm, fine. I need to go check my soup. I'll talk to you tomorrow."

She clicked off the call and closed the lid of my laptop.

And sat in my chair staring at my wall. Imagining the giant map of the world she'd been mentally projecting there for the past several days.

Her plan wasn't going to work. Colorado wasn't going to work. She'd been fooling herself all along.

She heard the front door open. Great. Not even a moment to herself.

"Audie?" my mom called. "We need to talk."

The last thing Halli needed right now was some big, dramatic, heart-to-heart talk with a mother she didn't care about.

Halli pasted on her smile. "Coming!"

33

I had mother troubles of my own.

"We expected more from you, Herr Schroeder," Halli's mother was saying to a head that hovered above her tablet. The head was bald, with crooked teeth, and it looked worried. "Are you aware of your competition?"

"*Ja*, Doktor Markham, but as I explained—"

"No more excuses," Halli's mother said. "You either have it for us by the end of the day, or your contract is cancelled."

"But it will not be ready—"

"Then consider it cancelled now. You're relieved of your duties, Herr Schroeder. We won't be using you again."

Halli's mother punched her finger against the side of

her tablet and disconnected the call. Herr Schroeder's head disappeared. I still wasn't used to the 3D effect of those comm calls. I was staring at the air when Halli's mother looked over at me and caught me awake.

"Halli, dear," she said sweetly, "how are you?"

I looked around the room. Just as I suspected, there was someone else in there. A nurse I hadn't seen before was messing around with one of the monitors behind my bed. Of course Halli's mother felt the need to perform in front of her.

"How are you feeling?" she asked me. "You gave your father and me quite a scare."

"I'm fine," I said. "Just thirsty."

Halli's mother snapped her fingers at the nurse, then pointed at me.

"Yes, Dr. Markham," the nurse said. She quickly stopped what she was doing to help me take a few sips of water.

As soon as it looked like I was done, Halli's mother ordered the nurse to leave us.

"But Dr. Rios's orders were to—"

"Go," Halli's mother said.

The nurse nodded and fled the room. I wondered if Bertrise would have been that intimidated.

"So," Halli's mother said, turning to me, "what is all this about?"

"What do you mean?"

"Why was I forced to leave one of the most important negotiations in the history of your father's and my company, and fly over here in the middle of the night to supervise the care of my attention-seeking daughter?"

"Attention-seeking?"

"Well, you've certainly gotten that, haven't you?" she asked. "History reporters clustered outside the hospital, people calling us day and night—I told you that you represent us now, Halli. You were supposed to be discreet and dignified when you came over here."

The woman was just so hard to like. I understood every single harsh thing Halli ever had to say about her mother. I could add a whole list of my own.

"So tell me, Halli," she said, "what were you doing locked in some room with a young man I've never met?"

This was laughable for two reasons: first, I only *wish* the door had been locked. That would have kept everybody out, and I wouldn't be in this situation in the first place.

Second, Halli's parents had ignored her for the first sixteen years of her life, and Halli had ignored them for the past year as they tried to barge back into her life. Halli could have had eighty boyfriends at the same time all around the world, and I doubt she would have introduced a single one of them to her parents.

I chose to say nothing. I believed that's what Halli would have done—just stared blankly back at her mother and chosen silence.

"I'm waiting," Halli's mother said.

"I have nothing to say."

She glared at me through squinty eyes set in a puffy face. She smelled a little like wine. Her makeup had melted into her greasy face. Her teased hair looked flat and unkempt. Her business suit was wrinkled. She looked like she really had flown all night.

But since I'd now flown twice on one of their company's private jets, I knew very well how luxurious it could be. She could have slept in a real bed, eaten gourmet food, taken a shower—brushed her teeth, for goodness sake—generally done a lot better job taking care of herself so she wouldn't look as hagged out as she did right then.

It felt good to have those thoughts about her. Secret, mean thoughts. They even made me smile.

But at the same time, it was hard to look at that woman and not miss my own, pretty mother. To imagine what it might be like to have her there with me now, holding my hand, showing me genuine concern, and not acting like my being in a hospital was some hatched-up scheme to inconvenience her and gain a bunch of publicity for myself. I mean, come on.

"Where's ... everybody else?" I asked. I didn't want to name names, so I left it open-ended.

"If you mean Jake," Halli's mother said, "he's lucky he still has a job. We fired him at first, but once he explained things..." She flicked her manicured hand. "The mess you've gotten us into."

"What mess is that?" I asked, sitting up a little straighter. It was hard to be confident and Halli-like when I was slouched down in a bed. Plus, after days of being immobile, I wasn't feeling all that spunky.

Halli's mother listed them off. "Reporters, board members, business competitors who would love any hint of scandal. You may enjoy all the attention, young lady, but your father and I have carefully nurtured a certain reputation over the past seventeen years—for ourselves and for our company. We don't appreciate being dragged into the spotlight by some uncontrollable teenager."

I suddenly felt very tired—tired of her voice and tired of the insults. That woman was exhausting enough to deal with when I felt strong. It was time to ask myself the most basic question for dealing with my current situation: *What would Halli do?*

"As you may recall, *Regina*," I said, using Halli's mother's first name, the way Halli always did, "I came to London to inspect the facilities here so that I could become more involved with the company. I am a forty-nine percent shareholder."

Halli's mother didn't like me reminding her of that.

"You may also recall," I said, "that it wasn't me who invited that reporter along—you did. I didn't invite

Jake, either—you did. I didn't create any scandal—Jake did. I was minding my own business—"

"With some young man whose parents run a very questionable history organization—"

"Where is Daniel anyway?" I asked. "I'd like to talk to him."

Halli's mother smirked. "I'm sure you would. But once Jake explained the situation to us, we took appropriate measures."

"Then it's true," I said. "You won't allow him to visit me."

"We need to contain this situation immediately," she answered. "Any more publicity needs to be carefully managed. You're not in control of this anymore, Halli. We are."

Before I could say any more, the doctor came in. I'd seen glimpses of her over the past few days as I faded in and out, but this was the first time I really got a good look at her.

She was tall, fit-looking, with thick black hair cut in a perfectly straight line falling just above her shoulders. And even though I distinctly remembered her speaking English to me with some kind of slight accent, this time she spoke in a language I didn't understand.

"*Beni terk annene sormak ister misiniz?*" She gave me a meaningful look.

I gazed back at her in confusion. Then she said

something else I didn't understand, in what sounded like the same language.

When I still didn't answer, the doctor picked up my wrist to check my pulse, and switched back to English. "How are you feeling, Miss Markham? Your color is so much better today. You're looking well."

She stood in a way that blocked Halli's mother from seeing my face. The doctor raised her eyebrows at me, but I still didn't understand what she was trying to signal.

"I have to examine her now, Dr. Markham," she told Halli's mother. "If you would wait outside."

Her voice was deep, kind of throaty, and I still couldn't place the accent. But I liked the way she spoke with authority. Halli's mother wasn't going to be able to push her around.

"I want a full report," Halli's mother told her.

"Of course. But I need to speak with my patient now, so you have to go."

Halli's mother frowned, but she did as she was told. She slipped her tablet into her briefcase and shouldered a fancy purse that I'm sure cost a fortune. Dr. Rios stood placidly waiting for her to leave the room.

Then she turned back to me and smiled.

"I'm sorry," Dr. Rios said. "I thought I read somewhere that you spoke Turkish."

"Oh ... um, I kind of ... I mean, you know, it's been a while." I was sure Halli did speak Turkish—along with all her other languages. But I certainly wasn't equipped to fake that.

"What did you say to me?" I asked her.

"I wondered if you wanted me to ask your mother to leave," Dr. Rios said. "I hope you don't mind that I took the initiative and told myself yes on your behalf."

"No, I don't mind," I said with a smile. "Thank you."

Dr. Rios went over and closed the door to my room, then drew the curtains across the windows so no one could see inside from the hall. Then she returned and sat on the edge of my bed. She looked at me with an expression that was both friendly and direct.

"Now, Miss Markham," she said. "Are you ready to tell me the truth?"

34

"What ... truth?" I asked. I could smell a stale kind of perspiration start leaking out of my pores.

"I've found when a case is truly frustrating," Dr. Rios said, "sometimes it's best to start with the patient. So tell me, Halli, what do *you* think happened? Why are you here?"

"Um ... because I had a headache?"

"Let's define our terms, shall we?" she said. "On a scale from one to ten, with ten being the worst pain you've ever experienced in your life, how severe would you say that headache was?"

"Um ... a ten? No, maybe an eight." Ten was the true answer—in fact, on a scale from 1 to 10, I would have called it a 50—but since my goal was to get her to stop drugging me and let me out of there, I figured I'd better downplay it.

"Worse than the pain of a broken bone?" Dr. Rios asked.

"Um ... no."

"Worse than the time you nearly lost your toes to frostbite?"

Wow, that sounded interesting. I would have loved to know the story behind that.

"No, I don't think so."

"Worse than a snakebite?"

I didn't know whether she was making this stuff up, or actually reciting from some list of injuries Halli really had.

Then I realized Halli's medical records were probably accessible to any doctor who wanted to look at them. They were probably encoded into that microchip hidden beneath her collarbone.

So I needed to give Dr. Rios some explanation for what had happened. Something that might have actually occurred, but not necessarily shown up in any of Halli's medical records.

"I get really bad headaches sometimes," I improvised. "I used to get them when my grandmother and I went mountain climbing. I think it was the altitude." Then I thought of a better, more general reason. "And sometimes I get them because of stress. I've been under a lot of stress lately."

"Hmm." Dr. Rios didn't seem convinced. "Let's look together, shall we?"

She pulled out a small, wallet-sized tablet from one of the pockets in her white coat. She swept her finger across the screen, then poked it a few times. When the lights started swirling above it, she set it down flat on my bed.

The lights quickly formed themselves into an image. A 3D image of a brain.

"We surveyed it when you first came in," Dr. Rios said. "I've looked at it from all angles. I can't find a single thing wrong with it."

I couldn't have been happier to hear that. The way Halli's head hurt sometimes, I wondered if maybe I'd broken something in there.

But I had to play it cool. Like there was never any question in my mind.

"That's because I'm fine," I said. "It's just a temporary thing that hardly ever happens anymore."

"Yes, but why at all?" Dr. Rios asked. "A headache of the type you experienced—something so severe you were rendered unconscious—should leave some physical marker within the brain. If you bruised your skin, for example, I would find subtle indications of it: a pooling of blood, a warmer temperature at the site. We took images of your brain immediately when you arrived. There should still have been some remnant of whatever caused the effects you were feeling."

I didn't know what to tell her. In part because I didn't understand the headache myself.

"I feel perfectly fine right now," I said, "except I can't stay awake. Am I on some kind of drug?"

"We are giving you medications, yes."

"Well, I really wish you'd stop," I said. "I need a clear head. I don't like feeling fuzzy like this."

"I can understand that," Dr. Rios said, "but we don't want to wean you from them too quickly, in case the pain returns in full. Perhaps another day or two."

"That long?" I said. "Please. I don't need them. I'm fine—really."

"I'm glad you're feeling better," Dr. Rios said, "but you have to understand. You're my patient, and I dislike it when my patients suddenly scream out in pain. Call it a personal issue of mine," she added with a smile. "Selfish, I know."

Then she became more serious. "I have to tell you the truth, Halli. You've been a very difficult patient for me."

"Oh, I'm sorry—"

"No, no," she waved away any apology. "What I mean is I enjoy puzzles, but this one has been much more difficult than I am accustomed to." She smiled. "I like to know everything, you see. Top student. Best in class. So when I can't find an answer…"

All I could say again was, "I'm sorry."

"Despite that," she said, "I am thrilled to have the

chance to meet you, even under these circumstances. I've followed your career since the beginning. I have a younger sister who adores you and wishes she were you."

I could relate. I felt the same way when I first started learning about all of Halli's adventures.

Now that I *was* Halli, of course, I felt a lot different about it. I hadn't realized before that with any adventure comes risk, and so far all of my risks had led me exactly where I was. I doubted Dr. Rios's sister would have admired the weakened Halli Markham currently lying helpless in a hospital bed.

"So when can I leave?" I asked.

"Not for several days. Perhaps not until next week."

"Next week?" Impossible. Horrible. I needed to get out of there. "Why?"

"Halli, I don't think you understand how much pain you were in. You blacked out several times. Your screams could be heard down the corridor."

Ooh, that didn't sound good. And it especially wasn't good that I couldn't remember that. Maybe something really was wrong with me.

But no—I knew there wasn't. The only thing that was wrong was the interruption in my session visiting my real body. If I could have come out of that experience gently, at my own pace, I'm sure everything would have been fine.

If I couldn't convince her to let me go now, maybe I could at least persuade her to do something else.

"I have a friend," I said. "His name is Daniel Everett. Have you seen him here?"

"Yes," Dr. Rios said. "A nice young man. He was very attentive to you the first few days. It was only after your mother told us to exclude him that he stopped coming."

"I need to see him," I said. "Very badly. Is there any way you can help me with that?"

"You're under eighteen," Dr. Rios said. "I have to abide by your mother's wishes unless it's a matter concerning your medical care." She paused and raised her eyebrows. "Is this a matter concerning your medical care?"

"Yes," I said, taking the hint. "Absolutely. Daniel was there with me when it happened. He was ... helping me meditate. He knows these relaxation exercises—mental exercises—and when I felt one of my headaches coming on, I asked him to help me. We were doing really well, but then some people interrupted us, and ... you know the rest. But if I could see him again, I think we could get rid of any pain once and for all. I'm pretty sure. We could just try."

I was saying too much. I needed to stop talking. But I was nervous. And Dr. Rios didn't look convinced.

I thought of something else.

"Meditation is very important to me," I added. "My grandmother taught me to do it when I was little. We used to meditate all the time." That much was true—Halli had told me so herself. "But I can't do it when my mind is all muddled. The best thing for me would be to get all the drugs out of my system, then let Daniel come here to talk me through a meditation."

Dr. Rios shook her head. "I respect the power of the mind," she said, "but I have more respect for the power of medicine. I can't eliminate your medications—not yet. And I'll have to think about whether to allow Mr. Everett to visit. There are strict guidelines about when we can overrule the wishes of a parent."

"But she doesn't understand," I said. "My mother hardly knows me. The only time she's seen me in person since I was a baby was last weekend. She doesn't know anything about me."

All true. And, I hoped, persuasive.

"Well, the fact is," Dr. Rios said, "you, not your mother, are my patient. I must do what is in *your* best interests. So let me think about what you've said."

She shut off her tablet and the hologram of Halli's brain disappeared.

"I'll speak to you about this later," Dr. Rios said. "Right now, you should get some rest."

I groaned. "All I do is rest. And sleep."

"As you should," Dr. Rios said. "It promotes healing. You're far better off now than when you first arrived."

That was because the effects wore off, I wanted to

tell her. I felt fine after the first time I got ripped out of my body, too. All it took was time.

Dr. Rios headed toward the door, but before she opened it she asked, "Would you like me to tell your mother that you're sleeping?"

"Yes, please. Thank you for that."

She smiled. "I have a mother, too. With a similar personality. You and I should compare stories one day."

"Why," I said, "did your mother abandon you in India when you were an infant, too?"

"No, Turkey," Dr. Rios said. "With my father. My mother is a surgeon in Spain. And yet despite that, I still became a doctor. Though not a surgeon—I still have my rebellion."

Dr. Rios and I smiled at each other. She really did understand Halli's situation.

"I'll consider your request," she said. "Now I have other patients I must see."

"Thank you, Dr. Rios."

"My pleasure, Miss Markham."

She softly closed the door behind her. Against my will, I could feel the drugs pulling me back into sleep. I tried to fight them, but as usual it was no use.

My eyes were fluttering closed when I saw the door to my room open again. I thought maybe it was one of the nurses, or worse yet, Halli's mother.

I wish. It was Jake.

35

He shut the door behind him, then rushed to the bed.

"You're awake."

"Not for long," I answered truthfully.

"This is the most awake I've seen you since they brought you here."

His smile would have melted the heart of any conscious girl in any universe. "Oh, Halli, I'm so glad you're all right."

He leaned forward and gently gathered me into his arms. And then, even though my tongue felt flaky and my lips were as dry as dust, he seemed to have no qualms trying to kiss me. I turned away. And not just because my mouth felt so disgusting.

"I saw you hit Daniel," I said. "Why did you do that?"

Jake looked at me with disbelief. "*That's* what you have to say to me? After all this time? Halli, I've been waiting at your bedside day and night. I thought you might die. Don't you understand what that did to me? I love you. You know that. I can't even think about losing you."

The way he looked at me...

But I couldn't let that sway me. He had made a mess of everything. If only he had done what I asked and left me alone for a few days. Trusted me with Daniel—

—okay, even though it's true my feelings for Daniel seemed to intensify by the hour the more time we spent together —

—and you could also argue that Jake might be rightfully confused about where things stood between us, since at one point I did tell him I loved him back, but that was before all of this happened, and now it wasn't true anymore. Maybe it never was. Maybe my judgment was always so clouded when we were together because he was the parallel version of Will in this world, and he was always kissing me, and looking at me that way, and telling me he loved me...

"Where's Red?" I asked, trying for a more neutral topic. I felt so sleepy, but thought I might still have a minute or two left in me. That poor dog had been on my mind. I wanted to at least find out if he was all right.

"He's with them," Jake said. He seemed to have

trouble saying the name. "Daniel and his family. I couldn't watch the dog and be here with you, too—"

"No, it's fine," I said. "Thank you. I just wanted to know."

I couldn't stand the look on his face. He seemed so disappointed. Clearly this wasn't what he expected from our reunion. And I guess I couldn't blame him. I didn't doubt that he'd been at my bedside all those days and nights. He was certainly there every time I briefly regained consciousness. Maybe I was being too hard on him.

"Thank you," I said. "For being here all the time. That was really nice."

"Nice?" he said. His eyes softened and the edges of his mouth turned up into that smile I could never seem to resist. "Halli, I would give my life for you. I don't think you understand what it's been like, seeing you in pain, hearing you scream—"

"Yeah, okay," I said. I really didn't want to hear about the screaming again. It made me very uneasy. And somehow made my head throb with the memory.

I needed to change the subject. I said the first thing that came to mind. "I heard my parents fired you."

"Briefly. It didn't matter. Nothing matters right now but you." He picked up my hand. Halli's hand. I liked the way he held it. Then he lifted it to his lips and kissed it. Come on.

I was losing focus. Fast. And I still needed something from him.

"Could you do you do me a favor?" I asked. "Please?"

"Of course. Anything."

"Do you think they'll let me see Red? I miss him so much."

"Of course they'll let you see him," Jake said, as if the answer should be obvious to me. Maybe everyone in that universe took for granted that dogs got to fly next to their owners on commercial airplanes—Halli told me they even had their own seats—and also sit with them in their sickrooms until their owners healed.

And now for the trickier part of the request.

"Then can you ask Daniel to bring him? Just for a while?" I asked it as innocently as I could.

But Jake wasn't falling for it. "I can get you the dog myself. I'll send a car for him right now. The driver can bring him straight here."

"But Red doesn't do well with strangers," I tried. "It would be better if Daniel just could bring him—"

"He can't," Jake said. "Your parents don't want him here."

Because of you! I almost said, but I stopped myself. It seemed smarter to keep him on my side. Maybe if I acted like I didn't care whether or not I saw Daniel, Jake would eventually relax and tell Halli's parents it was okay for him to visit.

A big maybe.

It was more likely I'd have to get out of the hospital first before I ever saw Daniel again.

But all of it was too exhausting to think about. That dull headache I'd felt earlier was gone now, but in its place was the heavy lethargy I'd come to associate with an extra dosage of drugs. It was as if the drugs themselves sensed even the slightest hint of pain, and then immediately pumped themselves into the bloodstream. For all I knew, that was one of the medical advances they'd come up with in Halli's world.

"Okay then," I said sleepily. "Just Red."

Jake leaned over and kissed me. "He'll be here when you wake up. So will I."

Maybe he wasn't so bad, I thought as I drifted away. Although Daniel was better, wasn't he? I knew I had reasons for being mad at Jake and wishing Daniel was there instead. Lots of reasons—good ones.

I just couldn't remember what they were.

36

Halli awoke on Thursday morning with a renewed sense of mission.

She'd gone to bed unhappy. First, because of the conversation she had with Professor Whitfield and Albert where they pointed out to her that she couldn't just run off and do whatever she wanted in Colorado. Not if she wanted the college's money. If she was going to live there on my scholarship, she would have to be a physics student, just like me. Which was the last thing Halli wanted to do.

And second, because my mother had her own point of view about the radical choices I was making lately—quitting my job, treating everyone so insensitively, acting like staying there and going to school and spending time with my mom during my senior year was suddenly so awful, and why was I acting this way, was something wrong, please, why didn't I just tell her, we could work it out together, we've always been a team, what's going on with you, Audie? Et cetera, et cetera. Accompanied by more tears, which left Halli with a pounding headache and a panicky feeling that she just had to get away as soon as possible, no matter what.

But in the light of morning, things were clearer again.

Halli lay in my bed looking at the ceiling. Thinking about her life before. Thinking about Ginny.

"Are we going to cross that?" Ginny quizzed her one day as they stood on the bank of a river deep in the jungle.

Halli was eight. She looked at her grandmother, hoping for a clue, but Ginny kept her face impassive.

Halli gazed again at the water. The current looked fast, but they'd crossed faster ones in the past. She thought they could probably do it.

"Yes," she told her grandmother.

"So you think we should cross it right now?" Ginny asked. She lifted her foot as if she were about to stride straight into the river right then.

"Wait!" Halli said.

Ginny pulled her foot back.

"I need to test it first," Halli remembered.

"Good," Ginny said.

Halli searched around for a rock that was heavy enough for the job. Then she tossed it into the center of the river and listened.

The rock made a distinct *ker-plunk* sound. That meant the river was deep. And dangerous.

"What should we do?" Ginny asked her.

Halli considered their options. "We'll go together," she said. "Walk slowly, side by side, and use our hiking sticks to brace ourselves."

"Which way do we walk?" Ginny asked.

Halli pointed. "At an angle, slightly downstream."

"And what if one of us falls?" Ginny asked.

Halli thought about that. "We'll tie ourselves together with rope first. Then whoever's still standing can pull the other person back up."

"Or the river will pull us both down," Ginny said, "and since we're tied together we'll both drown."

Halli nodded, taking that in. She'd learned not to get frustrated when she didn't know the answer right away. It helped that Ginny always let her take her time to work through the proper solution. Even if it didn't seem like they had the time to spare.

"We'll link arms instead," Halli said. "And shuffle our feet sideways."

"What if the water's too deep to wade?" Ginny asked. "What if we have to swim?"

What if, what if, what if...

The answer was never, "Well, I give up. Forget it.

This is hopeless." There was always something they could try, always some action they could take to move forward.

Halli never forgot that.

Or at least tried not to.

There was a period after Ginny died when she let the darkness consume her. Halli didn't know what to do next—not for a long time. She made her way back to Colorado from India, but then didn't leave there for a whole year. She didn't want to. She holed up with Red and only went out every day because she didn't want to cheat the dog. Red needed his walks, his hikes, his runs in the snow while Halli skied. If not for the dog, she might have stayed in bed for a year and rarely bothered to get up.

She hated that period of her life. She didn't feel like herself. And she knew Ginny would have been so very disappointed.

But it was Ginny's own fault, Halli reasoned at the time. If only her grandmother had left her a note, left her some guidance—not just sneaked off without saying anything to Halli, even though it was clear Ginny knew she was going to die. It's no wonder Halli lost her footing. No wonder she felt lost.

Until I came along. At least that's what she told me. Somehow my showing up out of the blue one day reignited something in Halli. By the time I saw her last, hiking in the Alps, she looked happy. Energized. Alive.

Until, that is, she died.

But that reignited spirit was still in her. Something had shifted in Halli over the past month, and she felt like herself again. Like the girl her grandmother had brought her up to be. And that girl didn't give up. Not ever.

So what if?

What if you're stuck in someone else's universe, and you're stuck in her life, and she's stuck in high school studying things you know nothing about?

You learn those things or you leave.

But what if you're not interested in learning those things, and you can't leave unless you pass a test?

You pass the test.

But what if the place where you were going to escape to involves more school and more studying things you know nothing about and aren't interested in? What if all you really want to do is get out and explore this new world from top to bottom and use all the skills you already have?

Then you figure something out.

Like what?

I'm working on it.

37

It was working.

In Algebra I that morning, Halli could see she understood. The equations Ms. Gonzales wrote up on the board actually made sense to her. Halli nodded as one of the girls in the front row called out the right answer.

Ms. Gonzales saw that.

After she wrote the next equation, she called on Halli. "Audie? Want to give it a try?"

If it had been me, I would have been all tongue-tied, sweating. Even if I thought I knew the answer. Algebra brings out a kind of panic in me.

But Halli was calm and cool.

She gave the correct answer.

Winslow Henry twisted in his seat and gave her a

bitter smirk. "Great," he muttered, like she'd just turned traitor, like one of the inmates had suddenly become friendly with the guards.

"It's easy," Halli whispered when he turned around again. "I can show you."

"Yeah, right," he snorted, then shrugged like he didn't care.

In Mrs. Arnold's English class two periods later, Halli offered again. "I can teach you in ten minutes."

"Shut up," Winslow said.

Halli wasn't going to beg him to let her help him. She'd done the decent thing by offering, and now he was on his own.

As soon as the bell rang for the start of class, Mrs. Arnold picked up a stack of notebooks from her desk and started handing them out.

Someone groaned. "Not journaling."

"Yay!" said a girl in the back.

"It's been a while," Mrs. Arnold said. "Would you rather have this or a pop quiz?"

"This," came the chorus in return, and Mrs. Arnold continued distributing the notebooks. She handed Halli the one with my name on the front.

Finally, Halli thought. Some activity at that school that she could actually enjoy.

She had spent the past few days in Mrs. Arnold's listening to the class discuss a book Halli had never heard of and had no intention of reading. She tried pulling out the algebra worksheets to work on instead, but Mrs. Arnold shut her down right away.

"Audie, your thoughts on Benjamin's decision? Do you think he was right or wrong?"

"I don't know."

"Do you think he was too impulsive? Or was he brave?"

"I don't know."

A few more back-and-forths like that, and finally Mrs. Arnold gave up. But she still made Halli put away the math worksheets, and Halli hadn't tried since.

But if they were going to write in there instead, then maybe it wouldn't be so bad.

Halli hadn't written anything in a very long time. Not since the day before Ginny died. People asked her to, begged her to—"*Tell us what you're doing! Tell us how you are!*"—but Halli always resisted. It wasn't anyone's business how she felt about what happened. And she knew she wasn't living the kind of life anymore that anyone might find interesting.

But it wasn't surprising that people still wanted to hear from her, whatever she might want to say.

Over time, her field reports had become wildly popular—even more popular than Ginny's. It had something to do with the style Halli developed of always downplaying whatever was going on. The more dramatic something was in real life, the more casual she tried to sound about it.

Brief visit to village doctor. Agreed bite not serious. Probably won't lose arm. Ginny happy, since means I can carry more gear. Doctor says rest tomorrow and chew herbs she gave me. Taste like rancid worms. Might chew off arm instead.

Whenever they got back to civilization, Ginny and Halli would write up longer, more detailed descriptions of their trips. But people always seemed to prefer Halli's day-to-day reports from the field.

Fingers and feet so frozen, decided to shave head to stuff hair inside boots and gloves. Ginny said stupid idea. Waiting for her to fall asleep so I can shave her head instead.

"Eli?" Mrs. Arnold called. "I think you're next."

A guy two rows over from Halli got up and shuffled to the front of the room. Mrs. Arnold held out a paper bag in front of her. Eli reached in a pulled out a slip of paper, which he handed to Mrs. Arnold.

"Okay, let's see what today's..." She read the slip and smiled. "Good. This is a good one." Eli returned to his seat.

Mrs. Arnold used her Magic Bag of Topics as a way of tricking us into writing essays. At the beginning of the semester, she had us all write out provocative questions on a slip of paper. Things like, "Would you rather be deaf or blind? Why?" or "Would you rather be ugly but smart, or good-looking but stupid?"

Every few weeks Mrs. Arnold would have someone reach into the bag and pick out one of the topics. Then we'd have five minutes to speed-write out our answer in essay form: topic sentence, two paragraphs of body, conclusion. It was a lot better than always having to write things like, "What was the theme in *Old Man and the Sea*? Discuss."

"Here's your question," Mrs. Arnold said. "Ready? 'If you could have any two special powers, what would they be, and why?' You have five minutes. Go."

Halli thought about it for a few seconds, then she started writing. She didn't stop until Mrs. Arnold called time.

Halli wished she could have written longer. It felt good to exercise that muscle again. And what she'd written ... surprised her. She hadn't expected to say exactly what she said.

Mrs. Arnold gathered up the journals, then told everyone to pull out their books. She spent the rest of the class period droning on about fake characters Halli didn't care about. She was still thinking about what she'd written:

If I could have any two special powers, they would be the power to go back in time and bring back people who have died.

38

Something cold against my face. Something wet. Something with a particular, familiar smell...

Then the hot breath, the wagging, wriggling body, and I knew without even opening my eyes that Halli's dog was lying practically on top of me, licking me frantically, and generally having an ecstatic meltdown because he was finally reunited with the girl he thought was his.

"Red," I breathed out happily, lifting my hand to scratch behind his ear. That wasn't enough for him. He let out a sound that was half bark, half moan, and kept bumping his head into my arm until I finally got the message and hugged him tightly around his neck. Then he nuzzled in as close as physically possible, and continued licking me on the ear. If he could have climbed inside my skin somehow, I'm sure he would have done it.

I felt this giddy sort of happiness. Like I might want to bark and moan myself. I hadn't realized what a relief it would be to see and feel that dog beside me again. To hug him and smell his fur. To be the object of so much affection and pure love. To feel something warm and comforting there in the midst of the cold, strange features of the hospital.

And equally welcome, the human face I saw smiling down at me with both delight and concern.

"Halli Markham, please tell me you're alive."

"I'm alive," I said, smiling back.

"No, *really* tell me," Sarah said. "Something that only you would say if you really were all right and everything hadn't gone so horribly wrong."

"I'm fine, Sarah. Really. Thank you so much for bringing my dog."

"Ha!" she said indignantly, plopping down on the dog-free side of my bed. "As if that chauf*feur*, or whatever his credentials are, were simply going to march into our home and collect the dog and drive away with him! 'Master Demetrios's orders,' indeed! I said, 'Look, you tell your *master* that *I* am the mistress of this dog—temporarily, at least—and it will take an order from the Queen for me to release him to the care of anyone other than Halli Markham herself.'"

A little dose of Sarah, and I was already feeling much better.

"Well," she went on, "the driver could see he wasn't getting past *me*, no matter how unthreatening I might look in my pink bathrobe, and since apparently he was under orders to deliver Red to your bedside within the hour, he simply had to wait while I changed into something more presentable, since I wasn't parting from that dog under any circumstances no matter what *orders* your boyfriend Jake might concoct—"

"He's not my boyfriend—"

"Well done, you," she bubbled on, "since that was to be topic number two: his general overall unsuitability and demeanor, hitting my brother in the face like that, telling your mum not to let us visit you anymore—your mum!" she paused to exclaim. "That's topic number three—but eventually Red and I rode comfortably in the back seat of a *very* large sedan, and here we are, and may I say I can now safely die of happiness, having seen that you're all right."

She reached down and picked up my hand and pressed it against her cheek. "Oh, Halli Markham, you don't know how *awful* it's been. We've all been absolutely mad with worry."

"I'm sorry about that," I said. "But really, I'm fine."

"I hope you're right, because if anything happened to you..."

Her voice trailed off. Sarah turned to the side and

made a hiccupping sound. Much to my surprise, I realized she was trying to hold back a sob.

"Sarah!" I squeezed her hand. "Look at me. I'm fine now. Everything's going to be all right. They said they'll let me out soon."

Not exactly true, but I couldn't let the sunniest girl I know sit there looking so upset.

Sarah sniffed and gazed at me with misty eyes. Her voice was very quiet. "Halli, tell me the truth. I know I had something to do with it—with your being here in hospital—and if I did, if I somehow caused this..."

"You didn't," I assured her. Another lie. She had everything to do with it. But I never wanted her to know that. "Don't cry. Everything is fine."

Sarah nodded and wiped her eyes.

"Is ... Daniel here, too?" I thought I knew the answer, but I had to ask.

"No, and I tell you he'll crack apart with jealousy when he finds I've been to see you. Mum and Dad, too. But of all days, the three of them left this morning on some errand to Oxford. I don't expect them until this evening."

"Oh. That's too bad." I smiled as if I didn't really care that much, even though inside I was the one cracking apart at the thought that I could have seen Daniel, but didn't. Maybe this was the one time any of them might have been able to sneak in. Maybe he'd never get that chance again.

But agonizing about it wasn't going to help me.

"How has Red been?" I asked Sarah, changing the subject for my own sake.

It wasn't a casual question. Red has separation problems. I saw that for myself the one time Halli came over to my universe to visit me. When she returned, her campsite was in shambles. Red had gone practically berserk looking for her. Then once I took over her body, I got to experience for myself the kind of connection those two have. Red never left my side.

"Oh, he's been lovely, of course," Sarah said. "Poor thing."

She reached over and patted his side. But I noticed she avoided looking me in the eye.

"Sarah...?"

She sighed and met my gaze. "Well ... there was a bit of destruction that first night."

"What kind of destruction?"

"My bedroom, my brother's bedroom, our living room, half of the kitchen—"

"Oh, Sarah—"

"Not to worry!" she said cheerfully. "All in a good cause. That poor dog was the most pitiful creature I've ever seen. After the medics took you away, he sat on the pavement howling as though someone had stolen his very soul. It was terrible. Then we finally coaxed him into a car and brought him home, but he was still so distraught, and ... well, it took some time for him to calm himself.

"But after that," she went on quickly, "once he'd exhausted himself, poor thing, he was quite sweet and pathetic. And now he can't bear to let any of us out of his sight. Mum and Dad let me miss school a few days, just to keep him company."

I kissed the top of Red's head and gave his neck an extra squeeze. "Poor boy. I'm so sorry to have done this to you." He licked my cheek and thumped his tail on the bed.

"And we got the house all sorted again in time for the party," Sarah said, "so no harm done."

"What party?"

"My dad's fiftieth—you probably don't remember—"

"Oh, of course I remember! I'm so sorry I missed it. I really like your dad."

Sarah and Daniel's father is a history producer. Their mom is an archaeologist. They were the only people besides Daniel who knew the truth about who I was and where I'd come from. And they'd tried to help me find the real Halli again. Which I did. It just hadn't worked out the way I hoped. Not yet, anyway.

"So how was it?" I asked Sarah. "Did you all have fun?"

"Not really," Sarah said. "Everyone was fairly mopey. Daniel especially. He kept saying he should be here with you, not drinking punch and eating sweets. He's been very devoted, my brother. He obviously feels a great bond, because of Audie. I think he pines for her a great deal."

"Yes, um ... right..."

Now it was my turn to keep control over my tears. It was hard to hear Sarah talking about me behind my back, telling me that Daniel missed me without realizing she was telling *me*. For some reason it meant more to me than if she had told me to my face.

Even though she just did.

I cleared my throat and blinked my eyes a few times. I turned my head to the side and coughed. And then accidentally kept on coughing.

Sarah stood up in alarm. "Are you all right? Should I call someone?"

"No, I'm fine—just some water..."

Sarah filled a cup for me and helped me with the straw. I took a few sips and used all that time to gather myself.

"So..." I said, searching for a safer topic, "have you had the pleasure of meeting my mother yet?" I remembered Sarah had a very poor opinion of Halli's parents, since she knew all about them abandoning Halli as a baby.

"No, and I shan't, thank you very much," Sarah said indignantly. "She's already gone. One of the nurses told me."

"Gone? As in..."

"Back to America. Didn't you know?" Sarah studied my face. "She didn't tell you, did she? That wretched woman. Not a jot of maternal instinct. I know one shouldn't speak ill of another person's mother, but honestly, that woman just makes me so, so…"

"Trust me," I said. "I agree."

"Whereas *my* parents have been absolutely sick with worry," she went on. "They've even been trying to locate your cousin, I think. Something I'm surprised your mother didn't do—"

The back of my neck tingled. "What do you mean, they've been trying to locate her?"

"Well, don't you think she should be here?" Sarah asked. "Clearly no one has informed her. I'm certain Audie would fly to your bedside if she knew about your condition."

"Yes, I'm sure." I sat up straighter in bed. "But what do you mean they're trying to locate her? What have they done?"

"I'm not privy, you understand—no one feels the need to include *me* in their secret plans, as though I'm not a member of this family, when clearly I love your cousin nearly as much as you and Daniel do—"

"Thank you," I said, delighting in that statement more than she could have known.

"All this whispering," Sarah went on. "Audie this, Audie that. I suppose Daniel must have confessed some sort of love sickness for her, because my parents seem very sympathetic every time he mentions her name."

Oh, Daniel. I could imagine what those conversations might be. Not about any love sickness, but strategy sessions among the three of them about what might have gone wrong, and how they might be able to help me.

Maybe that was why they all went to Oxford. Did it have anything to do with me? Or was I just being self-centered, thinking everything in the world had to be about me? It was perfectly possible they went there because Daniel will be graduating next spring. I suppose that even in the midst of a crisis, you still have to deal with your university applications.

Which was a weird thing to think about. Because I realized I hadn't been thinking about my own university application—not for a long time. Getting into Columbia University was as insignificant to me now as whether I got a good grade on the last paper I turned in to Mrs. Arnold. That whole prior life of mine seemed so remote. So irrelevant, in a way. Even though my main goal at that moment was still to get back to my old life as soon as possible.

"Are you all right?" Sarah asked. "Did I say something wrong?"

"No, not at all," I said, shaking myself out of my stupor. "Sorry, I just ... faded out there for a second."

The door opened and Bertrise came in.

"Ah, your friend is here!" she said.

Sarah jolted off my bed, looking very guilty. "Sorry, I only came to bring the dog—"

Bertrise clicked her tongue and patted the air in a soothing way. "Don't trouble yourself. Who is this beautiful animal?"

"Red," I said, and the dog thumped his tail in greeting.

Bertrise came over and stroked his head. "Did you miss your mama?" she asked the dog, pressing her nose right against his. Red wagged in response.

"I know how my girls would miss me," Bertrise said. "Agnes and Coco, my little kittens. How they would cry and cry if I went away..." She shifted her attention to me. "How are you feeling, Miss Markham?"

"Better," I said, "now that Sarah's here."

Bertrise wagged her finger at Sarah. "I remember you. So sad. But look! Your friend is nearly well."

"Completely well," I corrected her.

"Only the doctor can say." Bertrise smiled and patted my arm. "But you have good color today—red rosy cheeks. Your dog and this young lady are good medicine."

Sarah looked very pleased. And also relieved that she wasn't going to be kicked out.

But that relief only lasted a second.

"What are you doing here?" came a voice from the doorway. "Who let you in? You're not supposed to be here."

"Hello, Jake," Sarah answered bitterly. "Back again so soon?"

39

For a generally polite girl, Sarah had a lot of very impolite things to say to Jake.

Bertrise pretended she had a lot of work to do on my monitors, my bedding, swabbing my forehead—anything to get to stay in the room while the whole drama played out.

"As if WE are the problem," Sarah shouted at one point, "banning *my* family instead of yourself! When *you're* the one who insisted I show you and Bryan where I thought Halli Markham and my brother might be. Now I see they were hiding with good reason! Daniel told me everything about it. We had no business barging in there like that, just so you could satisfy your prurient suspicions about what they might be doing—when I've already *told* you Daniel fancies the cousin—"

"There is no cousin," Jake said. "Halli's parents don't have any siblings. So I don't know who you think this Audie person is, but that's beside the point. What did your brother say the two of them were doing in there? I'd really like to know."

As if I weren't in the room, sitting right there listening. Jake and Sarah were too wrapped up in their own fight.

"Planning something very romantic, I can tell you that," Sarah said haughtily. "Something involving the *cousin*—and yes, she exists, I've met her, you fool—and if you hadn't forced me to interrupt them, then all of this might have ended happily..."

I don't know what Daniel told Sarah the two of us had been plotting. Something romantic involving me? The real me? That sounded much more fun that what we were actually doing.

"You're delusional," Jake said.

"And you're a disgrace," Sarah answered. "All I'm asking is that you allow my family and me to visit Halli Markham whenever we please. We're her *friends*—we have no wish to harm her."

"Sarah, I don't have anything against you," Jake said.

"Humpf!" she answered.

"But I do have something against your brother," he continued. "I don't care what he says he was doing, whatever it was obviously put Halli in danger. It's my duty to her parents—to everyone—not to let anything else happen to her. Look where we are!" he told Sarah. "Do you think I want her to be here?"

"Do you think *I* do?" Sarah returned. "I love Halli Markham with all my heart! If I thought Daniel had anything to do with her condition, I'd bludgeon him on the head myself! But clearly my brother didn't cause any of this. It was us—you and Bryan and me—banging into the room like that and causing some sort of brain episode from the shock—"

"That isn't what caused it," Jake said.

"Oh, you know so much," Sarah answered back.

Throughout the whole argument, Red had continued happily snoring at my side. The poor dog probably hadn't slept the whole time we were apart. Now he was making up for it. Occasionally if the shouts grew too loud, he'd snort and shift and bury his nose a little deeper under my arm. I admired his concentration. Especially because I was starting to feel an exhaustion like that, too.

I wanted to stay awake—fought for it—but as the noise continued it also started hurting my head. And just like I suspected before, once I reached a certain threshold of pain—not very much, so they must have had the whole thing adjusted very low—I could feel a druggy sort of haze seeping behind my eyes. Like clouds closing in before a storm.

"Guys..." I murmured at one point, and even though

they didn't hear me, Bertrise did. She came around to the side of my bed where I could see her.

She bent over and spoke softly, probably so she wouldn't interrupt the very juicy fight she was enjoying so much. "Sleepy, Miss Markham?"

I nodded. I licked my lips.

"Thirsty, too? No wonder, all the heat in this room."

I didn't think the room was particularly hot, but I did need a drink. Bertrise poured water into my cup and held the straw for me while Sarah and Jake kept arguing.

"He is yours, no?" Bertrise whispered to me.

"My what?"

"Your young man."

"Oh … kind of…" I mumbled. "I don't know…" I felt one step from passing out. My tongue and eyes felt so heavy.

"Be careful," Bertrise told me. "You sleep and they stay awake."

"Huh?" I wrestled with my eyelids to keep them open just a few seconds longer. I wanted to understand what she was saying.

Bertrise held up her index finger from one hand, then her index finger on the other. She brought the two fingers together, pressed side by side. Then she gave me a significant look.

I tried to see what she was seeing—some sort of connection between Sarah and Jake?—but it was all too much for my medicated head. Let the two of them do what they wanted. I was too busy being unconscious.

"You're despicable," was the last thing I heard Sarah say.

Jake said something equally rude, and then it was lights out for me.

40

It was Thursday afternoon back in my world, and Halli was currently kneeling on a yoga mat, head bent backwards, hands gripping my ankles so she could arch my chest higher toward the ceiling in another one of those impossible yoga poses I could never see myself doing. But apparently I was wrong.

Lydia came over every now and then during the class to help Halli make some slight adjustments to what she was doing: straightening a leg here, lengthening an arm there, tucking my hips at one point so Halli could stand even taller.

And that's what was really amazing: how tall Halli looked inside my body. Like she'd found an extra inch or two somewhere just by standing straight and relaxed instead of always slouching the way I didn't even realize I was doing. It's like seeing someone else wear an outfit of yours and thinking, "Wow, that looks so much better on her."

When the yoga class was over, Halli once again left sweating and smiling. She stepped outside for a few minutes to cool off in the fresh air.

"I don't get it," Lydia told her when she came back in. "You're a complete natural. Are you sure you haven't secretly been doing this at home?"

Halli repeated what she'd said before. "You're a really good teacher."

"That wasn't me," Lydia said. "You were perfect all on your own."

Halli shrugged and changed the topic. "Any word on Gemma's brother? Has he come to town yet?"

"No, he's supposed to get in some time tomorrow. Why?"

"Curious," Halli said. "And hoping he's the opposite of her."

"I don't know about personality," Lydia said, "but he is cute. Gemma showed me some pictures of him last night."

"Hm," Halli answered noncommittally. She thought Daniel was attractive enough, but he wasn't really her type. She liked guys with dark hair, dark features—more like Will, as a matter of fact.

Plus, it was hard to think of Daniel as cute when she

knew he was already taken—by me. She wasn't in the habit of poaching other girls' boyfriends.

"Let's talk about Saturday," Lydia said.

"All right." Halli wiped a towel across my face, then draped it around my neck.

"My house or yours?"

"Excuse me?" Halli asked.

"Getting ready," Lydia answered, as if it were obvious. "I don't know what I'm going to do with your hair now that you cut it—maybe I have some combs or something we can use. Or I might crimp it. You should probably come over in the morning so we can try a few things in case you need to wet your hair down again before we really do it."

Halli gave my head a quick shake of confusion. "Lydia, what are you talking about?"

"Your *hair*. And your makeup." Now it was Lydia's turn to look confused. In the past, I'd always willingly turned myself over to her on the few rare occasions when I actually agreed to attend some party or other event. She knew I was completely incompetent when it came to making myself look presentable. I never wore makeup in my regular life, and the most effort I ever put into my hair was shampooing it, putting a little conditioner on the ends, and then letting it air dry while I went on to more important things like eating breakfast or finishing my homework.

But a fancy ball? Where I'd have to wear a fancy

dress and might even have a chance to impress Will for once? Of course I would have wanted Lydia's help—I would have begged her for it if she hadn't offered. It's just that Halli didn't feel that way at all.

She patted Lydia on the arm. "Thank you, but I think I can manage."

Lydia gawped at her. Then she laughed. "Audie, you're not going to try to do this on your own? Come on!"

And now a kind of coldness crept across my face. Halli never appreciated an insult—even when it was aimed at me, not exactly at her.

"I can take care of myself," she said. Then she forced on a smile. "But I'd love a ride from you that night, if you don't mind."

Lydia's eyebrows furrowed. She probably couldn't believe Halli was sticking to her no. But she must have sensed enough about Halli's mood not to press it any further.

"Of course I'll give you a ride," she said, looking down as if she were suddenly very interested in the carpet. "You think I'm walking in there alone?"

"Good," Halli said. "Thank you."

Having eased the tension, Halli asked Lydia for a ride home from yoga, too.

"Sure," Lydia said. "But I need to clean up first. If you don't mind waiting."

"I don't mind," Halli said, and proved it by settling

into one of the chairs in the lobby and pulling out a stack of algebra worksheets from my backpack.

Lydia stood there for a few seconds more, like she might want to say something else, but whatever it was, she let it go and went about her work. Pretty soon Halli could hear her running the vacuum in another room while Halli ran through her new studying routine:

Do a worksheet, do ten pushups. Another worksheet, then ten squats. She had a whole series worked out now so she could build my body at the same time she got ready for the test. It was a lot better than just sitting in one place and whipping through worksheet after worksheet.

She didn't hear Lydia come back into the room. Right then she was in the middle of doing jumping jacks.

"Who are you?" Lydia asked again, just like she had that first day after yoga.

This time Halli wasn't caught off guard. She stopped jumping and gave Lydia a smile. "Ready?" She gathered up her worksheets.

"I'm serious, Audie. Are you ever going to tell me what's really going on?"

Halli gave her the standard answer. "I just want to make some changes."

"I guess," Lydia said. "Like an entire personality transplant, if you ask me."

"Do you really think I'm that different?" Halli asked.

Lydia snorted. "Let's see: telling off Gemma, telling off my brother—yeah, I heard about that—advanced yoga poses, voluntary exercise, voluntary *algebra*, of all things—so yeah, I think you're that different."

"Haven't you ever wanted to change anything about yourself?" Halli asked.

"Of course!" Lydia answered. "But not overnight. You might want to change something, but it's not like it's just that easy."

"What would you change?" Halli asked. She was genuinely curious.

Lydia rolled her eyes. "Come on. I have a paper to write for Mr. Varney's class." She headed for the door.

They walked together across the darkened parking lot. A cold breeze made them hurry to get into Lydia's car. I've always appreciated October, because it finally starts getting cold enough to wear sweaters just before Halloween. It's such a relief after what feels like a six-month summer.

As soon as they slammed the doors, Halli asked her again. "Tell me one thing—one thing you think you would change."

Lydia sighed. "Really? Just one?" She started the car. "Okay, but you're going think it's really stupid."

"I doubt that."

Lydia shook her head, like she still wasn't sure she wanted to confess it, but as she drove out of the parking lot she finally spit it out.

"I'm sick of this problem I have about guys."

"What problem?" Halli asked. I would have asked the same thing. Because even though Lydia and I have been best friends since we were little, we never really ... talk. It's weird. But it's like neither of us wants to get too personal.

I understand it from my side, since the only boy I ever could have talked about was Will, and I wasn't about to reveal all my feelings about him to his twin sister. But I've never really understood why Lydia doesn't like to talk to me about the various guys she's had crushes on over the years or dated. It's like I'm allowed to know the basic facts—"James and I went out last night"—but then she doesn't want to tell me much more. Not about how much she might like a guy, or how the date went—any of it.

But maybe I've never asked her the right questions. Because now if she was going to tell Halli—

Lydia tapped her steering wheel. Like she was stalling, trying to decide how much to say.

"Okay, so this thing with Colin," she blurted out.

"Colin? Gemma's brother?"

"Yeah. I haven't met him, right? But already I'm all..." Lydia took both her hands off the steering wheel and waved them in the air and spoke in a high falsetto. *"Oh, Colin's coming! I'm so excited! He's the one for me! It's going to be so great! We'll get married, and we'll live in a castle—"* She dropped her hands back on the steering wheel and dropped her voice back down to normal. "Know what I mean?" she asked Halli. "I build things up in my mind, and then I'm always disappointed. It lasts a few weeks, at most, and it's over."

"Why?" Halli asked. "Because of you or because of him?"

"Either," Lydia said. "Both. It varies. But it's always the same."

I've noticed that, too, of course, but she's never wanted to talk to me about it.

And the truth is, I've never been brave enough to ask.

It hasn't felt like it was my business. I've always assumed if she wanted to tell me, she would. So I've just been waiting all this time.

"I've had that happen," Halli said.

"*When*?" Lydia answered. "Who have you ever even liked? Besides my brother, I mean."

Oh. So she knew. Oh.

But Halli handled it well.

"He's the perfect example," she said. "I can make up a whole story in my head about how things would be, but do you ever see me act on it? No. Because it could never live up to the dream."

"Trust me," Lydia said, "Will is no dream. You've never had to live with a boy—they're disgusting. But I'm glad you're finally willing to admit you like him. It's been ridiculous."

"We're not talking about me," Halli said. "We're talking about you."

"So you'll see," Lydia said. "This Saturday. I'll be all googy-eyed about Colin, and probably fall head-over-heels for him, and we'll probably make out somewhere, and then he'll leave, and we'll write..." She said this all in a bored tone, like it was predictable and inevitable. "And he'll be telling me from afar, '*Oh, I love you so much. I can't live without you,*' and I'll already be over it because that's just how I am."

Halli gave a little snicker.

"I'm serious," Lydia said. "You watch."

"Or ... you could do something different," Halli suggested. "Just this once."

"It's no use," Lydia said. "Even when I'm not trying, it always goes the same way. I get all hepped up, the guys are all infatuated, then *blip, bing,* never mind. Over."

They had reached my house. Lydia shifted the car into park while Halli got my backpack out of the back. Before she left, Halli leaned in and offered Lydia a useful piece of advice:

"Break the habit," she said. "Colin is here for only a short time, right? So don't go after him."

"It won't matter," Lydia said. "He'll probably go after me." She didn't say it arrogantly, but just factually. She's obviously been through it enough times before that she knows how guys react to her. And I've seen it, too:

Lydia is very beautiful, and she's always had plenty of attention.

"Still worth a try," Halli said. "I've always found I can turn it on or turn it off. If I feel like making a connection, I do. If I want to be left alone, I am."

"Yeah, Audie, whatever you say," Lydia answered with a laugh. "Guess you've been off for what, almost eighteen years now?"

It was pointless, Halli knew. She could tell Lydia didn't actually want advice. She just wanted to complain about the problem.

And maybe Lydia didn't even see it as a problem—not really. Maybe she liked things exactly as they were, never having to spend more than a few weeks on any one relationship. Halli knew people like that. Sometimes she *was* a person like that. She'd been happy enough to have just a week-long fling with that guy Karl. She told me at the time she didn't plan on keeping in touch with him once we all left the Alps. So Halli understood Lydia better than my friend could know.

Which made everything that happened after that so much stranger.

41

I woke up not knowing what day it was, what hour, even whether it was day or night. The windows of my hospital room were covered, and the lighting was the same it always was.

I pushed my way up through the fog. It wasn't as bad as it had been in the days before, but it still had a weight to it, tugging on my mind and trying to keep me from thinking clearly. But enough was enough. Halli's body felt doughy and sluggish, her mouth was constantly dry, and whatever there was of me inside her was sick to death of always feeling wrong—off—drugged into this kind of mental lethargy that made me feel stupider by the hour.

I enjoy my brain. I always have. I wanted to enjoy Halli's brain, too, if they'd just let me.

"Hello?" I called out. I wasn't sure if anyone could hear me, but sure enough, within a minute or so a friendly young nurse appeared at my door.

"Yes, Miss Markham? How are you feeling?"

"Do you have coffee or something?" I asked. It was the only thing I could think of. "Or tea?" I knew the British loved their tea, but so far it hadn't given me the kind of kick a strong cup of coffee did—especially the way Halli brewed it for me a few times. I didn't have that option, of course, but I'd take what I could get.

"I'll bring a tray," the nurse said. Then she pressed the button on her collar. No doubt summoning someone higher up to say whether she was actually allowed to give me what I asked for.

So I wasn't that surprised to see Dr. Rios coming in with the tray herself.

"I understand you've asked for my speciality," she said, pronouncing it with an extra *i*. "I keep my own supplies, for special patients. Have you ever tried Turkish coffee?"

I shook my head no. Even though Halli probably had.

"Then just a little, I think," Dr. Rios said, pouring out half a cup. "Not so much to shock the system. But first have some bread. Your stomach needs a base."

So I ate a few bites of the soft, sweet bread she offered me, then took a sip of the coffee. Then another, then another. It tasted like mud, like dark, earthy medicine, but it also felt like life. Like the opposite of whatever they'd been dripping into Halli's veins.

"Thank you," I said after I'd drained the whole cup. "That feels really, really good."

"Have some more bread and I'll give you some more," she promised. Then she pulled out her tablet and set it on the bed.

"I have a mystery to discuss with you," she said.

"Uh-oh, another one?"

"This one much simpler, I think." She swooped her fingers over the screen, poked it a few times, and the familiar lights started swirling above it.

But this time, instead of the lights forming themselves into a 3D image of Halli's brain, they organized themselves into a graph, with lines spiking and dipping from left to right.

"The red," Dr. Rios said, pointing to one of the lines, "is the automatically-delivered pain medication. The green is your blood pressure. Blue is your pulse. Black is the activity in your pain receptors."

She tapped the screen once, and the lines rose and fell in a slow, steady rhythm.

"These are the days you've been with us," Dr. Rios said. She pointed to the mountains and valleys of the graph. "Your pain peaked on the first day, lessened within twenty-four hours, reduced in the days that followed, but see here—" She pointed to a couple of areas of the graph with very noticeable spikes. "Do you know what was happening during these times?"

"No."

She pointed to the first spike. "This was a visit with your mother." She pointed to the second one. "This was a visit from Jake. This was your visit from Miss Everett—"

I started to protest, but Dr. Rios held up her hand.

"This is the beginning of your visit with Miss Everett." She pointed to a nice long valley on the graph. "Your pain levels were almost non-existent. Then later in the visit..." She pointed to the spike. "Do you know what was happening here?"

I briefly explained about the fight between Jake and Sarah. Dr. Rios nodded. "You see the pattern, don't you?"

"Yes. If I'm relaxed, no pain medication. If I'm stressed..."

"So we know what we have to work on, don't we?" Dr. Rios said.

Sure. Just cut out all the stress in my life. Good luck with that.

"I've been considering your request," Dr. Rios said. "About Daniel Everett."

That made me sit up.

"The visit from his sister and your dog was, I think, healthy. Therapeutic. Would you agree?"

"Oh, definitely."

"Until the argument," she said.

"Right."

"In fact," Dr. Rios said, "one might look at these results and conclude that it is in the best interest of my patient to allow her certain visitors—her dog, for example? And perhaps one human visitor each day to bring the dog to her?"

My eyes must have lit up like sparklers. I could see where she was going with this, but I didn't want to jinx it by speaking.

"We must be careful," Dr. Rios said, "not to overwhelm you. I'm still concerned that you have any pain levels at all. But I would like to attempt this experiment, if you are willing."

"Yes, please," I said as calmly as I could.

"Good. Then we'll begin this afternoon, shall we?"

"So Daniel can come? Is that what you're saying?"

"If he brings your dog, yes. That is his primary purpose, you understand?"

"I understand." Boy, did I. Dr. Rios was giving me the best gift she could have. I wasn't sure why, exactly, but I wasn't going to ask too many questions. I didn't want her to change her mind.

But I couldn't help asking this: "What about Jake, and my mother, and the people on her list?"

"I'll answer for that," Dr. Rios said. "But your responsibility is to remain calm, do you understand?"

"Yes. I will. I promise."

"Then perhaps we can lessen the medication," Dr. Rios said. "Let us see."

She shut off the swirling lights and got up off the bed.

"Dr. Rios, I really appreciate this."

She smiled. "I know you think we enjoy having you here as our guest, but I prefer to see you out in the world."

"I prefer that, too," I said.

"Tell me something," Dr. Rios said. She sat on the edge of my bed again. "Weren't you ever frightened, out there with your grandmother, just the two of you all alone in so many life-and-death circumstances?"

"Of course I was." I felt like it was all right to make that admission. Obviously I would have been a hundred thousand times more scared than Halli ever was, but I couldn't imagine she was never scared. She was a human, after all, not a robot.

"Which do you think was the most frightening?" Dr. Rios asked.

Now that was trickier. I quickly scanned my memory for any and all of the stories I'd ever heard about Halli, whether from her or from Daniel or Sarah.

"Probably the sharks," I guessed.

"Ah, yes. A very reasonable thing to fear. Although I'm certain the polar bears were just as unnerving." She smiled and patted my foot. "I have other patients to see.

But I'll ask the duty nurse to call Mr. Everett and pass along the good news, shall I?"

I smiled back. "I think you're my favorite doctor."

Dr. Rios laughed. "A high compliment! I happen to know some of my colleagues who have treated you over the years—Dr. Montrose, for example, who set your leg in Kenya. But I'll try not to allow it to overwhelm my ego."

She left and I settled back onto the pillow. And for once, felt hopeful. Daniel was coming. Daniel would help me fix everything.

It's not that I expected him to understand any of the complicated physics—that wasn't it at all. But what I valued most was his clear-headedness. His analytical mind. His calm reasoning in the face of utterly crazy circumstances.

Okay, that wasn't the only thing I valued. Or even what I valued most. Now that I was lucid again—or at least lucid for that moment, without the brain-muddling effects of the drugs—I could remember very clearly how much I liked him. Maybe, if I wanted to be honest, even loved him. I missed his honesty. His decency. The warmth and kindness I felt whenever I was with him.

Maybe he didn't have that same irresistible charm that Jake did, but Daniel didn't need it. He was the kind of person who grew on you. And then once he did, you never wanted him to go.

And there was this: he knew who I was. He wasn't like Jake, thinking the lips he kissed belonged to the real Halli Markham—to the girl he'd had a crush on since he was a kid. No, when Daniel looked at me he saw the same Halli exterior, but he also saw beneath it to the person I really was.

And that was the person he preferred. Talk about irresistible.

Between Daniel's calm rationality and my knowledge of physics, the two of us could figure this out. I had faith in us. And I had a reason to keep trying:

I wanted me back. Daniel wanted me back. And Jake wanted Halli Markham.

If I worked at it hard enough, maybe I could give all of us our wish.

42

"Feeling better, luv?" It was one of the day nurses, Laura, who seemed to trade off most often with Bertrise. I liked her, but the two of them were very different. Laura didn't coddle me the way Bertrise did. Instead, she had this kind of efficiency about her that made me feel like I should sit up a little straighter, wipe the gunk out of my eyes, ask for a toothbrush. Which I did.

"Feeling a little sour?" she asked, smacking her own mouth like she'd just eaten something nasty. "Not surprised. We'll fix you right up."

I was happy for the chance. If Daniel really was coming—maybe within a few hours, if I was lucky—I wanted to at least feel presentable.

Nurse Laura helped me to the bathroom and set me

up with some grooming supplies while she changed my sheets.

As I stood at the sink splashing my face and brushing my teeth, I was surprised Halli's legs didn't feel weaker. I hadn't used them in days. But the treatments the nurses were giving them must have helped. They rubbed some kind of gel on them every few hours and then encased them in long thigh-to-ankle cuffs that were filled with gel, too, like squishy shoe inserts. Then the cuffs would start pulsating, very gently, squeezing different parts of my legs at different times, making them feel like toothpaste being pushed around in a tube. The sessions I was awake for felt weird, but also very relaxing.

Laura came in to check on me. "Now then, feeling up to a proper wash?" She pointed to the shower in the corner of the bathroom.

"Oh, my gosh, I would love you forever." Considering that I couldn't remember the last time I'd taken a shower—five days? More?—you bet I wanted one. It's not like I was filthy—the nurses had been wiping me down with warm, scented water—but standing under a stream of hot water sounded so delicious, I could hardly wait.

She set up a chair for me just so I wouldn't overtire those legs, and I sat under the hot water for as long as I could, just feeling the clean. When I was done, Laura helped me into fresh pajamas and back into bed.

"There now, quite an improvement, eh?" she asked.

"Quite," I agreed.

"Would you like some holey?"

"Excuse me?"

She pointed into the air just above my bed. "The holey. Thought you might like a change."

"Oh ... okay." I still didn't understand what she was talking about, but so far all of Laura's suggestions had made me start to feel human again. I wasn't going to say no.

She reached for a device hanging from the side of the bed, swept her thumb across it, and activated some 3D projector that had lights swirling above my bed exactly where she'd pointed moments before.

It was a holograph. I should have realized. The same way some British people in my world might call television "the telly."

"Which History, luv?" Laura asked.

"Which ... history?"

"Which channel?" She was starting to look at me like I was stupid. She stood with her finger poised over the device, waiting.

"Oh, um, which do you think? Actually," I interrupted before she could answer, "is there an adventure one?"

Finally, I thought, I might have a chance to see some of the footage from Halli's and Ginny's travels that I'd heard so much about. I knew there was no guarantee a program about them would be on at that moment—I mean, really, the chances were pretty slim—but I thought it was worth a try.

But as soon as the lights formed into an image, I could see it wasn't them. Instead it was a small man, about the size of a two-liter bottle of soda, floating above my bed, dressed in full winter gear, and painstakingly climbing up a frozen waterfall. I could hear some sort of commentary in the background, but the volume was too low. It didn't matter, though, I could get the idea just from the action.

Laura watched for a moment, then shook her head. "You people are mad, the things you come up with." Then she pointed her finger at me. "And don't you go getting any fresh ideas from this, Miss Markham. I'll never forgive myself if we patch you up and you leave here in the pink, only to go strap yourself to the wing of an airplane or some such lunacy."

"I promise." What I didn't tell her was that I agreed with her completely. Even though I knew the real Halli probably would have thought that scaling an icicle waterfall or riding the wing of an airplane were both perfectly fine pursuits.

"I'm off to swap more bedding. You all right here for a bit?"

"Sure," I said. "Thanks."

She handed me the remote control, or whatever they called that device, then bustled out the door.

Meanwhile, the small holographic man continued his climb. He wore spiked boots and held two curved spikes that almost looked like extensions of his arms. He'd swing one back behind him and catch it in the ice above him, then step up with one of his spiked boots. Then he'd swing the other arm, drive that spike in, and take a step with the other leg.

It was slow going, and I felt a little hypnotized by the steady motion. He made it look so easy. But then suddenly he slipped. One of the spikes he'd just swung didn't stick, and then suddenly he lost his balance, and his boots were scrabbling against the ice, and he was just hanging there by one arm. I could hear some of the low commentary in the background—something like, "...incredibly dangerous, Mike, especially if he..."—and then I couldn't make out any more.

I was watching the whole ugly scene, worrying for the miniature climber who was about to plummet from the ice onto something not nearly as soft as the bed he was hovering over, when suddenly I remembered my own spikes: the ones on the graph Dr. Rios had shown me. I probably wasn't helping my stress level by watching this disaster unfold. And even though the man just then got one boot planted, then the other, and finally his one swinging arm, I knew I needed to watch something more calming.

Laura still hadn't come back, so I was on my own. I swept my thumb down the device, vertically, and for the first time *ever* since taking over Halli's life, one of the devices in her universe worked for me! A new image formed above my bed—a man who looked oddly familiar—and I settled back to try to remember who he was.

"Hmpf, that'll put you to sleep now, won't it?" Laura said when she returned.

"Do you know who it is?" I asked.

"It's one of those old scientists, isn't it?" she said. She reached for the device and increased the volume.

"… come to my second law of motion. The greater the mass of an object, the greater the force needed to act upon it for acceleration…"

"Is that … Sir Isaac Newton?" I asked. The person looked vaguely like the pictures I'd seen of him, and since he was the one who first defined the three laws of motion, it made sense. But he lived in the 1700s, so unless someone in Halli's universe had invented holographic recording back then, it had to be an actor portraying him.

"Who knows," Laura said. "I've always hated this channel—puts me back in school. Fancy a look around?"

She changed to another science channel, this one showing a woman who looked considerably more modern.

"… bacteria found within the well of an active volcano…"

Laura had no patience for that, either.

She passed by several more channels: World History, Art History, and finally came to rest on Celebrity History.

"There now—look familiar?" she asked. "They must play this every other hour, I've seen it so many times."

It was Halli—the real one. Stepping up on some platform and waving to a crowd. And stepping up beside her, Ginny Markham. Looking like my Grandma Marion, but much fitter and younger and happier.

Halli looked younger and happier, too. Maybe fifteen years old? I tried to think when I looked like she did.

"Turn it up!" I said.

"... just returned from their successful expedition to Antarctica," a British narrator was saying. "Within a year, Ginny Markham was dead, and Halli Markham left to carry on alone."

The scene then cut to a distant 3D image of Halli outside her house in Colorado. There was snow on the ground. Halli carried in an armful of firewood. She paused as if she heard something, then looked directly into the camera. Then she scowled, hurried back into the house, and slammed the door.

Then a more recent scene.

"... captured by a customer at a florist's in London. Mystery man revealed now to be Daniel Everett..."

I stared in fascination. It was Daniel and me. Talking in between two rows of plants. And even though the customer's camera hadn't recorded what we were saying, I knew. I could almost read Daniel's lips as they formed the words that had burned into my brain:

"You're not the girl I'm in love with. And I'm willing to do anything to get her back."

I would have loved to stay there, savor that moment in the image hovering above my bed, maybe even play it back again if I knew how, but whoever had put that program together was already on to something else: me being rushed into an ambulance, chaos all around me. Red trying to follow. The medic kicking him. Jake jumping into the ambulance.

Then the camera shifted to a young man sitting off to the side, being tended by another medic: Daniel, his face bleeding.

Then cut to another house I recognized: Daniel's family's.

"... history producer Sam Wheeler, his wife, archaeologist Francine Everett, daughter Sarah, son Daniel."

Then Sarah—dear Sarah!—coming out of the house and hurrying toward a waiting car. In answer to the shouts directed at her, she yelled back, "I have nothing to say. You vultures can return to your nests. This is our private business."

"Miss Everett!" one of the reporters tried again. "Are your brother and Miss Markham in a relationship?"

Sarah stuck her hand on her hip and frowned. "As if I'd tell you! Mind your own business and leave our property at once."

Then she hustled into the car and it took off.

Then cut to a different location: outside a school somewhere, young men hurrying down brick walkways between classrooms.

And suddenly another face I knew: Martin. Daniel's friend—the one I met hiking with Daniel and Sarah in the Alps.

"No, I told you, he fancies the other one—the cousin," Martin said, sounding exasperated. "Now stop bothering him—and me."

Martin huffed off, and the camera found another target: Daniel again, this time from afar. He didn't seem to know they were watching him. He walked along, head angled downward, a very serious expression on his face.

Poor Daniel.

Someone called to him, and he turned, giving the camera a better look at his face. The picture froze there. Daniel's kind, handsome face hovered above my bed.

"He is a nice looking bloke, isn't he?" Laura said. She smiled at me. "Nice fella, too. Very polite."

"You met him?"

"First day I was on shift. But then not after. Once he was on 'The List,'" Laura said dramatically.

"I know," I said. "But Dr. Rios said he can come back and bring my dog. So I'm hoping he'll be here today."

"That'll be lovely," Laura said. "Both of them here."

Then she shushed herself so we could listen to the rest.

"... Mr. Everett continues to refuse to comment," the narrator said. "But sources say there is no evidence of any cousin in Miss Markham's family tree. So who is this mystery girl? Or is she a fabrication? Why would Halli Markham's friends lie to protect her?"

The narrator answered that question for himself by showing the next two hovering heads: Halli's parents.

"Could it be that the titans of hydroenergy do not approve of their wayward daughter's choice?"

"Wayward daughter...?" I repeated.

"Is there a suitor they'd perhaps prefer?"

Then Jake's face, smiling. Smiling at me, as a matter of fact. It must have been film taken by that reporter Bryan Stewart when he was following us around. I didn't know he'd filmed us at that moment, but I remembered exactly when it was: Jake and I had just secretly sneaked off for another one of our quick makeout sessions. We'd just come back looking rumpled and guilty.

My life—Halli's life—really was looking more complicated by the moment. No wonder they were so interested. A celebrity like Halli, with potentially two hot young suitors? I'd probably watch that show.

Then back to the frozen image of Daniel looking toward the camera.

"What really happened in the upper room at the History 14 Studios?" the narrator asked. "Is Daniel Everett responsible for the mental and physical breakdown of Halli Markham?"

"What?" I answered back. "I haven't had a breakdown—"

"... Why is our strong, courageous, resilient Halli M. currently lying in a hospital bed, comatose and unable to communicate? Anonymous sources—"

"I'm not comatose!" I yelled at the holograph. "And I'm communicating—see? You big fat liar."

I could feel something, something far away, and I tried to ignore it. But I knew: drugs were seeping into my system again. Too much stress.

"... will, of course, update you as we receive more information," the narrator continued.

Calm down. Calm DOWN.

"Nurse!" came the voice from the doorway. "Why are you letting her watch that?"

43

Jake raced over to Nurse Laura and snatched the remote control device from her hand. Within seconds, Daniel's head disappeared and the narrator's relentless lies were gone.

"Are you all right?" Jake asked me. He peered intently into my face.

"I'm fine," I said, feeling irritated, but also ... a little relieved. He was right. I shouldn't have kept watching that once I knew how bad it was.

Jake sat on the edge of my bed and reached out to smooth away a section of hair lying limply against my face. "Halli, you need to be careful—always. Didn't the doctor tell you that? She told me."

"I'm not a child." But the second I said that, I knew I

sounded like one. "I'm perfectly fine," I tried again. "Aren't I, Laura?"

"Perfectly," she agreed, her mouth pinched with disapproval. Anyone could see she didn't like being spoken to or treated the way Jake just had.

He saw it, too.

"I'm sorry," he said, "but obviously my first concern is for Halli. You know what the doctor said about triggering her headaches."

"Do you have a medical degree?" Laura asked.

Jake could have continued the fight with her, but he had the good sense to defuse it. "Like I said, I'm sorry. I probably overreacted."

Laura sniffed and turned her back on both of us while she checked the monitors behind my bed. Jake and I exchanged a glance. He smiled that way he has of smiling at me.

At Halli.

"Everything in order," Laura reported. "As I expected," she added for emphasis. "I'll leave you to it, Miss Markham, unless you need anything else?"

"No, but thank you, Laura. You've been great. Thanks for the shower especially."

She smiled at me, frowned at Jake, and bustled out of the room.

Jake reached for my hand and brought it up to his lips. "Mm, you do smell good." Then he leaned forward and took a good whiff of my neck and my hair. "Very good."

It was hard to think straight when he did things like that, but I had someone else on my mind. When Jake went in for the kiss, I shifted so he landed on a cheek.

Which was a good thing, because in the next instant a mass of yellow came barreling toward the bed and jumped on top of me.

And Red's escort stood in the doorway staring at Jake and me.

"Interrupting something?" Daniel asked.

Jake answered, "Yes," just as I answered, "No," and practically pushed Jake away.

Daniel looked ... great. I don't know how else to put it. If someone had been looking at my stress graph right now, I'm sure they would have seen it plummet to the bottom. It was just such a *relief* to see him standing there. So solid and safe and steady. I locked eyes with him and gave him the simplest of smiles. He seemed to relax then, too.

Laura stood triumphantly behind Daniel. "You know Dr. Rios's new rule," she told Jake, obviously pleased to get back at him after he'd yelled at her that way. "One visitor at a time. Plus dog." She swept her hand behind her like she was inviting him to the door.

But Jake wasn't easily intimidated. He leaned forward and brushed his lips against Halli's ear, then whispered, "See you soon," loudly enough for Daniel to hear. Then he took his time striding toward the doorway and out past Daniel and the nurse.

Meanwhile, a certain someone demanded my attention.

"Yes, boy, yes, I missed you, too," I told the wriggling, overjoyed Red. He had been crawling closer to me by the second, until now his face was level with mine and his tongue lapped at any skin it could find. I held him tightly around the neck and felt the bed shake with each thump of his tail.

I stole another look at Daniel. It was hard not to openly stare. He just looked so ... great. Not because of what he wore or how good-looking he naturally is, but just because it was *him*. There in the flesh where I needed him. But still standing too far away.

I glanced over at Laura and caught her grinning at me. I smiled back. Then I buried the rest of my smile in Red's neck fur so I wouldn't make such a fool of myself in front of Daniel.

"Oh, listen," Laura said, theatrically holding a hand to her ear. "I hear someone calling. Best be off then." She winked at me before closing the door behind her.

Then Daniel was to me in three quick strides, and I sat up and reached for him, and he pulled me into his arms and held me so tightly I almost couldn't breathe. I squeezed him back with the kind of strength I didn't know Halli's arms had anymore. I could feel his heart beating against Halli's chest and I was sure he could feel hers. And for the moment it felt like that heart was mine.

"Audie, are you all right?"

"Now," I said.

I choked back a cry I didn't realize was there. But it felt so good—so *right*—to be with him again. Like being back in my own body for even a short time after all that time away. If you want to know the science, it was chemical. Biological. And as much a mental as a physical fact: Daniel was the one for me. I would never doubt that again for a second.

But I wasn't the one for him. Not anymore and not yet. I still had work to do. I had to get her back.

"Tell me everything," Daniel said. He sat on the only section of my bed not currently occupied by a blissed-out yellow Lab.

"No, you first. Mine is boring—I mostly just lie here and sleep. Have you found out anything?"

"Perhaps," he said, in that proper British way of his. "My parents know someone at Oxford—a professor there. We visited him yesterday."

So they really were there for me—it wasn't just my egotistical imagination.

"What did he say?" I asked.

"He wants to meet you. To speak with you. I tried to explain as best I could, but obviously you can do it much better. So as soon as you can leave here..."

"Whenever that is," I said. "I don't know, the doctor said maybe next week."

"Next week isn't soon enough," Daniel said.

"I know—it's driving me crazy to be stuck in here."

"No," Daniel said, looking at me with a grave expression on his face. "I mean next week might be too late."

"What do you mean, too late?" I asked. My nerves suddenly felt very cold.

"He thinks the longer you stay here, in Halli's body, the greater the risk of ... deterioration."

I didn't like the sound of that. At all. "What kind of deterioration?"

"Mental. Physical. All aspects."

Daniel and I stared at each other.

"So what you're saying..."

"You could die," Daniel said. "Halli, too. If we have any hope of reversing the process, it needs to happen soon. Quickly."

I swallowed against a dry mouth. My heart was fluttering, and not in a good way.

"I could die."

"You both could," Daniel answered.

Red snuffled into my neck just then, reminding me of other times when I'd relied on petting him to help calm myself. Right now I didn't think any amount of petting would do the trick.

"But ... how does he know, this professor?" I asked, hoping it was just speculation. Maybe it was just a wild theory that wouldn't prove true in my case.

"He said he's seen something like it before."

"What?" That seemed impossible. "When?"

"It's a long story," Daniel said. "It would be better if he told you himself."

Daniel looked behind him to make sure we were still alone.

"Audie, I can't stress enough how urgent this is."

"No, believe me, I get that."

"I'd take you out of here right now if I could."

"Well, can't you?" I asked.

He shook his head. "Your parents—sorry, Halli's parents—have forced the hospital to institute certain measures. Your tracking is linked to a security system. If you leave, everyone will know."

"So what?" I asked, my face suddenly feeling hot. "I'm sick of this. There's nothing wrong with me—" Considering what he'd just said, though, I knew I had to change that. "There's nothing wrong that they can fix here. Do you really think that professor can help me?"

"I don't know," Daniel said. "But I also don't know of any other alternatives at this point."

"Well, if I can't go see him, can we at least call him or something?"

"We could, but the man is ancient. He's practically deaf. We'd have to shout, and even then I think it would be difficult."

I could just imagine that: the Oxford professor's head hovering above Daniel's tablet, and the three of us shouting back and forth about how it was I came to be stuck in Halli Markham's body and what I was going to do about it now. Anyone listening outside my door would get an earful.

"I feel like a prisoner," I said.

"You are one," Daniel said. "For the moment."

We both sat in silence while the truth of that settled around us.

"Maybe I can try something," I said, saying it out loud before I'd really thought through a plan. "My doctor— Dr. Rios—she's the one who let you come here today. Halli's parents didn't want that, but she overruled them. So maybe if I can think of some way to convince her to let me go..."

But then a second thought occurred to me.

"No. If your professor is right, I don't need to get out of this hospital, I just need to get out of this body. I don't need him for that—you and I can do it ourselves. Just like last time."

"No," Daniel said. "Absolutely not."

"Why?" I couldn't believe he didn't see the brilliance of that solution.

"Because it *would* be just like the last time," he said. "We're not alone here. Someone could come in at any moment, and then ... no, Audie, we can't risk it. Not again."

I could feel my stress rise. Could imagine the spikes on my graph. Could picture exactly what Daniel was afraid of, the pain shooting through me again, Halli's head feeling like it had split wide open—

"Then what?" I said. I had run out of ideas.

Just then Laura came in. Daniel let go of my hand. He gave me a look that said, *See?*

Laura caught the movement. "Oh, don't mind me, luv!" she told Daniel. "Be out in a flash."

I'll have to admit my heart sank. Daniel was right: even a small interruption like this one could ruin everything. I'd feel the ripping, the agony, then all those drugs would flood into my system and I'd be out of it again for days...

Unless —

"Laura, can you send for Dr. Rios?"

Daniel gave me a quizzical look. I ignored him for the moment.

"Trouble, luv?" she asked. "Everything all right?" She leaned over me to check.

"I'm fine," I said, "but if you could find her right away, I really need her. Please, Laura. Right away."

She nodded and hurried out.

I turned to Daniel. "We're going to talk to her, you and me. And we're going to lie."

45

"Dr. Rios, this is Daniel Everett."

"I remember," she said, coming toward us with a look of great concern. "What is it?" she asked me. "Are you in pain?"

"Not yet," I said, "but it's coming. I can feel it."

Dr. Rios quickly whipped her tablet out of her pocket and called up the graph of my vitals. All three of us looked at the various spikes and valleys from the past hour. My stress level had just peaked again about five minutes before.

It was one of the reasons I wanted Dr. Rios to come so quickly. Because I knew that the drugs in my system were already sensing trouble, and were seeping into my blood.

"I need you to take these out," I told the doctor,

pointing to the tubes in my arm. "If I'm ever going to learn to control this on my own, I have to do it when I'm under stress. And Daniel just told me something about one of our friends that has me very distressed. So now seems like a very good time to use meditation."

Dr. Rios looked very skeptical. "If you need pain medication, you should have it."

"I need to try, Dr. Rios. That's why Daniel's here— remember? He's the one who was leading me through a meditation before all this happened, and I know it was working. But then those people interrupted us, and that's how I ended up here."

Dr. Rios shook her head. "I don't want to risk it."

"Think about my life," I told her. "I will always be under constant stress. I live dangerously. I like it that way. I can't spend my life in this hospital being drugged day and night. You have to let me try to manage it on my own."

Before she could argue, I added, "And this is the perfect setting. You can monitor my graph every minute and make sure I'm safe. But I need you to order everyone to stay out of here for as long as it takes. It might be an hour, it might even be more. Please, Dr. Rios, I can feel the drugs. I don't want them anymore!"

I was close to tears, and I wasn't faking. Dr. Rios looked from the graph, to my face, back to the graph.

"One hour," she finally agreed. "But only if you're

stable for that hour. If I see anything that concerns me—"

"One hour," I repeated, feeling my heart still racing. I wondered how I was ever going to calm down enough to make good use of the time. It might take me an hour alone just to bring my mind to some kind of peaceful condition.

But if that was all I had, it was all I had, and at least it was a start.

Daniel hadn't spoken the whole time, but now he piped up. "If there's any problem, I'll alert you. I care about her as much as you do—more."

He squeezed my hand, and boy, did I want that right then. I forced myself to breathe slowly. I needed to start calming down right away.

Dr. Rios moved behind my bed and shut off whatever switches or buttons or valves controlled the drugs moving into my veins. Then she picked up her tablet from on top of my bed, but she didn't shut it off. She carried it with her, the graphs still rising above it in their vivid blues and greens and reds.

"One hour, Miss Markham, Mr. Everett. You have it, beginning now."

I did what I knew how to do. Calmed my mind, calmed my breath, pictured myself flying over the vast sea of vibration, feeling for any kind of sign of Halli, some hint of energy, a tug, a ripple, anything to tell me she was there.

Nothing. She was lost to me. As lost as I was to her.

It didn't matter that I had one hour of complete peace. Didn't matter that Daniel lowered the lights, that Red soothed me with his steady snores, that Daniel held my hand when I asked him to and sat there beside me protecting me and making me feel safe. I did everything I could think of, but still none of it worked. I couldn't make the connection no matter what I tried.

Finally I had to admit defeat.

Daniel turned up the lights again, then came back to

sit at my bedside. We didn't need to speak. We both looked at each other with the same kind of grim expression.

"I think I need to talk to your professor," I said.

Daniel nodded.

I pressed the button above my bed. "So get ready to lie again."

47

When Halli walked in on Thursday night, my mom was already home from work.

"Audie! Where have you been? I've been calling you for the last two hours!"

"I was at yoga with Lydia."

"Well you could have told me!" my mom said. "I've been worried sick! How long would it have taken you to simply call me and say where you were?"

Halli's expression darkened. My mom could have no idea the effect of her words. They reminded Halli too much of her own mother.

I'd witnessed a few of the comm calls between Halli and Regina. Halli was always tense, snappish, quick to end the call. And with good reason: after ignoring her for sixteen years, suddenly Halli's mother started checking up on her all the time, asking her where she was, what she was doing. It drove Halli crazy. She'd never had to answer to her parents before, and she had no intention of starting.

Her answer to her own mother had been a cold, "Watch my dot." Then she'd ended the call. Once I learned about the microchip and the ability of parents to track their children, I understood what Halli meant.

But this was my mother she was speaking to, not hers, and so she forced herself to remain pleasant.

"I'm here now," she said. "Shall I make us some dinner?"

"I've been waiting to order us Chinese," my mom said. "It's almost time for our show. Or don't you care about that anymore, either?"

From her tone, it seemed like my mother was looking for another fight, but Halli didn't take the bait. She couldn't endure another night of my mother crying and asking her what was going on.

But Halli also had no intention of doing what my mother wanted, which was sitting on the couch eating Chinese takeout and watching some stupid sitcom that my mom and I happen to love. The week before, back when she was trying to be a better sport, Halli had given up at least ten minutes of her precious time to watch what we consider entertainment. After that, she pretended she was still feeling sick, and escaped to my room.

Now that I've seen what passes for entertainment in Halli's world, I can understand her reaction. She had no experience with sitcoms or mystery shows or dramas or anything like that. Not even reality shows, the way we're used to them. Her "reality" shows are actual pieces of history: events filmed while they're going on or reenactments of the past. So it's no wonder Halli had no patience for the exaggerated acting and fake laugh track of the show my mom and I like to watch. She wasn't about to give up another minute to nonsense like that.

"You go in the other room and relax," Halli told my mother. "I'll make us some pasta. It won't take long."

"You sure you don't want to order Chinese?"

"Not tonight," Halli answered with her insincere smile. "Maybe next time."

She could hear the TV blaring from the living room while she chopped up tomatoes and zucchini and garlic to make a sauce. But the noise didn't distract her. She was very, very focused on something else.

There was no tracking in my world.

She knew that, of course—I'd told her—but she hadn't really thought about what it meant to her.

What it meant was freedom.

My mother had just proven that: She'd never know where Halli was if Halli didn't call. Sure, my mom could have taken certain steps—called the police, called Elena, driven around the neighborhood looking for me—but she couldn't do what Halli's parents could by just accessing some real-time map showing exactly where Halli was on the planet.

It was glorious. It was sublime. Halli felt lighter than she had in days.

She boiled some pasta, drained it and tossed it with the cooked vegetables, then brought a bowl of it out to my mother.

My mom patted the couch beside her. "I'm recording it. We can start it from the beginning."

"I have to work," Halli told her. "But you enjoy it. I hope you like the pasta." Then, ignoring the hurt look on my mom's face, Halli picked up her own bowl and headed for my room.

She was just closing the door to my bedroom when she heard my mother call out.

"Audie, please..."

Halli closed her eyes and waited a few seconds before answering. She needed to sound sincere.

"Next time, all right?" she called, knowing that if everything went the way she hoped, she would be out of that house before the show ever came on again.

My mother waited a moment before answering, too. And it sounded like she, too, was trying to appear nice. "Sure, honey. Next week will be fine."

Halli escaped into my room and shut the door behind her.

She booted up my laptop. No surprise, there were three messages from Professor Whitfield.

She called him back and kept her voice quiet.

"Audie's mother is in the next room, so we have to keep this short."

"Have you talked to her about coming here?" Professor Whitfield asked. "I can get tickets for you for next weekend."

"I haven't told her yet. I'll do it tonight."

"Good," he said. "And I've arranged to have someone escort her around campus all day so we have plenty of time together."

"Right," Halli said. But she was distracted. "Listen, Professor, I've been thinking about what you said before—about me having to attend classes there until Audie can take over again. But I have to know: what if? What if we can't get her back?"

"I can't let us think like that," Professor Whitfield answered.

"I understand," Halli said, trying to keep the irritation from her voice. She hated when people wouldn't face facts—wouldn't prepare for disaster when disaster was just around the corner. "But I need to know. What will happen to me if we can't reverse this?"

"What do you mean, what will happen to you?"

"Financially, for one thing," she said. "How long until I'd lose whatever money your college will give me?"

"If you at least tried," he said, "went to classes, tried to do the work, we could probably stretch it out for the first semester."

"Which is how long?" Halli asked.

"Middle of May if you start here in January."

"And what about if I come there now?"

"Then maybe ... December, depending on how well you can fake it."

Halli sat for a moment, silently absorbing the information.

"So it will only be for a few months, no matter what I do."

"Yes," the professor admitted.

That was all Halli had to hear. Because that answer, too, was freeing. She didn't have to worry about losing the college's money, because she was going to lose it anyway. Which meant she didn't have to try to play by their rules.

Halli heard the sound of the toilet flushing. "I should go. I hear her mother. She might come in."

"Okay, but ask her about the trip next weekend—"

There was a knock on my door. Halli's instinct had been right. She snapped my laptop closed and called for my mom to come in.

My mother stood in the doorway and looked around. "I still can't get used to how clean your room is."

Halli smiled politely.

My mom seemed nervous and shy. Halli didn't care, but it would have made me sad to see my mother acting that way around me.

My mom cleared her throat. "Did I hear you talking to someone?"

Halli thought quickly—lie or don't lie? Might as well get it over with.

"That was Professor Whitfield," she said. "He said he can fly us up to Colorado next weekend, if you want to go." She studied my mom's reaction. "Do you?"

My mom tried to look very brave. But anyone who was her daughter could have seen her heart was breaking. She smiled as best she could. "Sure! Fine. That's a good idea. When did you say?" Her voice was abnormally high. Clearly she didn't want to deal with any of this.

"Next Friday."

"And miss school?" my mom said.

"If everything goes well, I'll be finished anyway," Halli said. "I plan to take the algebra test next week."

My mom's eyes welled up with grief. "Next ... week? Already?"

"I'll be ready to leave by the end of the month," Halli told her. "You should be ready for that, too."

48

"No, I'm sorry," Dr. Rios said. "I won't allow it."

We'd been going around and around the subject for the past fifteen minutes. But the doctor wouldn't budge.

She pointed to the graph again. To the rise and fall of the spikes. They were small, but they were there. Despite what I thought, I hadn't been perfectly calm over the previous hour. I'd had moments of it, moments when my graph leveled out and my pulse and breathing looked perfectly mellow, but then the lines would rise again— probably every time I wondered, "Why isn't Halli here? Why isn't this working? Why can't I find her?"

"It's the hospital," I tried to explain again. I remembered seeing some news report once about how some people's blood pressure goes up whenever they have to have their blood pressure checked in a doctor's office. It's called the White Coat Syndrome or something.

But apparently Dr. Rios had never heard of it.

"You are my patient," she said for what seemed like the hundredth time. "My duty is to protect you."

Daniel squeezed my hand, probably trying to send me some signal to give up already. But I had to try at least one more thing.

"Maybe like a day pass?" I asked. "Just let me go somewhere with Daniel for the day, and I swear I'll come back that night."

"And what if you die?" Dr. Rios said. She hadn't used the D word before, but maybe she was as frustrated with me as I was with her. "Do you think I can console your parents with the knowledge that you were out of my care for only one day?" She shook her head. "I'm sorry, Miss Markham." She was back to calling me Miss Markham—that wasn't good. "I will not discharge you until you are well."

"Can we try another meditation?" Daniel asked quietly. I think he was concerned about how heated the conversation had gotten. He didn't want to see those spikes on my graph, either.

Dr. Rios considered that for a moment. "I don't see any harm," she said. "So yes. I will agree to that."

So at least that was something.

"But allow some time," she said. "Obviously Miss Markham has become agitated again."

"Which means I should do it right now," I said. "Isn't that the point?"

"Not today," Dr. Rios said with a note of finality in her voice. "You need rest. Your visitors are restricted for a reason—" And before I could complain about Halli's parents and their stupid list, she continued, "—and that reason is your safety. I have no objection to Mr. Everett visiting you again tomorrow, but for now, you need rest and quiet."

Considering the pain creeping into my head, I couldn't exactly disagree. Dr. Rios hadn't flipped the switches or valves or whatever they were to turn the pain medication back on, so I was going to have to deal with my headache myself.

My eyes widened with the realization.

No pain medication.

"You're probably right," I told the doctor. "I should rest now. But Daniel can come back tomorrow?"

He gave me a strange look. He probably wondered why I was giving up so easily all of the sudden.

"He can come again tomorrow," Dr. Rios confirmed. "For a short visit. I have no objection to that."

"Okay, good," I said. "So I'll see you tomorrow," I said to Daniel, trying to signal him with my eyes that everything was okay, I had a plan, and he should leave.

I'm not sure I got all of that across, but Daniel still took the hint.

"Tomorrow, then." He patted Red, then pried the reluctant dog off my bed.

He was about to leave when he turned back. Came over to me and leaned down for a hug.

"You're all right?" he whispered so softly I was sure Dr. Rios couldn't hear him.

I shifted the hug so that my mouth was right next to his ear. "No drugs. She forgot. I'm going to try again."

Daniel pulled back and gave me a look of concern. But he knew as well as I did that we didn't have the luxury of waiting another whole day. Not if the Oxford professor was right. If I had another chance to find Halli, I had to take it.

"See you," I told Daniel.

He gave me a nod.

When the door closed behind him and Red, Dr. Rios stood up to go.

"I'll look in on you later," she said.

"Mm-hm," I answered, trying to look innocent and calm.

A smile tugged at the edge of Dr. Rios's lips. "I didn't forget, you know."

"Forget what?" But I was pretty sure I knew.

"Your medication," Dr. Rios answered. "As I said before, I enjoy having you as a patient, but I prefer seeing you out in the world. I'll have someone check on you every hour. If you don't need the medication, I'll continue to suspend it."

"Thank you, Dr. Rios. I really appreciate that."

"But if you feel any pain," she added, "you *must* tell someone. Do you understand?"

I nodded.

"This isn't the jungle or the Arctic, Halli. If you need help, you can have it. There's no reason to be stoic. And in fact it's dangerous if you need help and don't ask for it."

I knew the real Halli probably would have tuned out the lecture, but I heard every word.

Until recently, I doubted anyone would ever apply the word "dangerous" to my life. Halli was used to it—she'd been raised for it. But me? The only kinds of lessons drilled into my head when I was a little girl were to say *please* and *thank you*, to always do my home-work, to brush my teeth at least twice a day.

But if that Oxford professor was right—if my condi-tion really was "deteriorating"—then I was in more danger than Dr. Rios realized. And since she couldn't offer me a cure for mishandled body swapping or being trapped in the wrong universe, it wouldn't really have done any good to explain it to her.

I was on my own. I liked it better when Daniel was there, but the truth was I had to do this by myself. He could hold my hand all I wanted, but it was my mind that had to find Halli out there in the waves, my mind that had to resonate with hers somehow so that maybe —*maybe*—I could build some sort of bridge that she could use to follow me back. Maybe Professor Whitfield was wrong before. Maybe I really could figure out a way for Halli to take over this body, even if her real body was dead.

My head throbbed just a little bit harder. That was no good. That was the opposite of what I needed.

I took a deep breath. Then another. The most important thing right now was getting the drugs to seep out of Halli's brain.

Then I'd try again and keep trying until I found Halli and fixed this.

49

"I enjoyed your journals," Mrs. Arnold told the class on Friday morning. "Some very inventive answers there. Being invisible was your top choice—"

Cheers went out from people who had picked that.

"—with the ability to fly, second—"

More cheers.

"—and incredible strength, third."

"That's me," one of the guys shouted. He flexed to prove he was already there.

"Some of your answers, though," Mrs. Arnold said, "were unusual. I thought you'd like to hear from a few of your classmates. Samantha, would you come up and share yours?"

As Halli watched Samantha Grabel walk up to the front of the class, looking both shy and pleased, Halli felt a strange kind of dread. She had no reason to think Mrs. Arnold might call her up there, but the possibility made her uncomfortable. She thought what she'd written was private. It wasn't like the kinds of things she wrote during an expedition with Ginny—she knew those would all eventually find their way to strangers.

But this particular journal entry was one she'd written off the top of her head, and she'd been so happy to write something again, she let her guard down. The only risk she saw was that it would be read by some English teacher she would never see again as soon as escaped from school. She wasn't counting on having to read it out loud to a room full of strangers.

But Halli sat there calmly, listening to Samantha read aloud, and telling herself there was no reason to expect the worst.

"If I could have any two special powers," Samantha began, "they would be that I could speak to animals and I could turn myself into any of them I wanted."

The essay was a cute one—I've always thought Samantha was a good writer—and people chuckled as she read it because everyone knows she's absolutely crazy about animals of every kind. Everything she owns—clothing, backpack, notebooks, purse, water bottle, jewelry—has some kind of animal on it. Horses, dogs, cats, elephants, lions, birds, dolphins—you name it, she'll wear it.

The class applauded as Samantha returned to her seat.

Then Mrs. Arnold looked at Halli.

"Audie? Would you come read yours?"

Halli thought about saying no. But then, did she really care what any of these people thought? She was never going to see any of them again. It wasn't worth making a scene by refusing.

She strode to the front of the class and accepted the journal from Mrs. Arnold. Then she turned to face my classmates.

"If I could have any two special powers," Halli began, "they would be the power to go back in time and bring back people who have died."

"Cool," someone murmured in back.

Halli looked up for a moment, then went back to the page.

"I used to have a grandmother," she read. "She was the greatest person I've ever known. She was strong, brave, wise, fearless, and above all, reliable. No matter what we were doing, I always felt safe when I was with her. I thought nothing bad would ever happen because she would always find the solution and she would save me, no matter what.

"The day she died was the worst day of my life. I couldn't believe it was real. The person who told me had to say it three times before I finally nodded and then started sobbing."

Halli paused and cleared her throat.

"I've thought about that day so many times. I've thought about what I wish I could have done differently. Maybe if I hadn't eaten breakfast, I wouldn't have felt sick, and I could have gone with her and saved her. Maybe if I noticed she was acting strangely that morning, I would have asked her what was wrong and would have kept asking until she told me. Then I could have forced her to let me help.

"If I had special powers, I would go back to that day last year and I would save her. Someone else I know died a few weeks ago. I wish I could go back in time and save her, too.

"My grandmother and I had a happy life together. I wish it could have gone on forever."

The room was very quiet. Halli stood there looking at my journal, not ready to meet anyone's eye. She wasn't used to feeling shy, and she didn't like it. So she forced herself to stand up tall and gaze out over the class.

She caught Winslow Henry giving her a quizzical kind of look, but when she scowled at him, he changed it to an approving nod.

"Very good, Audie," Mrs. Arnold said, and as soon as she clapped the rest of the class did, too. But Halli didn't care. She felt exposed in a way she hadn't since coming to my life and taking it over. She didn't like the feeling. It wasn't any of those people's business how she felt about Ginny or anything else.

Halli took her seat and tuned out the rest of the class. A few more people read their essays, and she didn't care. Mrs. Arnold went over vocabulary for an upcoming test, and Halli didn't care. All she wanted to do was leave. She couldn't believe she had wasted five days already being at that school. There was no reason for her to be there.

On her way out of class, Mrs. Arnold complimented her again on her essay. "That was very well done, Audie. Your writing has really improved."

Halli gave a single nod of acknowledgment, then kept on going.

She thought about leaving, right then and there. Just go out the double doors, and start running as far as she wanted to go.

She forced herself to stop. To reassess. To stand there in the hall and review her ultimate plan.

Once when she and Ginny were in Peru, getting set to climb the Andes, they met another group of climbers led by a man Ginny knew. He had a lot of ideas about the best route to take, the right gear to bring, how heavy the packs should be, what food they should eat—all of it.

Ginny listened politely, then told the man, "Good luck." She didn't argue with him, didn't share any of her own opinions, she just went on her way.

When she and Halli were alone again, Ginny told her what she really thought. "Thorne has always been an idiot. He never listens to advice. I gave up ever offering any. But so far he's killed five people on his expeditions, and he doesn't seem to learn from any of it."

"Why didn't you tell any of the other people?" Halli asked her. There had been a group of eight, ready to follow Thorne up into the mountains.

"Tell them what?" Ginny asked. "That their leader has more guts than sense? That they shouldn't trust his decisions?"

"Well, tell them that people have died."

"People die all the time," Ginny said. "Maybe all those people will live. We can't prevent anything from happening. All we can do is look out for ourselves."

Halli hadn't liked that answer. She walked along side Ginny for several minutes, saying nothing.

Ginny finally broke the silence. "You think I'm being callous."

Halli nodded.

Ginny stopped and looked at her. "You are the only person in this world I care about. I would give my life to save you. I will always do everything in my power to keep you safe and alive. Do you understand that?"

Halli nodded.

"That is my only job in this world," Ginny told her. "Everyone else has to look out for themselves. You have to learn to decide what's most important to you, and then let everything else go."

Halli stood in my high school hallway, oblivious to the stream of people going by. They didn't matter. School didn't matter. Had she gotten so caught up in succeeding at this plan of graduating early and moving to Colorado that she'd lost sight of what it really was she wanted—what it was that was really important?

She had been offered a clean slate. A new universe where nobody knew her. She could go wherever she wanted, do whatever she wanted, and still keep with her all the knowledge and experience she'd gained from almost eighteen years of her other life. Why was she wasting any part of this opportunity? Why was she living so small?

Ginny had six rules for an expedition. Rules that were meant to keep the two of them safe and healthy:

Sleep enough.

Eat enough.

Know where you're going.

Respect the weather.

Take care of your partner.

Be willing to change your plan when you know it's the smart thing to do.

Halli was face-to-face with rule number six. Was she just being stubborn, hanging on to the plan she'd made on Monday? Had she just been wasting time this week, going to classes, going to yoga, doing endless algebra worksheets, when she could have been taking positive, tangible steps toward the life she really wanted?

She thought she had set out along the right path, but maybe she was wrong. Maybe she'd taken some detour, and now she was further from her goal than she ever meant to be.

Ginny taught Halli not to dig in. Not to insist on continuing up a particular path just because they'd already put so many miles into it already.

Stop. Look at the map. Look at terrain around us. Are we lost?

And if the honest answer was yes, they had to be willing to backtrack all those many miles, and start up the right path again.

Halli heaved a huge sigh. "All right," she said to herself. The bell rang for the next class, but that was irrelevant to Halli. Halli Markham was not me, and she didn't actually care about any of this. It was time to head back down the trail.

How far back she'd have to go before finding the right path, she didn't know. But she wasn't going to get anywhere just standing still.

50

On her way out the doors Halli heard someone call my name.

It was Will. He'd obviously been heading for first lunch when he saw her leave the building.

Halli kept going. She had a plan in mind, and it didn't involve wasting time talking to Will.

"Audie," he called again, and jogged over toward her. Halli resisted the urge to take off running in the opposite direction. She wasn't in the mood to be scowled at or scolded by Will. Still, he had been generous once, giving her that refurbished phone. Halli knew she owed him at least some courtesy. If he could behave, she'd give him a few minutes.

"Where are you going?" he asked. He knew I had the

same lunch as his sister and Gemma, after fourth period. I should be in class right then.

"Away," Halli answered.

"Away ... where?"

"I have some things to do," she told him. "I need to go."

Halli turned to leave, but Will reached out and grabbed her arm. "Hold up. I just ... I wanted to tell you something."

Whatever it was, it was of as little interest to Halli as the World History class she was missing.

"Yes?" she said, trying to hold back her impatience. Ginny always said there were two kinds of people: the ones who wanted to help you spend your time, and the ones who wanted to waste it. School was a waste. And as far as Halli was concerned, so was talking to Will.

"I know ... we didn't really have a chance to talk the other day," he said. "At the office, after you quit. I was ... pretty shocked. I think we all were."

Halli didn't say anything. She just looked at him blandly.

"What I'm saying is," Will continued, "I don't really understand what's going on with you right now. You're different. Very different. I'm not saying it's bad, I'm just saying it's ... noticeable."

"Thank you for your observation," Halli answered. "I have to go now."

She slipped the loose strap of my backpack over her other arm. Any second now, she'd take off at a run.

"Wait—" Will seemed to struggle for what to say next. He was acting as shy and nervous around Halli as my mother did the night before. Apparently Halli had that effect on people.

"I just want to say … I don't mind it," Will said. "You know? I mean, after I got over the shock. And what you said to me in the car. You asked me if I liked it. And I guess … it's different, but not bad."

"I'm so happy you approve," Halli answered. "Enjoy your day."

She pivoted in the grass and started loping toward the street. She could hear Will call something after her.

She turned around and continued jogging backwards. "What?"

"I said I'll see you tomorrow night," he called again.

"What?" Halli shouted.

"At the ball."

She turned around again, then picked up her pace. As she ran away from that school for what she planned on being the last time, she shook her head at the ridiculousness of it all. As if Halli Markham, world explorer, were interested in attending some ball put on by the family of that overpreening girl Gemma.

Although there was still the fact that her brother would be there. And that could be interesting. Entertaining, even. In terms of wasting or spending time, it might actually be worth an hour of Halli's life to satisfy her curiosity about what some parallel version of Daniel would be like. Then if she ever did see me again, she'd be able to give me a full report.

A big if. She hadn't heard from me in a week. But it had been a week before she heard from me the first time, so maybe it was possible I was on some kind of schedule. Maybe I'd show up tomorrow morning as she set off on a jog, just like the previous Saturday. It could happen. She had no idea.

"'I'll see you tomorrow night,'" she mocked under her breath. "'At the ball!' Yes, and you'll be there with your bossy girlfriend, bowing and scraping to please her. What did Audie ever see in you?"

But we've all had our strange alliances. Parallel universes will do that to you. Halli just didn't realize it yet.

51

"Halli, what are you doing?" Professor Whitfield asked later that afternoon.

"What do you mean?" she said, but she could guess.

"I just got a call from Mark McKuen over at Bear Creek Mountain Guides. He said you tried to get a job with him?"

"Yes."

"He said you made all sorts of claims about your experience, but you couldn't give him any references except me. He was calling to see if you really had done everything you said you've done."

Halli sighed. The afternoon hadn't gone well. She'd contacted a dozen different outdoor companies in the area around Mountain State College, asking if they could use her for any upcoming winter excursions. So far all she heard was no.

"Halli, it's not going to work that way," Professor Whitfield said. "For one thing, you can't tell people your name is Halli Markham."

"I thought that would be better than saying Audie," she answered. "You said it would be easy to check up on Audie and find out she'd never done any of that."

"But it's worse to have no record," the professor said. "Remember that social security number you memorized? That means something here. You need it if you're going to get a job. Halli Markham doesn't exist. Audie is the only one with identification."

So she wasn't as free in my universe as she thought. We might not have microchips and tracking, but if she had to give people a number just so she could get a job —

"Can I get a number of my own, then?" Halli asked. "In my name?"

"Not without a birth certificate," Professor Whitfield said. "I'm sorry, Halli, there are just certain rules over here."

Halli got up from my desk and paced around my bedroom. She felt trapped. She hated the feeling.

"Let me make a suggestion," Professor Whitfield said. "I told you Mountain State has an outdoor education program. The guiding companies hire a lot of our students. Why don't I enroll you—as Audie—in some of those classes? Then you can participate in some of the activities and go out on job interviews—"

"It's all taking too long!" Halli said. "I don't want to have to go to school. I don't want to take some algebra test just so I can leave town. I have more experience in the mountains than probably half of those guides I talked to today. And forget about the mountains—I could probably crew a two-person boat as well as anyone else, and help someone sail around the world. Why should I have to stay here and rot away? Help me, Professor!"

He rubbed a hand over his face. "Look, Halli, I understand your frustration—"

"Do you? What if I told you *you* had to sit in a room day after day and wait for someone else to decide whether you can leave and go live your life? I didn't ask for this. You and Audie—"

"Saved your life," Professor Whitfield interjected. "Remember that."

"Did you?" Halli returned. "I thought the two of you were fairly sure that isn't the case. If I'm really dead, Professor, then I want my freedom. I should be able to start over here and rebuild whatever I can. I'm asking you to help me. Please."

Halli had a hitch in her voice. It was the first time Professor Whitfield had seen her this discouraged. And this desperate. Maybe he didn't realize what life was like for her. He'd been so busy trying to dig himself out of the hole he and Albert found themselves in.

"Let me make a few calls," Professor Whitfield said. "I can't promise anything, but maybe I could get you on as an assistant of some kind. Then once you have your foot in the door, you can show them what you know.

"But you have to be Audie," he added. "I'm sorry, but that's just a practicality. It won't be so bad," he said, looking at Halli's disappointed face. "You can be great in both physics and outdoor guiding. We'll figure it out. I promise. Okay? I'll help you—Albert and I both will. Whatever it takes."

"Whatever it takes," Halli muttered under her breath.

"And don't forget," the professor said. "You're assuming this is permanent. I don't assume that. In fact, I'm hoping that when you come here next weekend— you are coming here, aren't you?"

"Yes. Audie's mother isn't happy about it, but she said we can come."

"Good. Perfect," the professor said. "So once you're here, we'll spend as much time as we can coming up with some answers. Okay? So don't give up."

Halli ended the call and then lay back on my bed. The day had worn her down. She wasn't used to that. Even after long, grueling days in the wilderness, she always seemed to have energy to spare. But dealing with life in my universe was exhausting in other ways.

Rule number 1: Sleep enough.

Fine, then. If she couldn't do anything useful for herself at the moment, she might as well take Ginny's advice. Maybe everything would become clearer once she rested.

Maybe.

Stop. Look at the map. Look at terrain around us. Are we lost?

Yes, Ginny, I'm lost. Now what am I supposed to do?

52

"Hi." Jake saw my eyes open. He leaned over and kissed me warmly on the cheek.

I looked around the room. We were alone. And my head gave off a dull ache.

Which was good news, as far as I was concerned. It meant no one had turned back on the pain meds.

"What time is it?"

"Around two."

"Afternoon?"

Jake nodded. "I talked to your parents a while ago."

"Great," I answered sarcastically. The dull thud in my head seemed to amp up a little.

"They want you to come home."

It took me a moment to process that. I might be drug-free, but I still felt a little groggy from the nap.

"Come … home? What home?"

"Their home," Jake said, as if it were obvious.

"When?" I still wasn't exactly tracking the conversation.

"As soon as they release you. Your mother is sending one of the planes."

"Oh." I blinked my eyes hard a few times, hoping that might reset my brain. It didn't really help.

"Dr. Rios told them she might let you out as early as next week. They'll have a nurse waiting at the house to help take care of you."

Something about all of that sounded really bad. I just couldn't put my finger on it.

But then I remembered: Halli didn't live with them. Halli had never lived with them. "Home" wasn't on their private island, it was in the house Halli had inherited from Ginny. The one in Colorado.

But there was something else—someone else. Mrs. Scott. I knew I didn't remember everything about her visit, but she'd said something that mattered. Something I wanted to ask her about. And she had invited me to stay with her. I was sure of it.

"I'm not ready to leave here," I told Jake. "I mean London—not the hospital. I'm definitely ready to leave the hospital. But I have to stay here."

Why did I feel so slow-headed? So loopy? Like it was an effort to think of the right words. Something wasn't right…

Jake squeezed my hand. "You're tired," he said. "We can talk about this later." He stood up and kissed me again, this time on the forehead. That felt strange, too.

He hadn't tried to kiss me on the lips. Not even once. Maybe Jake didn't like me anymore. Not that I cared, but I did, sort of. It seemed like the kind of thing I should know. Maybe Bertrise was right. Maybe he liked Sarah.

"Do you like Sarah?"

"What?"

"Do you like Sarah? I think you like her."

Jake stared at me, his expression laced with concern. "Halli, you know I love you. Only you."

"It's just that you seem to like her—"

My tongue felt thick. My brain did, too. I've never had a drop of alcohol in my life, but right at that moment I felt drunk. Something was definitely wrong.

Jake noticed it, too. He reached up and pushed the button above my bed. He held on to my hand while the room started to move. I couldn't watch it anymore. It kept spinning.

"Halli? Halli—"

And then the colors burst inside my head.

53

Saturday morning. Halli wasn't a superstitious person, but she wasn't above following a ritual that seemed to work.

And since the last time she'd seen me—or really, felt me, heard me, there inside that same body and brain— was the Saturday before, it made sense to try to duplicate all the same conditions.

So she wore the same clothes. Wore the same sneakers, even though she'd bought new ones in the meantime. Left the house as close to the time she thought she'd left it before. Bent over to retie one of the shoes. Then took her first step toward setting off on a run.

Nothing.

She backed up, leaned over, untied and retied that shoe, then took a big leap forward, as if maybe she hadn't emphasized it enough before, hadn't been dramatic enough.

Still nothing.

So. There it was. That had been the last thing she thought she could try.

Now she really knew.

No use waiting, no use pretending anymore. She was free to think only of herself.

It was sad, really, she thought as she jogged along. The morning was beautiful, crisp, the body she'd inherited felt alive and well—Halli couldn't help but feel sorry for me in that moment. Sorry that I wouldn't ever get to feel what it was like to be me anymore.

It was the same kind of regret she'd had for me just a few days before.

She had been gathering up her things at the end of the physics class when Mr. Dobosh called to her.

"Audie, do you have a minute?"

Halli felt a moment of discomfort. She'd been getting along pretty well in my classes with her polite *I don't know*s, but maybe Mr. Dobosh was about to make an issue of it. And then she'd have to deal with that somehow.

"Is everything all right?" he asked her.

"Yes," she said. "Of course." She stood relaxed and confident and gave him one of her standard smiles.

"I only ask because ... you seem less than engaged in class lately."

"I've had a lot on my mind," Halli answered truthfully.

Mr. Dobosh smiled. "Well, maybe this will help."

He handed her a sealed envelope.

"What it is?" Halli asked.

"My letter of recommendation for your Columbia application."

I had been waiting for that letter. You hate to bug people when they're doing you a favor, but I wondered whether Mr. Dobosh had forgotten. If it had been me in that body right then, I would have gone crazy with appreciation.

But Halli simply accepted the letter and gave him a polite thank you.

"You can read it," he said. "I expect you will anyway."

"Thank you," Halli said again, then turned to go.

"I really think you're an exceptional student," Mr. Dobosh told her. "I've said that in the letter, but I think you should hear it directly from me. You may be one of the brightest students I've had in a long time."

This time Halli's smile was genuine. Because she liked hearing such a warm compliment for me. It made her feel good on my behalf. And it made her like Mr. Dobosh.

"Thank you, sir," she said. "That's very kind of you." *I'll be sure to pass it along if I ever see Audie again.*

She could imagine how I would have felt if I had heard it. And it made her feel sorry for me. Sorry that I was missing out on some of the pleasures of my own actual life.

She knew it probably wasn't any easier for me than for it was for her. In fact, she guessed she was probably doing better, simply because she'd been trained to deal with harsh circumstances.

But she hoped that the life I was living instead had its compensations: plenty of money so I never had to worry about that; a big friendly dog to keep me company; the kind of freedom and independence I probably never felt before with a mother and all those teachers breathing down my neck.

Little did she know that at that moment I would have been happy living her life, my life—anyone's life.

Because what life I still had seemed to be hanging by a thread.

54

I t was different this time. Different from when I tried to save Halli.

When I threw myself in front of that avalanche, I ended up in some kind of holding pattern. In some strange, formless, timeless mush that held me in between my former life and this one. I couldn't have said whether I was dead or alive or being reborn. I just was. And also wasn't, at the same time.

But now, I definitely *was*. I knew there was a me in here, and I wanted to save her and protect her and not let her slip away.

But I could feel myself losing the grip.

I know they were working hard, up there in the light, in the hard physical world where my body—and face it, it was my body now, I'd been in it long enough there wasn't any use in pretending anymore—lay pale and limp on the bed. I knew Dr. Rios with all her brain power and her science understood the practicalities of a life on the edge of blinking out. She might not understand the cause, but she could see the effect: me unconscious, unresponsive, seemingly beyond her powers to revive me. My heart still beat strong, my brain made waves along her graph—but *I*, the I inside the body, was somehow gone.

Where? I wish I knew.

In time, I followed the thread back. Like a bungee cord reaching the end of its tension, then snapping back with incredible force. I gasped and sat up and started screaming my head off.

Because the pain in my head seemed worth that.

Dr. Rios shouted out orders to the nurses, had them drug me, sedate me, do anything to calm me down. Jake looked ashen white. He stood in the corner of the room staring at me, watching me try to press all the agony out of my head, and as the nurses pulled my hands away, held my arms down, I could imagine then how things had looked to Jake as he rode with me to the hospital a week before and then sat desperate and worried by my bedside until the day I finally woke up.

For all his faults—and really, isn't the main one just jealousy? Is that so much of a crime when you're in love with someone? I couldn't blame him for loving Halli Markham—the real Halli Markham. I only wished he had really met her. I think she would have liked him—despite any faults, I admire him for being brave. Because I couldn't have stayed in that room with me if I didn't have to. Not for one minute, not the way I was.

And luckily I didn't have to. Because with the heavy dose of pain medication and sedatives they pumped into me, the world, blessedly, went black.

55

"So, are you ready?" Albert asked Halli.

"No." She had changed out of her sweaty running clothes and taken a long, hot shower. Now she finally faced the conversation she knew she'd have to have. But since her mind was firmly made up, saying no was easy.

"I'm not taking the test," she told Albert.

"You mean ... not today?"

"Right," she said. "Not today."

She didn't feel compelled to tell him the full answer, which was, "Never."

Not everyone needs to know what you think, Ginny once explained to Halli after they'd finished being interviewed by a reporter who asked a lot of personal questions. Halli was used to it, and was also used to being as honest as possible. If someone asked her a question, she somehow felt bound to answer it.

But she'd listened to Ginny give short answers or no answers to some of the reporter's more probing questions: What did Ginny think about her fellow explorer, Mr. Manning? Did she think he fell to his death because he was careless, or because the conditions on the mountain were too dangerous? Did she think he was a skilled mountaineer? Had she talked to his widow yet?

Ginny had no trouble just sitting and looking at the reporter and saying nothing. When he didn't get an answer, he went on to his next question, and the one after that. Finally Ginny said, "We're done." Then she and Halli got up to leave.

"Miss Markham?" the reporter called out to Halli. "Did you know Mr. Manning? Did you like him?"

"He was ... nice," Halli said, even though the truth was she thought the man was an arrogant bully. But it wouldn't look very good for her to say that.

"Not everyone needs to know what you think," Ginny told her as they continued walking. "Remember that. Your thoughts are completely your own, and they are as private as you want them to be. You never have to tell a person a single thing about yourself, or what you think or feel, if you don't want to. Do you understand?"

"It's just so hard when they ask us questions—"

"They can ask," Ginny said. "Anyone can ask away all day long. But *you* are the owner of your thoughts. Only you decide whether to give them away."

"So ... maybe some time next week, then?" Albert asked. "We can really do it any time. It's just the practice test. You can take the real one whenever you're ready."

"Right," Halli said. "Great. I'll let you know."

Then she ended the call.

And went back to searching the Internet for the information she needed to help her plan her escape.

56

By 4:00, Halli had some solid ideas. Enough of them that she finally felt she could see her way in front of her—at least the next several important steps—instead of wandering so much in the dark.

So when Lydia called to ask if she was getting ready yet, Halli actually didn't mind taking a break.

"Not yet," she said.

"Not even a shower?"

"Not yet."

"Well, get in there!" Lydia said. "I'm coming over in an hour. I don't care what you say, I'm doing your hair and makeup. You can thank me later."

Halli didn't feel like arguing. And another hot shower sounded like a great idea. She'd been hunched over my laptop for far too long, and needed to loosen her muscles.

But first she needed another run. In part for the exercise, but more important because she needed to run a certain errand. After that she could be in and out of the shower in ten minutes, dressed in five. How long would it take to get ready for something that only involved a dress and simple shoes? It wasn't as if she were suiting up to climb Everest.

"Shouldn't you be getting ready?" my mom asked when she saw Halli head for the door dressed in shorts and a long-sleeved T-shirt.

"I will," Halli said, then took off before she had to hear any more. Why did everyone in my life think they could boss me around? She didn't know how I could stand it.

She was in such a better mood than that morning. Progress did that for her. Planning and mapping did that for her. She felt the tension leave her body, felt the smile relax onto her face. She could do this. Would do this. A fresh start and a whole new world waiting for her to explore it.

She jumped in the shower at quarter to five, had her hair towel-dried by five-till, and wore the long blue sleeveless dress by 5:00 sharp. She took a lot of satisfaction in that. In being right.

And in doing things her way.

When Lydia arrived, she took a long, critical look, then told Halli, "Take off the dress."

"Why?"

"I don't want to get makeup on it."

"I told you, I'm not wearing any makeup."

"Come on, Audie, be serious."

"I happen to like this face," Halli told her. "Just as it is."

Which, when I think about it, is one of the nicest compliments anyone has ever paid me.

Lydia rolled her eyes and shook her head. But she didn't press it.

"And you're going out like that? With your hair all wet?"

"It will dry. We don't have to be there for a while."

"Can I at least do *something* with it?" Lydia pleaded. "Come on."

It was the last time, Halli thought. The last time she'd ever see Lydia. So why not let her have her fun? Halli would be gone from her life soon enough.

"All right," Halli said. "Sure. Go ahead."

Lydia grinned with delight. Then practiced her artistry, drying and styling Halli's hair, fluffing it, putting fancy combs in it, spraying it with some combination of holding spray and glitter.

"Isn't that nice?" Lydia asked, surveying her work. "Now don't you want at least some blush and some lip gloss?"

"The hair looks nice," Halli conceded. "Thank you. Keep your hands off my face."

Lydia touched up her own makeup, refluffed her own hair, until finally Halli called an end to all of it.

"Ready?" she said, motioning toward the door.

Lydia checked herself in the mirror one more time, then scanned Halli one more time from head to toe. "Are you sure?"

"Lydia, it's just a dance. Let's go."

Funny way to talk about an event that was about to change both our lives.

57

Gemma's mother had rented the largest ballroom in the fanciest hotel in town. It was up in the foothills where all the rich people build multi-million dollar houses on big desert lots, and then end up complaining about how many coyotes and javelina and rattlesnakes they have on their property. You see stories in the paper all the time about people's little toy poodles disappearing, or the fire department having to come out to "relocate" a diamondback rattler, or gangs of javelina that chase innocent people out walking their dogs in the early mornings. Nature is great, except when you think you're living in a city.

The hotel parking lot was already packed when they arrived, so Lydia had to take one of the far away spots at the bottom of a hill. The two of them got out to walk.

Lydia had bought a pair of ridiculously high platform shoes to go with her dress, and Halli couldn't help laughing to herself about how silly and impractical they looked. She'd hiked over enough boulder fields and river beds to appreciate the benefits of solid footwear. She couldn't imagine intentionally strapping on a pair of shoes like Lydia's that would make her wobble over uneven ground, in danger at any moment of twisting an ankle and going down.

They passed through the heavy wooden doors of the hotel lobby, where a uniformed worker greeted them. Lydia asked about the ball, and he directed them toward a room far down the hall.

Halli could hear music drifting out of the room. Violins, she thought, and a few cellos. Maybe even a soft horn.

Lydia took a breath. She seemed nervous as she stood before the closed door. Then she opened it and they went inside.

There were already fifty people, maybe more, scattered around the room. Most of them looked old, the age of Gemma's parents and even older, which made the few younger guests stand out.

Gemma and Will stood in a corner talking. Or at least Gemma was talking. She kept flipping her hair and clinging to Will's arm, and Halli could see her mouth moving without a rest.

Then Will looked up and caught Halli's eye. And for a moment he just stared.

Maybe it was the dress. It had a V neckline that showed more skin than I normally do. It wasn't crazy immodest—it's not like it showed any cleavage or anything—but it was definitely something more feminine than I usually wear.

As Lydia and Halli walked toward the two of them, Will continued staring. If it had been me, I would have been embarrassed by now, looking down at my feet, probably hunching over to make myself disappear.

But Halli didn't care at all. She walked with my body like she'd walk with her own, with that same athletic grace I was used to seeing from her, head up, shoulders back, feet confidently carrying her forward. Her eyes surveyed the room the way they might take in the view at the top of a mountain. Will meant nothing to her. He could look at her any way he wanted, for all she cared.

Gemma glanced sideways at her boyfriend. She pulled him in even closer and pressed her chest against his arm. Then she gave her long blonde hair an extra flick. Will seemed oblivious to all of it.

As soon as she was standing beside her brother, Lydia blew out a breath. Then she gazed around the room. Every man wore a tuxedo, some of them basic like the one Will had rented, some of them the more elaborate kind that had "tails," those long V-shaped flaps that extended further down the backs of their legs.

"You look nice," Will told the two of them.

"You, too," Halli said to both Will and Gemma, then she went back to staring at the one person she came there to see.

Gemma's brother Colin stood at the other side of the ballroom, engrossed in conversation with an older looking gentleman. Halli smiled at the familiar face. Colin wore his hair a little longer than Daniel's, but it looked good that way, not scruffy. He had Daniel's same athletic physique, and Halli noticed the tuxedo set it off nicely.

Lydia bumped Halli with her arm and stared in the same direction. "Yum," Lydia whispered. Then she asked Gemma, "Are you going to introduce us to your brother?"

"*Persona non grata*, you mean?" Gemma answered, giving her hair another dramatic flip.

"What do you mean?" Lydia asked.

"Well, if you must know, Colin and my parents had a terrible row last night."

"About what?" Lydia asked.

Gemma scoffed. "Well, apparently Colin has been sneaking around the past year while we've been living here, engaging in some very seedy activities, indeed."

"Like what?" Halli asked.

Gemma didn't even look at her, but continued

speaking to Will and Lydia only. "Last night he informed my parents he won't be going to Oxford—won't be attending university at all." Gemma folded her arms across her chest, and pursed her lips in a way that was both disapproving and smug. Like she'd caught someone in the middle of graffiti-ing the *Mona Lisa*, and couldn't wait to be the one to tell on him.

"What does he want to do instead?" Lydia asked, stealing another glance at Colin the way she'd been doing ever since she and Halli walked in.

"He wants to *travel*," Gemma sneered. "As if that's any substitute for education, or a profession. Daddy is livid, I assure you."

The story was getting better and better, as far as Halli was concerned. "Travel where?" she asked.

"What does it matter?" Gemma snapped, waving her arm in a circle. "The *world*. He seems to think he can make a living at it, well good luck to him. He'll end up on the streets like a beggar, and Mummy and Daddy will *not* rescue him, I assure you, and I for one am glad of it, the audacity of him using a plane ticket here, paid for by our parents, to pursue his own agenda, exploring 'the wild west,'" she said, doing air quotes with her fingers, "rather than spending time with his family, whom he hasn't seen in a year, not that *we* would matter to someone so selfish as my brother—"

"Where's he going?" Halli asked.

"The Grand Canyon, among other places," Gemma

answered impatiently, still not looking directly at Halli. It must have been hard for her to want so badly to tell on her brother, but at the same time want to ignore Halli. "He rented a car behind my parents' back and he says he's spending the rest of the week 'on tour.'"

"When is he leaving?" Halli asked.

"Tomorrow, apparently," Gemma said, "and the sooner, the better, after the way he spoke to all of us last night—"

Halli had heard enough. Without a word, she left the group behind and strode purposefully across the ballroom toward Gemma's brother.

The private orchestra Gemma's parents had hired was playing the kind of old people's music that only old people know how to dance to. And even though there were plenty of them scattered all around the ballroom, no one was dancing yet. People just stood around in clusters, eating and drinking and murmuring like no one was quite sure what to do with themselves.

Halli was sure. She interrupted the conversation Colin was having with a stately-looking British man in a dusty-looking tuxedo, and reached for Colin's hand.

Instead of shaking it, she simply pulled him away, out toward the dance floor.

Colin looked surprised at first, but then his eyes traveled up and down the blue-gowned figure of the girl pulling him away, and he smiled.

"Do I know you?" he asked.

"You will in a moment," Halli said. "Audie Masters. I'm *not* a friend of your sister's. I hear you're a disappointment to your parents."

Colin frowned at that, but Halli still smiled.

"Good," she said. "Just the kind of thing I like."

Then she positioned him smack in the center of the dance floor, reached her arms up, and waited for him to take them.

Colin's mouth tilted into a smile. "Audie, you say?"

"Something like that," Halli answered. "Are you going to dance with me or not?"

58

"So," Colin said after they'd made a few turns around the dance floor, Halli easily managing whatever formal kind of dance step Colin was leading her through. It might have been a waltz, I'm not sure.

"So," Halli said back. "Here's what I know so far: you're a traveler, you're going to the Grand Canyon tomorrow, your parents think you're horrible, your sister agrees—what am I missing?"

"That I'm forbidden from writing any of my blogs anymore—"

"What blogs?" Halli asked. She knew the word by now, she'd seen it enough.

"I have three websites," Colin answered. "One on traveling in London—a local's perspective on cool places to go, cheap food, where to take someone you really want to impress."

"Good. Second one?" she asked.

"Second one on travel around Europe—same thing, find the cool places, how to get there cheaply—and now the third, beginning with my visit out here: traveling to America. Or at least to the Wild West."

"Gemma said that," Halli answered. "What exactly is the Wild West?"

"Cowboys," Colin said. "Tombstone—the shoot out at the OK Corral—that sort of thing."

Halli didn't know anything about that, but she kept her expression neutral.

"Europeans are mad about cowboy legends," Colin said. "You should see all the advertisements for Tombstone in the back of magazines. So when I found out my parents would be flying me out here for my father's party..."

Halli smiled appreciatively. "Traveling cheaply."

"Exactly. I'm here for a week, and I have it all planned out: first Bisbee, an old mining town, then Tombstone, a few other sites, then on to the Grand Canyon, then race back to the airport."

"Not spending much time with your family," Halli observed.

"The less the better, as far as I'm concerned," Colin said. "And they'd see it that way, too, if they were the ones who'd thought of it first."

The music stopped, and Halli and Colin reduced their waltz to a simple shuffle on the floor. Colin still held her by the hand and waist.

"You don't like your family?" Halli asked.

"I like them well enough," he said, "but I've known for some time—an entire year, in fact—that once I told them what I've been doing, they wouldn't be very friendly anymore."

"So you're really not going to ... wherever you were supposed to go? Oxford?"

"Total waste," Colin answered. "I'm already making a good living as a travel writer. I'd leave school now, but I know my parents would be deeply disappointed if I didn't at least stay through my A-levels. But as soon as I'm finished next spring, I intend to pursue travel writing full time."

"And you can make money at that?" Halli asked. "Enough to pay for everything you need?"

"If you do it right," Colin said with a smile. "And I do it right."

The orchestra had started up again, some kind of jaunty old-fashioned song no one under the age of 100 would know how to dance to, and Colin and Halli weren't really trying. A few couples had now joined them on the dance floor, but Halli barely noticed. At that moment she only had eyes for Colin, and from the way he was looking at her, the feeling was obviously mutual.

"Can you teach me?" Halli asked him.

"Teach you what?"

"How to do what you do?"

Colin pulled her in a little closer and brought his mouth to her ear. "How long do I have you?"

"You're the only person I'm talking to all night," she answered, stepping back a little. He was still Daniel, after all, no matter what name he went by in my world, and he was still, in her mind, my boyfriend.

"May I be honest with you, Audie?" Colin said.

"Always."

He swept her toward him again, and for the briefest moment laid his cheek against hers so he could murmur in her ear. "From the moment you crossed the room, my evening improved a thousand percent."

"Mine, too," Halli said, creating space between them again. "Now, start talking."

59

They were on their fourth dance when Halli felt a tap on her shoulder.

"Maybe other people would like to meet Gemma's brother," Lydia said. She smiled, but her lips were tight, like she had to force herself to seem polite to Halli.

Halli wasn't giving up easily. "We're right in the middle of something—how about in another ten minutes."

"Audie," Lydia tried again, but that was as far as she got before deciding to go another way. She reached her hand over Halli's dancing arm and said, "Hi, I'm Lydia. I'm Will's sister—you know, Gemma's boyfriend."

Colin briefly released Halli's hand to shake Lydia's. Then he held on to Halli again. "I'm sorry, I know it's very rude of me—"

"Rude of somebody," Lydia said, still smiling, but casting a pointed look at Halli.

"So I'll just finish this dance," Colin said. "Then I'd be honored to dance with you, if you'll have me."

Lydia looked very pleased. "Okay, I'll wait over there." As soon as she was gone, Halli said, "Lydia's nice—you'll like her. It probably is wrong of me to monopolize you all night."

"I don't mind," Colin said, sweeping her closer again. "In the least."

Halli patted his arm. "You'll like her," she repeated. "We're not done—don't worry. Dance with her for a while and come find me later."

The song ended, and Halli immediately let go of Colin and started to leave. He held lightly to her wrist.

"Audie..." Then he lifted her hand to his lips and kissed it. Halli gave him a pointed look in return.

"We're just friends," she told Colin. "Remember that."

"Of course," he said, bowing slightly and appearing very proper and formal. Except for the sly smile that went along with it.

By then Lydia was already standing between them, ready to claim her prize.

"Don't go far," Colin called as Halli threaded her way through the people on the dance floor. She waved a hand behind her without looking back.

Gemma and Will stood at the outer edge of the

dance floor doing small, shuffling circles, which was Will's version of a slow dance. Halli glanced over just in time to see Will watching her. He didn't look happy.

Neither did Gemma. "What do you think you're doing?" she asked as Halli passed by them.

"I'm going to the restroom," she answered, pausing. "What do you think you're doing?"

"With my *brother*," Gemma clarified.

Halli gazed back at her, expressionless and silent.

"Answer me!" Gemma said.

"You seem to think that just because you want something from me," Halli said, "I'm required to give it to you. I don't agree with that."

"What has he been saying to you?" Gemma persisted.

Halli turned and walked on.

"Answer me!" Gemma shouted after her.

Halli exited the ballroom in search of the bathrooms.

Five minutes later, when she emerged into the lobby again, she found Will waiting for her.

"Audie? Can I talk to you?" He seemed serious. Maybe even angry.

Halli sighed. "Is this about Colin? Because really, you and your girlfriend need to mind your own—"

Will cut her off. "Would you come talk to me, please?"

Halli wasn't in the mood to talk to Will or Gemma

or anyone else except Colin. But since she wanted to give Lydia a chance with Colin for a while, she couldn't think of a good reason to deny Will a few minutes of her time.

She followed him outside.

The night was cool, bordering on cold, but Halli didn't mind. She liked the crispness after having been inside the ballroom for so long.

"What did you want to—"

"Not here," Will said. He continued to lead her away from the hotel entrance, down the sidewalk toward the parking lot. The lighting was dimmer there, just lamps on the ground to light people's way to their cars.

Finally, Will must have felt they were secluded enough for him to round on Halli and say, "What are you doing with him?"

"What do you mean, what am I doing?" Halli asked calmly, even though Will didn't seem calm at all.

"You don't even know him!"

"Yes ... and that's what happens when you meet people," Halli said patiently. "You talk to them and get to know them."

"Well, it seemed like you two got friendly pretty fast," Will said. "That guy was practically drooling all over you."

Halli laughed. "Will, are your eyes all right? Because you're seeing things that aren't there." She rubbed her hands against her bare arms. The night was colder than she thought.

"Here," Will said. He took off his tuxedo jacket and handed it to her. Halli thanked him and draped it over her shoulders.

Then the two of them just stood there looking at each other.

"Well?" Will said.

"Well what?"

"Are you doing it on purpose?"

"I don't know what we're talking about here," Halli said. "But it's cold, and I'd like to go back inside."

Will groaned. "Are you trying to make me jealous?"

"Jealous?" Halli said with a laugh. "No, sorry, it hadn't occurred to me."

"You think I'm weak?" Will said.

Halli sighed. "Are you still upset about that? Look, you can do whatever you want—"

"Good," Will said, then he gripped Halli by the arms and pulled her to him, and crushed his mouth against hers.

Halli stomped her heel into the top of Will's foot and shoved him back a step.

"Wrong, cave man. You think girls like that? We don't. Don't take what isn't offered."

I've never seen a look like that on Will's face: frustration mixed with shock and humiliation.

"Audie, I'm ... sorry ... I'm really sorry." He was so flustered Halli actually felt sorry for him.

"You want to try that again?" she asked.

"What?"

She knew it was the last time she would ever see him. And if, against all odds, I ever really did come back to reclaim my life, the least she could do was teach Will how to treat me.

Plus she was feeling flirty, playful, daring. Her evening had been far more fun than she expected. It left her in a generous mood.

She stepped toward Will, wrapped one arm around his waist and the other behind his neck, and gently pulled him toward her.

"You say, 'Audie, you're wonderful.'"

"Audie, you're wonderful," Will repeated, his breathing shallow and almost cautious.

"Good." She kissed him lightly on the lips. "Now try, 'Audie, I can't stop thinking about you.'"

"It's true," Will whispered. "I can't."

"Much better," Halli said. Then she showed him how to kiss her: not crushing, not forceful, but starting off slowly and waiting for her to respond before building to something more.

He wasn't bad, Halli thought. Those warm, hungry lips, his warm breath and tongue, his hand cradling the back of her neck, the way he shifted his body to hold her closer, the sound of my name, carried on his next breath, "Audie—"

"Will!"

Will jerked away, but Halli didn't move. She didn't see a need to.

Gemma stood a few feet away, fuming. "What are you doing? Get away from her!"

Will took a half step back, but Halli held her ground. She stood casually relaxed, as if Gemma had just caught the two of them doing nothing more than discussing some issue about the office computers.

"What is going on?" Gemma demanded.

Halli reached out and patted Will's chest. "He's a great kisser. I can see why you like him. He's all yours."

Then she handed Will his jacket, swept past them both, and headed back to the ballroom.

60

Colin was still dancing with Lydia. But as soon as he saw Halli return to the ballroom he made eye contact and motioned for her to join him.

Halli shook her head and pointed to the food tables. Colin nodded. Halli headed over there, and within about a minute Colin and Lydia joined her.

"Having fun?" Halli asked Lydia.

My best friend smiled, breathless.

"You're a wonderful dancer," Colin told her.

"You, too," she said, still smiling her beautiful smile. Halli knew that any guy looking at Lydia would know she was the most gorgeous girl in the room.

"I need a dose of air," Colin said.

"Me, too," Lydia said.

"Audie?" he asked.

"No, I need a dose of food." She patted her stomach. "I'll see you two later."

Colin narrowed his eyes and seemed to be trying to communicate something. Halli gave a small shrug. "Soon," was all she said, then went back to filling her plate.

"I want to talk to you," said a voice behind her.

Halli continued piling fruit onto her plate.

"Don't ignore me," Gemma said, "unless you want a scene, right here and now."

Lydia and Colin had just been about to walk away, but now they turned and stuck around for the show.

Halli popped a melon ball into her mouth and gave it a few casual chews while Gemma continued to glare.

"Why are you trying to steal my boyfriend?"

"Is that what he said?" Halli asked nonchalantly.

"No."

"What did he say?" Halli asked.

"It's none of your business," Gemma answered proudly, obviously thinking she was giving Halli some of her own medicine by refusing to answer questions.

Halli shrugged. "This is boring. Go work out your own troubles. I'm hungry."

She started to turn back to the buffet table, but Gemma grabbed her arm.

"You're a plain, ugly girl," Gemma said. "No one would want you when they could have me."

"Gemma…" Colin warned.

"I'm sure that's true," Halli answered.

"He pities you, that's all," Gemma said. "He pities you for your poor manners and your nonexistent social life."

"All true," Halli agreed.

Gemma stomped one of her high heels. "Stop it! I want to know what you have to say for yourself!"

"I'm sure you do," Halli answered.

Since Will was nowhere to be found, Gemma appealed to her brother instead. "Colin! Make her answer me!"

"Answer you about what?" he asked.

"I caught her kissing Will!"

Lydia's eyebrows shot up. Colin raised an eyebrow himself.

"Did you kiss Will?" he asked Halli.

"He kissed me first," she answered.

"Did you kiss him back?"

"Seemed like the polite thing to do," she said. Then she chomped on a fat strawberry.

"What would you do if I kissed you?" Colin asked her.

Lydia didn't like that one bit. She widened her eyes at Halli, obviously trying to signal her that she'd better have the right answer.

Halli shrugged again. "Hard to say. Each situation is different."

Colin turned to his sister. "Sounds reasonable to me.

I think you'd better address this to your boyfriend, not Miss Masters. She seems like the innocent party."

"Innocent!" Gemma scoffed.

"I'm plain and ugly, and he pities me," Halli reminded Gemma. "You know Will has a good heart. It was probably his charitable act for the night."

"Can I speak to you?" Colin asked her. "Privately?"

"Can I finish getting my food first?"

"Certainly," he said. He stood there patiently waiting while Halli added some bread, a spoonful of jam, and a few more slices of fruit to her plate.

Meanwhile Gemma and Lydia both stood with their arms crossed over their chests, glowering at Halli.

She turned toward Colin and said, "All right, where to?"

"Ladies," he said to his sister and Lydia, giving them a polite bow. "I'll go sort this out with Miss Masters and return with a full report. If you're not satisfied after that, you can question her further, sister dear. Come along, Audie."

He gently took her by the arm and escorted her from the ballroom. Will was just coming through the door as they were leaving.

"Audie?"

"I'm being questioned," Halli said, and she kept on walking with Colin.

Then once they were clear of the ballroom, out into the lobby of the hotel, they both looked at each other.

"Where to?" Colin asked.

"Feel like a long walk?"

He glanced down at her long dress. Halli pulled up the hem to show him her very practical shoes.

"Won't you be cold?" he asked.

"You're going to lend me your jacket."

"Anything else?" he asked, clearly amused by her attitude.

"If you kissed me, I wouldn't kiss you back," Halli said.

"Are you certain about that?"

He made a move toward her like he might try.

She gently placed a hand against his chest. "You're taken."

"I'm not."

"You are, even though you don't know it," she said.

"By whom? Your friend Lydia? She's a nice girl, but I'm not interested."

"It's hard to explain," Halli said.

"Try," he answered.

Halli smiled. "Maybe when I know you better."

Out of the corner of her eye, Halli saw Will standing nearby, watching them. She didn't care. She was done with him. She threaded her arm through Colin's and led him to the outer doors. "Now, we were at the part where you were explaining how you can get free travel gear from companies that sponsor your websites."

"Are you trying to distract me?" Colin asked as they

pushed through the doors. The cold night air hit them both in the face.

Halli released his arm. "Your jacket, please."

Colin took it off and helped her put it on. His hands lingered on the lapels as he folded them closer to her face and looked into her eyes.

Then he leaned forward again, and Halli stepped back.

"I can't," she said. "And I can't tell you why."

Colin kept hold of the jacket and gave her a disappointed smile. "Never?" he asked.

"Never is a very long time," she said. "I've learned to stop trying to predict what might happen next."

She lowered her hand to his and squeezed it. "Now come finish telling me everything about your life. And then maybe I'll tell you a little of mine."

61

You wonder if you'll know when you die.

You know.

At least I did.

I was as close to it now as you can be without taking that last, irrevocable leap. It isn't even a leap, really, just a small, conscious, deliberate step. Away from this, into that.

I wasn't afraid to take it.

Your body conspires, I think, to convince you that it's in too much pain, you'll be happier without it, you don't need it to keep living on. You know there's a you inside here, and it doesn't depend on bones and muscles and tissue to survive. It's a surprise, really, because all your life you've thought *that* was your life. But it turns out it wasn't. You were fooled.

I should have suspected—me, of all people. I was living proof that there was something about a human life that could live elsewhere, beyond its borders, take up residence someplace new like a hermit crab moving into an empty can.

And that *something*, that "me" was about to move on. To where, I didn't know yet. But it was done with that temporary body that looked like Halli Markham, and it wanted something new. Something healthy and whole, without all the drama going on with its head. The real me had better things to do than to live with so much pain.

We could have done it. We still had life in us and could have tried. But at some point the You and its body both agree, "What's the point?"

And it was at that moment, the instant when I gave up any struggle and any indecision, that suddenly everything became easy.

Then some automatic system kicked in. Maybe that's how the universe works, shuffling people and parts around to make sure everything returns to its proper place, nothing out of order—at least not at the very end.

I could feel the pull. The pull of my own body, my own world, and suddenly I didn't have to try for it, didn't have to work at it, I didn't have to do anything. I just relaxed into the inevitable and let it smoothly pull me home.

Back where I belonged.

Halli slept. I didn't wake her. I lay back against the base of my former skull like a shadow, no substance, no weight or form. Somehow I knew that if I kept still, didn't pour in any thoughts of my own, but just lurked there silently I could stay and not jostle either one of us out of the moment. I was safe. No ripping, no screaming, just safe and quiet and home.

And that's when the download began. Like I'd plugged into Halli's mind to sync up to my own. Everything that had happened since she took over my body poured into my own memory. Halli's memories themselves—anything that crossed her mind during the course of the last two weeks—poured in there, too, and it was like reading a book or watching a documentary, but it was instantaneous. Like a whole bubble of thought popping inside my mind, flooding it so that I had all the information at once and could watch it at my own leisure over the next several minutes, like a program I was fast-forwarding through but still completely absorbing at the same time.

I saw her life with Ginny. Her life as me. Felt her frustrations and her plans and her determination. Heard every conversation. Experienced every thought. All the way from the moment we switched bodies up to the start of her conversation with Colin as the two of them set off on their stroll.

I knew there was more, but that was as far as I got.

Because suddenly, abruptly, a sound cut in. Something that wasn't on the London side, but was on Halli's.

A soft knock. Then another, louder. Someone was knocking on my bedroom window.

Halli woke up immediately. And knew that I was there.

"Audie!" she whispered.

I could feel her relief, her joy. I felt it for myself, too. There was so much I wanted to say. And I had no idea how long we might have.

But there was that knock again.

"It's Will," I said. I didn't even have to look out the window. I knew.

Halli got up and peered through the blinds to confirm it.

"Audie?" Will knocked again.

"Ignore him," Halli said.

"We can't. He'll wake my mother."

"I'll get rid of him," Halli said.

"No, I will," I answered.

I knew why he was there, and I wasn't interested. Halli and I had things to discuss—*vital* things—and I wasn't sure how much time I still had. I knew the body I had just left was probably dead by now, and I didn't know what that meant for me. What would happen to me next.

Dealing with some guy coming to my house in the middle of the night just wasn't on the agenda.

I threw on a robe and quietly exited my bedroom.

Will heard the front door open. He came around from the side to find me.

"You have to leave," I told him. "I have nothing more to say to you."

It was harsh, but harshness was the only way. I couldn't get sucked into some long conversation.

Will reached for me. "I can't stop thinking about you."

"I'm sure that's true, but now you have to go—"

"I broke up with Gemma."

"Great," I said. "I'm happy for you. We can talk about it some other time—"

Will gripped my hand. "Audie, you know why I did it."

Yes, I suppose I did.

And a month ago, I would have been thrilled beyond belief. A month ago I would have had a hard time containing my joy. I would have thrown myself into his arms and finally taken those lips I'd been dreaming of for over a decade. I'd let him kiss me and never want him to stop.

But this wasn't a month ago. And I wasn't that girl. Not anymore. So much had happened. So much had changed.

Including me.

The words just sprang out of my mouth. And I

knew it was me working my lips, not Halli. "Am I supposed to be flattered?" I asked him.

Will tried to pull me closer. I resisted.

"I've been stupid," he said. "I get it. But I'm here now." Then he leaned forward like that was all it took, and everything was fine, and yes, Will, here's your kiss.

But no, Will, it wasn't.

"What changed your mind?" I asked, just out of curiosity.

"You," Will said. "Everything about you. I don't know why I couldn't see it before."

"I do," I said. *Because Halli was mean to you. Halli told you the truth about yourself. Halli didn't fall at your feet the way I always did and act like you were the greatest guy in the world. She didn't care about you one bit. That's why you like her. She's right: you're weak.*

But all I said was, "I have to go back inside." I turned toward the door.

"Audie, wait—"

I did wait. But only because I realized I had more to say.

"I've loved you for thirteen years," I said. "Do you know that? Thirteen years. And you never looked at me once."

"You're right," he said, reaching for my hand again. I didn't give it to him.

"What did you think?" I asked him, my voice tense

with the anger I could feel building inside. "That I'd just be so *grateful* whenever you finally decided to notice me? Forget it. You had your chance."

I felt the warmth of Halli's approval inside my heart. And it made me want to say even more.

"I've watched you date girl after girl who was incredibly pretty and unbelievably shallow," I went on. "That girl Lucy? Oh my gosh. Not to mention Gemma. And that Rachel girl from sophomore year, and the one who worked at Swenson's—"

"We barely went out—" Will tried to say, but I was having none of it.

"See, the problem with you, Will, is you have such a big heart. All those nice things you do for people—the ways you help everyone, all the money you give away—none of the girls you go out with ever appreciate it, do they? You know why? Because you always choose the wrong ones. I'm the only person who has ever seen everything you do in this world and thought it was amazing. And you know what? You're an idiot that you never saw that before."

"I know that," Will said. "You're right. But Audie, I'm telling you now I can see it."

"So what?" I said. "Too late. I've been here the whole time and you never even cared. Everyone has their limits, and I have mine. This was it. Goodbye, Will. Go back to Gemma. I'm sure she'll be glad to have you."

"Audie—"

"I mean it. I'm in love with someone else. His name is Daniel. Go away."

"Daniel?" I heard Will repeat, but by then I was already shutting the door. I locked it, too, not that he would have tried to bust in. I just wanted to hear the finality of the *click*.

As I walked back toward my bedroom, I could feel the tumult in my heart as Halli led up her own personal cheering squad. It felt good. *Great.* I finally understood what it was like to be strong. And not because I'd just skied to the North Pole or rowed hundreds of miles across an ocean or climbed some mountaintop. All I had to do was be brave enough to tell someone exactly what I thought.

"Tell me everything," Halli said once we were back in my bedroom. "What have you found out?"

I had to tell her I'd figured out basically nothing. That I'd been confined to a bed for the past week and could barely think that whole time. I did tell her about Mrs. Scott, and about the visit from Halli's mother, and about Sarah and Red—"How is the big guy? Does he miss me? (I lied and said he did. Even though he obviously thought I was Halli enough)—and about everything Daniel told me.

"That's it?" Halli asked. "He couldn't tell you more?"

"There wasn't really time," I said. "I was more focused on trying to find you again."

And I told her about my current situation. And what I thought it meant.

She silently took that in. The idea that we were both basically stranded at the moment in a single living body. Like the last two survivors of a shipwreck, washed up on shore.

"So now what?" she finally asked.

"I have no idea. I don't even know how long I can sustain this—being here, I mean. I have no idea if I get to stay or if ... I don't know."

"What are you going to do?" Halli asked.

"Wait until morning and then call the professor and tell him everything. Then I think that was a good idea you had about going back to see him. It'll be easier when we're all together again."

And my mother could come along with us. Even though we'd have to hide what we were doing from her, at least I'd get to be with her. I was even tempted to go wake her up right then, just to see her. But Halli and I needed to finish our business first.

And right now I could feel something going on with Halli. Something she didn't exactly want me to know.

Then images started flooding into my mind. Ideas that must have been there the whole time, but Halli had pushed them aside for a while as the two of us talked of other things.

My eyes instantly locked on the suitcase sitting in the corner of my room.

It looked full.

Then I glanced into the closet. I'd left it open when I went to get a robe, and it didn't really register with me how empty it was. I thought it was just clean. Organized. But the truth was it had been stripped to the bones.

"Where are you going?" I asked.

And then I saw another image: Halli on her last run that afternoon, the quick one she took before the ball. I knew she took a detour to the bank on the corner. I even saw her use my bankcard and my PIN to withdraw money at the ATM. But that memory had been swamped by so many others when I fast-forwarded through them, I didn't pay enough attention. Now that I really focused on it, I could see how much she took.

"Three hundred dollars," I said. "What for?"

It was *my* money. From my savings account. I thought she wasn't going to do that.

"I wasn't," Halli answered, hearing my thought. "But the situation has changed."

"How?"

"I'm still here. And I need a way out. I can't depend on Professor Whitfield anymore. You know that scholarship won't work. I have to do this on my own."

"With *my* money," I repeated.

"I'll pay you back," Halli said. "All of it."

"All of it? How much are you taking?"

But her answer merely echoed my question: *All of it.*

"Over two thousand dollars," I said.

"I'll pay it back."

Lights shined against my bedroom window. It was still dark outside—maybe only four in the morning—and some car had just pulled up in front of our house and shined its lights toward us.

"I have to go," Halli said.

She jumped off my bed and picked up the suitcase and headed for the front door.

"Where?" I asked. "Wait a minute! Where are you going? Who's out there?"

But it was obvious, wasn't it? It was Colin in his rented car. She was going with him. Running away. Touring the Wild West with a guy she'd just met that night.

"I was leaving today anyway," Halli said. "By myself. I had a plan. But now it's going to be easier because of Colin. He can teach me how to make money here. I need that, Audie—you know I do. Then he'll drive me where I need to go.

"And he's Daniel," she added, as if that would make me feel better.

"He's not," I said, "and this isn't the time to leave. We have to figure this out! I just got here!"

"And you might disappear again at any second," Halli answered. "You said so yourself." She quietly closed the front door behind her.

"Wait a minute," I said, desperate to hit Pause, to

make this whole situation slow down until I could catch up and do something about it. "You can't just leave. Did you tell my mother you're going?"

"No."

"Or the professor? Or Albert?"

Halli greeted Colin as he got out of the car. He took her suitcase and loaded it next to his in the trunk.

The resemblance was remarkable. But he wasn't Daniel. Daniel has a warmth about him, an innate goodness that you can just see when he looks at you. This guy was too sure of himself. Too confident. I could tell by the way he acted.

"You can't just leave and not tell her," I tried again. "Do you understand that? Go back. Wake her up. Tell her!"

Halli got into the car. "I can't have another four-hour conversation with your mother where all she does is cry and tell me I can't go. It's pointless. I'm not doing it again."

"Then I'll tell her!"

But I couldn't. Halli was too strong. No matter how desperate I was to see my mother after all this time, and to save her from the fear and heartbreak when she woke up and realized I was gone, I couldn't make my body do it. Couldn't force my hand to open the car door, or push my legs onto the driveway so they could run back into the house.

I wasn't in charge of any of it anymore.

"Please," I begged. "At least just leave her a note. You don't understand how she'll feel. Please just tell her where you're going."

"It won't matter," Halli said. "I'm not coming back."

"Ready?" Colin asked as he started the car.

"Ready," Halli said.

"You don't understand," I tried one last time. "I love my mother. I would never do this to her."

"No," Halli said softly inside my head, "you wouldn't. But I'm not like you, Audie. I can't be you. And if I stay here any longer, people are going to realize that. And then what? Can't you see that would be worse for all of us?"

"Then what am I supposed to do?" I asked. Colin had already pulled away from my house. I couldn't stop him. It was all out of my control.

"I don't know," Halli said. "All I know is what I'm going to do. I'm sorry, Audie, I really am. I hope you can sort this all out. But until then, I can't stay here anymore. I have to do what's right for me."

There was hardly any room for me in there anymore. Whether or not Halli was doing it intentionally, I could feel myself being squeezed out. There it was, my own brain, my own flesh and blood, and it had no use for me anymore. It's like I was a stranger.

So I took the easy way out, stopped fighting it, and rose above it instead. Surveyed the whole scene from somewhere outside. And once I had some distance, I could see it all with the sort of clarity I needed. I began to understand that what Halli said was true.

She wasn't me. She couldn't be me. Any more than I could keep pretending to be her. I'd twisted myself into knots for the past two weeks trying to do everything the way I thought she would want—and why? What good did it end up doing either one of us?

I'd been so busy being Halli Markham, I abandoned Audie Masters. No wonder my body rejected me—it knew I'd already betrayed it. Halli had the right idea: make the best of where you were, but don't stop being who you are.

Even if it meant not doing something simple and kind like leaving a note for my poor mom. I could forgive Halli for everything else, but I wasn't so sure about that.

But fine. I could deal with all of it, now that I knew the rules. My borrowed body back in Halli's universe was undoubtedly dead by now, but *I* was still here. The thinking, feeling me still had a lot of life in her, and all I had to do was figure out how to bring her back into the physical world.

After all, I'd done it once before.

This time I wasn't trying to save Halli, I was trying to save myself. And luckily I didn't need to race against an avalanche to do it. I had time. I could think it through. And try to remember exactly how I created a life for myself that seemed to skip ahead by three whole days.

If I could make it happen again, I knew this time it would be different.

Because if Halli could do whatever she wanted—

—then so could I.

Everything has to change.
My life depends on it.

Read the first chapter of
BEYOND THE PARALLEL

BEYOND THE PARALLEL

CHAPTER ONE

Walk, I have to keep telling myself. *Don't run.*

But the urge is so strong.

"Halli Markham!" Sarah shouts from the distance, and she's already racing toward me. Across this vast, polished lobby, toward the girl she thinks I am.

Walk, don't run. Stay calm. Stay in control.

I know this scene. I've been here before. It's Monday. I'm in London. I've just spent the day touring Halli's parents' headquarters, and now Sarah and Daniel are here to meet me.

I don't have much time.

"And Red!" Sarah cries, hugging me first, then the dog. "How are you, you handsome boy?" Red wags his tail so hard he might achieve liftoff.

I look past Sarah to where Daniel is still making his slow, steady way. He's limping a little, just like last time.

So far everything is like last time.

Which means by tomorrow night I'll be screaming. My head will feel like it's been split in two. I'll be rushed to the hospital, pumped full of drugs, unable to think or get away.

A week later, I'll be dead.

I want it so badly: to run to Daniel now, to throw my arms around him, hold him hard, and whisper urgently in his ear, *"It's me. It's Audie. Halli is trapped inside my body, back in my universe. This is me in here. We have to hurry. I need your help. We don't have much time."*

But I can't. I know that. Because telling him the truth right now—this day, this exact moment—started a whole chain reaction before, a chain that ended in pain and suffering and death, and I can't afford for the any of those things to happen this time. I can't take even one step down that same path. I have to do it all differently—*everything*.

My life depends on it.

You will never look at your life the same way again.
BEYOND THE PARALLEL
PARALLELOGRAM BOOK 4

Read all four books in the series

PARALLELOGRAM SERIES
RobinBrande.com

Mena's first week of high school?
DISASTER
But things are about to evolve...

**Riley is an expert with dogs.
With people? Not at all.
But maybe her dogs can help her
finally find her own pack.**

SPECIAL CODE FOR PARALLELOGRAM READERS

Treat yourself to a soft, comfy, custom-made T-shirt designed by Robin Brande herself, inspired by the *Parallelogram* series and her other books! You can see all of them at robinbrande.com/collections/t-shirts.

And here's a secret just for you: Use the discount code **AUDIE10** at checkout to get **10% off any items in the store**. That means books, T-shirts, hoodies, mugs—whatever! Go ahead and treat yourself. And high-five, book lover.

Ginny Markham's Motto

Embrace your nerd

Sleep-Read-Repeat

BOOK LOVERS
ARE THE BEST
I CHOOSE THE
BOOKISH LIFE
BOOK LOVERS
ARE THE BEST
I CHOOSE THE
BOOKISH LIFE
BOOK LOVERS
ARE THE BEST
I CHOOSE THE
BOOKISH LIFE

About the Author

Award-winning author Robin Brande is a former trial attorney, black belt in martial arts, Reiki Master, and wilderness medic. She writes in multiple genres, including young adult, mystery, fantasy, and science fiction.

She is also a designer and maker whose work celebrates the bookish life.

You will find all of her many books and designs at:
RobinBrande.com

9 781952 383236